ESCAPE PLANS

IN THE SAME BOAT

ESCAPE PLANS

SHERIE POSESORSKI

COTEAU BOOKS
WWW.COTEAUBOOKS.COM

Excerpt from *The Day of the Triffids* by John Wyndham, Penguin Books Ltd. 1983. © 1951 by the Estate of John Wyndham, Harmondsworth, Middlesex, England. Reprinted by permission of the Estate of John Wyndham.

Editor for the Series, Barbara Sapergia.
Edited by Geoffrey Ursell.
Cover painting and interior illustrations by Dawn Pearcey.
Cover and book design by Duncan Campbell.
"In The Same Boat" logo designed by Tania Wolk, Magpie Design.
Printed and bound in Canada by Houghton-Boston, Saskatoon.

National Library of Canada Cataloguing in Publication Data

Posesorski, Sherie.
Escape plans

ISBN 1-55050-177-1

1. Title.
PS8581.O758E8 2001   JC813'.54 C2001-911226-2
PZ7.P674ES 2001

10 9 8 7 6 5 4 3 2 1

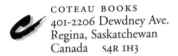

COTEAU BOOKS
401-2206 Dewdney Ave.
Regina, Saskatchewan
Canada   S4R 1H3

AVAILABLE IN THE US FROM
General Distribution Services
4500 Witmer Industrial Estates
Niagara Falls, NY, USA 14305-1386

The publisher gratefully acknowledges the financial assistance of the Saskatchewan Arts Board, the Canada Council for the Arts, including the Millennium Arts Fund, the Government of Canada through the Book Publishing Industry Development Program (BPIDP), and the City of Regina Arts Commission, for its publishing program.

PREFACE

JANET LUNN

"WHY AREN'T THERE ANY STORIES ABOUT US?" has been a heartfelt cry of Canadian children not descended from either French or English forebears for too long. In recent years, writers like Paul Yee, Leo Yerxa, Shizuye Takashima, and William Kurelek have created beautiful picture books and retellings of folk tales from the cultures of their ancestors. But there have been almost no children's novels, no up-to-date stories with which these children might identify.

Not more than a generation ago, this was true for all Canadian children. All but a small handful of their books came from Great Britain, France, or the United States. That is certainly not true now. Canadian children can immerse themselves happily in stories set in their own towns and countrysides, identify with characters like themselves, and be comforted and bolstered by a shared experience. This is what children of Japanese or African or indigenous North American descent have been wanting to do.

This series, In the Same Boat, was motivated by the desire of Coteau Books to do something about this. What a good idea it was! In these first five books for readers in their middle years of childhood, five writers, from five different backgrounds, offer the children who share these backgrounds stories in which they can recognize themselves and the way they live. At the same time, they offer all children insights into these diverse cultures.

These are five good stories, strong works of fiction, but what is perhaps more important is that they are all told honestly and with the authority that is only given to writers who truly understand what they are writing about.

For my parents,
Dora and Irving Posesorski

This is a symbol
for a Fallout Shelter

CAMP GRAVENHURST

"THEY'RE HERE! MUMMY AND DADDY ARE HERE! That's them! No," Becky Makowiecki's brother Jeffie said with a big, long sigh, "that's not them."

He'd said the same thing to her a dozen times at least, as car after car pulled up to park on the gravel next to Camp Gravenhurst's dining hall. Hanging above its front door was a huge banner: "Welcome Parents to Visitors' Day, August 19, 1962."

She and Jeffie were sitting at the bottom of the dining hall steps. Becky glanced at Jeffie. He didn't look so hot after ten days of camp. She should talk. Neither did she.

Both of them were covered with red, itching-like-anything spots, even more than when they'd had the chicken pox. In their first three days here, they'd used up all the insect repellent their mother had given them, and before you could say "Come and get it!" every mosquito and blackfly in Muskoka had feasted on their blood for breakfast, lunch, and dinner.

How come they were so much more tasty to mosquitoes

and blackflies than anybody else at this camp? Now they were bitten from right between their toes to right behind their ears.

So even though it was so boiling hot that most of the campers were wearing bathing suits all day long and were as tanned as the Malibu surfers in the *Gidget* movies, she and Jeffie were as packed up with clothing and as pale (except for the hundreds of red spots) as Arctic explorers. Both of them were wearing T-shirts under their sweatshirts, thick long pants, sweat socks, and the hideous, floppy, olive-green, kibbutznik hats her mother's relatives – who lived on a kibbutz outside of Haifa – had sent them.

Jeffie also looked pudgier. That had to be because of the tiny white-sugared doughnuts Becky kept buying for him at the tuck shop. Every time he felt bad and seemed like he was going to start crying, she fed him a doughnut to cheer him up.

Though, since yesterday, only with her left hand. Her right arm was in a sling. She'd sprained it when she'd tried to stop herself from falling off the horse she was trying to ride.

How come they couldn't have just kept going to Centre Island every Sunday in July and August like always? It was less than a half-hour away from their house, that was if they caught the streetcar, subway, and ferry, one after another without any boring standing around and waiting time. Centre Island was so close to Toronto that if Lake Ontario was land instead of a lake, you could walk there from the harbour in less than five minutes.

It had something for everybody in her family. Her father

got to play volleyball on the beach with his friends and then a game of poker under the big shady trees. Her mother got to lie in the sun on a beach towel like a lady of leisure as she gossiped with her friends. And she and Jeffie got to wear bathing suits, like normal people did in the summer, as they jumped into the waves of Lake Ontario and went on all kinds of rides in the Centreville amusement park. And everybody got to pig out on a picnic dinner before they took the ferry boat back to Toronto at sunset.

Instead they were stuck here! It was the worst place Becky had ever been stuck in so far. And she'd been stuck in some pretty crappy places. It was even worse than last year's Grade Six band class, where, when her eardrums weren't being attacked by the high-pitched squealing of clarinets and flutes, she was getting sprayed by the spit coming out of the end of somebody's trumpet. Whenever Jeffie complained about being stuck at home because he was too young to go to school, if Becky had brought her clarinet home to practise, she'd give an extra loud screech to remind Jeffie how lucky he was to be stuck at home and not in some lousy band class.

Jeffie hated being at camp and away from their parents. So did she. But all during July, she'd never built up the nerve to blurt out the real truth to her mother. Each time she'd been tempted, she'd remembered how happy and excited her mother had been when she'd told her that she and Becky's father were going to Crystal Beach on a vacation while she and Jeffie were at camp.

The minute she'd heard the word camp, she'd thought of the Siberian labour camp and the displaced persons camp in

Germany that her mother's family had to stay in during and after World War II, not of a camp for kids with tents, canoes, wiener roasts, and...swarms of insects out for Makowiecki blood.

And if being sent to camp wasn't bad enough, how come she had to go to a camp with a name like Gravenhurst, and not a camp named White Pines like her best friend Linda Friedman got sent to? Camp White Pines made Becky picture a camp surrounded by birch and pine trees and a wide blue lake. Camp Gravenhurst made her think of graves and hearses, and what was worse, she wasn't so wrong. Everywhere you looked in the camp you could see slabs of granite – on the hills, on the sides of roads, and tiny pieces of it were scattered all over the campgrounds. The Muskoka area was famous for its hills of granite, and in the summertime people came from all over Canada to see them. Why? Bad enough you had to look at granite in the cemetery, but who wanted to look at it for eighteen days of camp?

Her grandparents' gravestones were made of granite, and though she missed them, she still hated visiting them in the cemetery. Every time her family went, as much as she told her legs to walk slow, they started to speed up, and her father would then make some not very funny joke about how Becky was afraid the hands of the dead were going to grab her by the ankles and pull her under the ground. And what was worse, her father was right!

"They're here, Mummy and Daddy are here! That's them! That's them! No, that's not them," her brother Jeffie said with a big, long sigh for the thirteenth time as another car parked on the gravel.

"They'll be here soon. It's just taking them longer because they're driving from Crystal Beach. It's near Buffalo, so it takes more driving time than from Toronto," Becky said, with a big, long sigh herself.

Jeffie was sniffling like he was going to start crying any second and his bottom lip was thrust out like a plate to catch his tears. Grabbing her duffle bag with her good arm, she pulled out a cellophane package with three doughnuts left in it. "Want one?"

Jeffie nodded, and she handed it to him. Thank goodness their next-door neighbour, Mrs. Lepinsky, had immediately sent ten dollars after Becky had written her first kind-of-true letter. Her kind-of-true letters to Mrs. Lepinsky must have been more true than Becky had meant them to be, since Mrs. Lepinsky didn't stop sending money in all her letters. Becky guessed it was also because Mrs. Lepinsky knew that Becky was a city person, just like she was. Wild nature was for wild animals, not human beings, according to Mrs. Lepinsky. She liked nature only in parks and gardens.

Only in her letters to Linda did Becky write the real truth about camp. About how since she was the only new camper in her cabin she'd been assigned the bed at the back, next to the toilets and sinks. The smell was terrible, and the flushing woke her up several times every night. And about how all the old campers never included her unless the counsellor Ricki forced them to. And about how she spent the days hanging around with Jeffie and with Ricki, and wanting like anything to escape.

But to where? The camp was in the middle of nowhere,

surrounded by forests filled with poisonous snakes and hunters hunting deer, foxes, and rabbits. She wanted to escape with Jeffie, but not in a hearse after being bitten by a killer snake or shot by mistake by some hunter. So they stayed put.

"They're here, Mummy and Daddy are here! That's them! That's them! No, that's not them," her brother Jeffie said with a big, long sigh for the fourteenth time as another car parked on the gravel.

"They'll be here soon. Wait till you see what they brought us!" It better be good, otherwise Jeffie was going to tell them the real truth about how much he hated being at a camp. She had warned him not to say anything, because Mummy and Daddy had never had a vacation alone since they got married. And they really deserved one, especially Daddy who worked so hard at his job in the mattress factory. She had reminded Jeffie five times already that they only had eight days left, and then they would be home and never, ever, have to go to camp again. She hoped.

If he promised not to tell the real truth, she'd promised to buy him as many doughnuts as he could eat, and throw in as a bonus a couple of chocolate bars and red licorice. She'd promised she would play only with him and not with any of the other campers (not that Jeffie had to know that not a single one of the other campers had yet to ask her to do anything, anyway). If that didn't work, Becky was ready to prevent him with a giant pinch if he said one word of the real truth or cried and begged to be taken home.

In her letters to her parents, she had written hardly any truth. What was she going to write? That in a cabin filled with eleven other campers, she'd never felt so lonely in her whole life? That being at camp was like being trapped in gym class, and that the food was the worst, so she was hardly eating? So what could she do but write the shortest letters she'd ever written in her life.

"They're here, Mummy and Daddy are here! That's them! That's them!" Jeffie cried out. In the distance, she saw them get out of a green car.

As Jeffie leapt up, Becky grabbed him by the arm. "Remember what I told you. You like it here! You're having a good time!"

"Leave me alone, let me go!" Jeffie whined, squirming to get away.

"You're fighting already, and we're only here a minute," her father said as he bent over to kiss her, and then picked up Jeffie. "What's with all the clothes? I'm sweating in shorts and a shirt and you both look like you're wearing every single piece of clothing Mummy packed for you."

"Look, Daddy, look!" Jeffie said, pushing up one sleeve and looking in every direction to make sure no insect was ready to land for a quick snack. Becky shuddered. His arm was a mountain range of red spots, some even with pus. He quickly yanked it down again.

"We used up all the insect repellent. The tuck shop ran out too!" Becky explained.

"So you couldn't write? We would have bought you a couple of bottles," her father said.

Becky shrugged. Her parents were as sharp as Sherlock Holmes. If she'd written to ask for more insect repellent, they would have figured out she and Jeffie had run out and got bitten up, and so would have worried, like they did over everything. Each time she and Jeffie got a scrape or a cut, one of her parents would practically pour the whole bottle of disinfectant over it.

Why? Why? she'd asked her mother once when the stinging had lasted for almost an hour. Because, her mother had said, you never knew when a cut could lead to an infection, which could lead to gangrene, and then the doctor would have to cut off a finger or leg.

Becky glanced around. Where had her mother gone? She had just seen her.

"You want your mother," her father said, and from the way her father had said that it was like he was saying, your mother is the one you really want to see, not me. "She'll be here in a minute. She met an old friend from Krasnobrod she hasn't seen since she came to Canada."

Becky felt bad because that was kind of true. Not that she wasn't happy to see her father. She was. Her father looked good. He was tanned a nice brown, except for his nose, which was red and peeling. He looked rested too. At home after work, he mostly just looked totally pooped out.

"The food must very good here. How much weight did you gain?" he huffed, putting Jeffie back down on the ground. "You're eating the food and the insects are eating you." Staring now at Becky, he said, "Your arm! What's with the arm too? Some father I am. I didn't see it right away. What the heck is going on at this camp?"

Becky explained how during the riding lesson yesterday

she'd kept sliding sideways on the saddle and how it had made her so dizzy that she'd dropped the reins, and when she'd tried to grab them, she'd twisted her arm.

"You're okay? A doctor saw it?" he asked with concern.

"The camp nurse looked at it. She says I just sprained it."

"I don't know," he said, shaking his head. "Maybe we should drive you to Gravenhurst and get an X-ray to be sure. Maybe it's broken."

"No, no!" Becky hated getting X-rays. "The nurse was sure it was just sprained." The nurse had felt it up and down several times and had sounded certain when she'd said it wasn't broken. But maybe she was wrong. Now her father was making her worried. Maybe it was broken. No, the nurse would know.

"Only Cossacks ride horses," her father said, stroking her sprained arm. "The rest of us, we ride in rented cars like kings and queens. No more horses, promise."

That was an easy promise. There was no way she was going on a horse again. The riding lessons had been so awful she never wanted to see a horse again, even her favourite talking horse on television, Mr. Ed.

"It's hot like the tropics, so why are you two all dressed up?" her mother asked, coming up to Becky and hugging her, then Jeffie.

"Look, Mummy, look!" Jeffie said, pushing up one sleeve for a couple of seconds, then quickly yanking it down.

"Spots? Has every insect in Muskoka come for dinnertime only on my two children? And Beckelah, what happened to your arm? And Jeffie, you're so white. What are you eating?"

Her father gave her mother a fast explanation of the spots and the arm. As he did, her mother anxiously looked back and forth at each of them.

"Ira, maybe we should drive to Gravenhurst to get the arm X-rayed. What do you think?"

"That's what I said too."

"No, no!" Becky groaned, having just finished convincing herself that the arm was only sprained, not broken. "The nurse was positive it's a sprain."

"So she's sure?" her mother asked.

"POSITIVE!"

When her mother had hugged her, Becky had almost blabbed out the real truth about how they were having the worst time of their life at Camp Gravenhurst, but she stopped herself just in time. How could she do it? Her mother looked nice and tanned too, and relaxed. She was wearing a yellow sundress with daisies on it, and her sandy blonde hair was teased up like she'd just been at the hairdresser. Her parents were having a good time in Crystal Beach, and she wasn't about to spoil it.

"So really, do you like it here?" her mother asked.

"I'm having a good time," Becky mumbled as she eyed the tips of her dirty white sneakers.

"The camp's not what I expected," her father said, studying the campgrounds. "Look at those cabins. This is a children's camp? It looks like a displaced persons camp."

You know what? Becky thought, it did. The wooden cabins where the campers slept looked more like barracks than cabins. They were painted a dingy grey, and the grass

around them was patchy and worn out like an old carpet. There were no shrubs or flowers anywhere. The only decoration was those rotten pieces of granite that got stuck in the soles of her sneakers.

"Ira!" her mother whispered sharply.

"I want to go home. I don't want to stay here. I hate it here!" Jeffie wailed.

Becky moaned. If she pinched Jeffie to stop, he'd probably weep even louder.

"Ira! Look what you've done!"

Even through his tan, Becky could see that her father's face had gone white. He crouched down and held onto Jeffie until he stopped crying.

"Come, show me your cabin. Then afterwards, we'll go to the car. We brought you something, something you'll really like." Her father took Jeffie by the hand and they went off.

"So you're having a good time in Crystal Beach," Becky said. Maybe if she could get her mother talking about her vacation, she wouldn't have to answer too many questions about Camp Gravenhurst. Telling hardly any truth was hard enough to do in letters, but extra hard when the person was right next to you and was a mother who was better at discovering the truth than any lawyer or policeman.

"I have a picnic basket in the car, and a blanket. Let's get them and make a picnic over by that maple leaf tree."

After they spread the blanket under the tree, Becky and her mother talked about everything under the sun except camp. Finally, Becky got so tired having to be tiptoe-careful about what she said that she lay down on the blanket and fell asleep.

"Wake up, I come for a visit, and you sleep like Rip Van Winkle," her mother said, her face above Becky's.

Becky opened her eyes, then shut them. "Five more minutes," she slurred.

"You have tonight to sleep!"

Becky groaned. Yeah, next to the toilet with the flushing and smell. No wonder she was sleeping now, with the sweet smell of the grass and her mother's Evening in Paris perfume in her nose instead.

"*G'vald!*" her mother said, as she lifted Becky's head and shoulders off the blanket, then dropped them. "You're as stiff as a piece of wood. But not for long."

A second later, Becky felt her mother's hand slide under her sweatshirt and T-shirt and onto her stomach, and five seconds later Becky was squirming and laughing and coughing as her mother tickled her.

"See, from a piece of wood, I make a living girl. Your mother's a magician, no?"

"Yes, yes, just stop please!" Becky gasped. "I'm awake, I'm awake." She sat up and leaned back against the trunk of the tree.

"So what's going on here at camp?" her mother said. "The truth and nothing but the truth. Remember, you can tell me anything and everything because I'm your mother."

Becky gave her mother an anxious look. People always said they wanted the truth, but sometimes when you told them, they were sorry they'd asked for it. Becky was sorry sometimes. Like last year when she got her hair cut to her ears and it looked horrible. She'd asked Mrs. Lepinsky for the truth and Mrs. Lepinsky had given her the real truth. She'd said, since Becky had such nice, thick, wavy brown hair why should it be all over the floor of a beauty salon and not attached to Becky's head where it belonged? After hearing that Becky had measured her hair almost every day with her ruler to see if it had grown any since the day before.

If she told her mother the real truth, she would ruin her parents' vacation. Even if they did take her and Jeffie home, Becky knew she would be miserable with guilt. What was worse? To be miserable with guilt, or miserable at camp? Eight more days, she could take it...and so could Jeffie, as long as the tuck shop didn't run short of doughnuts.

Her mother lightly tapped on Becky's head. "If it takes you so long, it can't be the truth you're looking for."

Becky tried to smile, as if her mother was making a joke, but her lips wouldn't stretch too far.

"You call that a smile?"

So Becky tried harder, until she was showing most of her teeth and lots of her gums.

"That's still not a smile. Just teeth and gums. That you show to a dentist. So are you going to tell your poor mother how's camp?"

"It's okay," Becky shrugged.

"An okay place to stay or an okay place only for escape plans?" her mother asked.

Becky turned red. Ever since she could remember, she'd been making escape plans. She'd bet no prisoner on the island of Alcatraz had made as many escape plans as she'd made. Not that she'd ever escaped anywhere...yet. But an escape plan was good to have. It was like having a penlight in your pocket in case the lights went out, or streetcar tickets in your wallet in case you had to go somewhere quick. You never knew, so it was always good to have a plan ready, just in case.

"Come on, you can tell me. You know, my darling daughter, I'm a great escaper myself," her mother murmured. "Remember all the places my family tried to escape to."

Becky nodded. Before and after World War II, her mother's family had tried to escape from Poland. They'd tried to go to Argentina and to Barbados. Finally, finally, they had escaped to Canada – which they were all very, very glad about. Her mother had said that it had been *bashert* – that was the Yiddish word for fated – that her family had come to Toronto, Ontario, Canada in 1947. How else would she have met and married Mr. Ira Makowiecki and had two such children!

And besides, she'd added, who wanted to live in a country like Argentina run by that *meshugeneh* – that was the Yiddish word for crazy like a cuckoo – dictator Juan Peron? And Barbados, just forget it! It was too hot, too small, and had too many bugs! Her mother just hated any kind of bug. Becky and Jeffie had inherited that from her.

"You can't fool an old escaper like your mother. Please tell me," her mother said gently.

A bunch of girls from Becky's cabin walked past, giggling. Becky said hi and waved, but they looked right through her like she wasn't there.

"I don't belong here," Becky said, in a choked whisper, ashamed to have had her mother see how unpopular she was.

"So you feel like a displaced person here. Not an outdoors girl, hmm? What does Mrs. Lepinsky always say...?"

"If human beings were meant to live outdoors, God would have given them a fur coat like a bear and a taste for raw meat and vegetables like a wolf," Becky said.

"Right. So next summer, no camp. Daddy can rent a car and we can all travel around Muskoka, and Linda can come too."

Muskoka. Becky never wanted to see Muskoka again.

"Forget Muskoka," her mother said quickly. "We'll find someplace else. Sometimes it takes time to find the right place. The *bashert* place. I know this and you know this. You know how much I wanted to escape to Toronto."

If there was ever a time that Becky needed to escape into her mother's escape story, this was it. Her clothing was as glued to her as if she'd gone swimming in it and was rubbing on her bites. The ravioli she'd had for lunch had mixed together with the hard-boiled eggs and peanut butter from breakfast, and the stinky taste of both of them together kept churning up from her stomach into her mouth. Eight more days of crappy food, crappy campers, and crappy insects – she didn't know if she could take it. Suddenly the urge to scream out the real truth to her mother was overwhelming.

"Tell me your escape story, please, please, Mummy, right this second," Becky said in a rush of words, shifting so she was so close to her mother she could feel her mother's heart beating.

"Here? Again?"

"Please!"

And so without asking, why right now, because she didn't have to be a mind reader to figure that out, her mother began to repeat the story that Becky loved to hear about her magically miraculous escape from Krasnobrod in Poland to Toronto in Ontario in Canada.

KRASNOBROD

"IF I HAD KNOWN I WAS GOING TO BE SITTING AGAINST A tree with bark as sharp as fingernails, I would have worn a blouse with long sleeves and a big collar, and not a dress missing part of its back," her mother said, as she flung a towel around her shoulders like it was a mink stole.

Becky was so padded up that when she leaned back, the bark felt as soft as a pillow. But even though the branches of the tree were thick with shady green leaves, sweat still dripped worse than a leaky faucet off Becky's forehead into her eyes, burning like heck. She wiped it off with a sleeve.

"Never mind. Okay, so...." Her mother looked away from Becky and stared at a giant slab of granite on the side of the hill. She stared and stared, as if it were the outdoor movie screen at the Dufferin Drive-in and on it was playing a movie showing Krasnobrod just as it had been when she was Becky's age.

Becky cleared her throat loudly, but her mother didn't start. Becky tried coughing, but still her mother didn't say a word. So she decided to start telling the story herself.

"I'll never forget," Becky began. Her mother always began her stories with those three words. "Once upon a time, you, Hannah Simkovsky, were born in Krasnobrod, a tiny village in Poland with two thousand people, and a couple of hundred cows, horses, donkeys, chickens, roosters, dogs, cats, and creepy rats. There was no electricity and no running water, and there were no bathrooms."

"If you know my story so well, you tell it," her mother said, fanning herself with the edge of the towel. "I'll just rest."

"No, no, no! I like it better when *you* tell it," Becky said, sticking her left index finger into her mother's stomach when she said *you!*

Her mother smiled. "So where were you in my story? Okay, your Bubbe and Zaide, may they rest in peace, and my brothers Chaim and Rivem, we all lived in a one-room house."

Though Becky had heard her mother tell her story more times than she could remember, she still found it hard to imagine all the Simkovskys living together in one room. More than ever she appreciated having her own room back home, with a door she could close and lock. Who wanted to hear coughing, burping, scratching, talking, giggling, eating, and worst of all, flushing, from other people, all night long? A door was a necessity of life, just like air and food...and so were toilets, running water, and electricity. The Simkovskys had had an outhouse behind their house and had to get all their water from a river and carry it back to their house in barrels.

"There were only two beds in the house," her mother

remembered, sounding amazed herself. "I slept at the foot of my parents' bed, and Rivem and Chaim slept in a bunk bed. Zaide was a shoemaker, and he made shoes on his workbench near the front window. Every Tuesday he went to the marketplace in the centre of the village to sell them."

"Tell me about the marketplace," Becky said. The marketplace was one of Becky's favourite parts of her mother's story, even though her mother often sounded "nostalgic and melancholy" when she was telling it.

Years ago Becky had asked her mother why she sounded so sad. Her mother had said, using her newest night school words, that she was not sad but "nostalgic and melancholy." That meant that her mother was feeling not crying sad, but the kind of sad you felt when you missed something that was gone forever.

Her mother couldn't wait to use the new words she'd learned in her night school English classes at Harbord Collegiate. Every winter, once a week, her mother attended classes there. For someone who couldn't write, read, or speak English very well when she'd come to Canada, her mother was very proud now to do all three as well as a born-in-Canada Canadian. She read almost as many books a month as Becky did. How she managed, Becky didn't know, because she never saw her mother sitting down and relaxing. Even standing in line to pay for food, she did crossword puzzles, finishing them, one, two, three – even the hardest ones.

"Every Tuesday, in every city, town, and village in Poland, there was a flea market open for business," Becky said, answering her own question, she was so eager to get to this part again. "The marketplace was in a big courtyard surrounded by stores, and in the middle of it was a fountain with a statue. Everybody brought this and that to sell to everybody else. Farmers, bakers, booksellers, shoemakers, dressmakers, candy makers, and more, all of them would come to the marketplace, set up a table, and sell everything you can think of and a little bit more."

Her mother stroked Becky's hair. "And the little bit more was what I came for. Every Tuesday morning, Zaide would go to the marketplace with the new shoes he'd made. Every Tuesday afternoon, your Bubbe would cook up a soup for my Bubbe Faigeh, your great-grandmother, may she rest in peace, and send me to the marketplace with the soup.

"My Bubbe had a stand where she sold all kinds of candies and chocolates. Such a nice, gentle, kind Bubbe she was. Always a big kiss, always a big hug, always a big handful of chocolates and candies for my sweet tooth. But forgive me for saying this, God, the only reason I was bringing the soup to my Bubbe whom I loved very much, was so I could hear the singers who stood singing songs near my Bubbe's stand. I was just crazy about the singers. It was like an obsession with me."

Becky stared at her mother. As she stared, her mother got younger and younger right before her eyes. Her mother's short, sandy-coloured hair grew like the hair in Becky's old Tressy doll until it reached her mother's waist and was tied back in one long thick braid. Her mother's gold front tooth disappeared and instead she had a mouth full of her own teeth. She got much thinner and shorter, but what stayed the same were her big blue-grey eyes and the way that, when she laughed, she kind of looked Chinese.

Becky tapped her mother on the shoulder. There were times, like today, when her mother was telling her story that she spent as much time remembering in her head as she did remembering in words.

"Tell me about the singers," Becky said.

Her mother liked to remember things. Happy and even sad things. So did Mrs. Lepinsky, who was born in Minsk in Russia – who knew how many years ago, because Mrs. Lepinsky insisted that a lady never revealed her age. She could still remember what she and Mr. Lepinsky had eaten on their first date fifty-two years ago. Apple turnovers with two glasses of tea with slices of lemon. And she could still remember the face of her first baby, a girl who had died a few hours after being born, without any photograph to remind her.

Becky's father, though, liked to forget, which was bad and good. He didn't like to remember his life in Poland, and whenever she would ask him any questions, he would just say he had forgotten. But how could you, unless you had amnesia, forget twenty years of your life? You could only ask her father questions about his life after he came to Canada in 1948. If you asked him questions about his life before that, he would say in Yiddish, *a nechtiker tog!* which meant it's gone, so forget about it.

Still, sometimes it wasn't such a bad thing that her father liked to forget. Like when Becky hadn't turned down the volume on the record player even after her father had asked her six times to do it *this very second* because his head was splitting open with a headache, and Becky hadn't. The seventh time he'd ripped the needle off the record, scratching it but good, and then had really yelled at her. The next morning, though, he'd forgotten he was angry at her and acted like nothing had happened.

Becky liked to remember...but also to forget. Already, at age twelve, she had lots to remember...and to forget.

"The singers," her mother said, letting out a big breath of air. "The singers were a man and a woman. The man played the mandolin as they both sang together. After giving my Bubbe her soup, I would join the crowd of people listening to the singers. The singers would start singing near my Bubbe's stand, then move to another in the marketplace, and another spot, and another. Everywhere they went, I went too. One song they sang, I will always remember. It was a song that predicted the end of the world. After so many years, I cannot get it out of my head."

Hmm, her mother had never mentioned before that the singers had sung a song predicting the end of the world. What else new was her mother going to remember today? No matter how many times her mother told her story, it was never the same. New things were always popping up. That's what made her mother's story so very interesting to hear over and over. There was always more.

"What did the song say?" Becky asked.

"Tomorrow will come the end of the world," her mother sang. "It will come the end of the world. Everything came two by two, and everything goes one by one...." Her mother paused, then continued to sing the rest of the song to herself in Polish as she swiped at the tears in her eyes with the edge of the towel.

"Mummy, you okay?" she asked.

"Yeah, yeah. Silly to get tears," her mother said. "Who would have thought they knew? Anyway, enough with that."

What did the singers know? Becky looked at her mother with a worried expression.

"Ready to hear some more?"

Should she ask what the singers knew? Did she want to know or not? No, she wouldn't ask, she wanted this visitors' day to be a happy one. She had eight more days at camp to be miserable enough, without thinking about what the singers had known about the end of the world.

So Becky just nodded and looked away from her mother. In the time her mother had been telling her story, two other families had spread out blankets nearby and were having picnics, and she and her mother hadn't even noticed. It was always like that when her mother told her story. Sometimes, more than sometimes, Becky wasn't just listening, but felt like she was seeing and feeling everything as if she was there.

"After the singers, I would lose myself in the market. It was so busy. So many people. So many different stands selling food, clothes, jewellery, shoes, furniture, and books. I would look and touch, and look and touch, and Zaide could never find me and when he did, would he give it to me!"

"Did the marketplace look like Kensington Market?" Becky asked, wanting to make the picture in her mind perfect. Kensington Market was a market in downtown Toronto where her Bubbe and Zaide had sold shoes, first at an outdoor stand, then from a store.

"Not so much, because it was in an open space, and Kensington Market runs up and down on a couple of streets," her mother said. "So what do you want to hear next? The running away part or the beautiful Rachel part?"

"Oh, the beautiful Rachel part, please!" Becky said.

The beautiful Rachel was her mother's cousin. Just before World War II, when Becky's mother had been eleven, Rachel had been seventeen. She had long, thick, wavy blond hair, a peaches-and-cream complexion, and green eyes, and was such a beauty that everybody had to look at her. Becky imagined that Rachel looked like a combination of the actress Marilyn Monroe and Rapunzel.

"The summer before the war, Bubbe sent me to Zamosc to stay with her sister and her only child, Rachel. Both of them were real beauties. Rachel had lived in Warsaw for a year, as a nanny for a rich Jewish family. I thought she was a big success because she was living in Warsaw, a big modern city. To me, that was something, something. When the rich family emigrated to the United States, Rachel had to go back to Zamosc and was very unhappy about it. Who could blame her? Back in Zamosc, all she ever talked about was Warsaw this, Warsaw that. So when I came to visit, even though I was six years younger, she was very pleased to have a new pair of ears for her Warsaw stories."

Becky reached over and tugged her mother's left earlobe. "Fresh ears!"

Her mother laughed. "Yes, very fresh ears!"

"So after listening to Rachel, you wanted to go to Warsaw too?" Becky asked.

Her mother made a little face, then shifted. "Not exactly.

I was like you. Had too many never-never lands on the brain."

Her mother had had never-never lands on the brain? "You were like me?" Becky asked, amazed.

Whenever she remembered how she used to believe in never-never lands when she was much, much younger, she felt very dumb and silly. How could she have believed in all that stuff? She'd been trying to forget, but as hard as she tried, she couldn't erase it from her brain. It was as if it was written, not just in pen in her brain, but in thick, black magic marker.

Her mother sighed loudly. "Yes, I was like you. Every day after school, on the way home, I would go stand in the corner between a textile and a shoe store in the marketplace court-yard, watching people going here and there, watching carts going here and there, and all the time, hoping, wishing, dreaming that soon I would be going here and there and everywhere too. Where I wanted to go, what I wanted to do, I didn't know. I didn't have a place in mind. I only wanted to go away. Somewhere. Anywhere."

Her mother turned towards Becky and hugged her, and Becky hugged back. It felt so good to know that her mother too had hoped, wished, and dreamed about escaping. So Becky had gotten that from her mother.

Sometimes she felt left out when she saw her mother and Jeffie together, because they looked and acted so much alike. Jeffie had the same thick sandy hair, the same blue-grey eyes. One time when she'd been watching her mother and Jeffie playing dominoes, her father had snuck up on her and whirled her around, and wouldn't stop until she got rid of her *zoyer ponim* – which was Yiddish for sour pickle face.

When she'd started laughing, he'd stopped. Standing behind her, he'd rested his big hands on her shoulders, leaned over and whispered in her ear, "There's two peas in the pod, and we're two string beans. Now that's a family."

She'd turned around to face him. They *were* two string beans. They both had long pointed chins, though her father had a big scar on his. They both had wavy brown hair, though her father was missing some of his at the front and in the middle of his head. They both had brown eyes, though her father had good eyesight, while Becky sometimes had to wear ugly black secretary glasses to see things faraway. But since faraway ended up close-up sooner or later, she only wore them sometimes instead of most of the time like she was supposed to do. Both of them were skinny, even though they ate just as much as her mother and Jeffie. When Becky had seen how happy her father had been about her being a string bean just like him, she never again wished that she looked like her mother, because then her father would be all alone with nobody else in the world who looked like him, because his whole family had died during World War II.

Still, it was nice to know that she and her mother were like two peas in the pod in one way.

"So after visiting Rachel, you came home to Krasnobrod, and soon World War II began," Becky said, elbowing her mother to go on.

"There you both are," her father said. "I was looking all over for you. Come. Jeffie is singing with some other campers in a show for the parents by the lake." He stood at the edge of the blanket, his arms crossed against his chest. "So what were you two talking about?"

"Oh, this and that, nothing," her mother said, getting to her feet, then helped Becky up.

"Oh, this and that, nothing. Nothing must be good for the ears if it makes you smile and laugh, huh?" her father said sarcastically.

"You stay here and set up the picnic with Daddy. I'm going to hear Jeffie sing, and when he's finished, we'll eat," her mother said. "Okay?"

"Okay by me," her father said.

Becky was silent, not knowing what to say just in case she made him get even more sarcastic with her. The word sarcastic always made Becky think of the whizzing sound a swordsman made as he swished his sword in the air right before he stuck it through your stomach, and that's what her father's words felt like when he was being sarcastic.

Becky felt the flutter of her mother's lips beside her right ear.

"To be continued...." she whispered.

Becky turned toward her mother and whispered, "To be continued, the *Search For Yesterday* story of Hannah Simkovsky."

"Comedian!" her mother said, a little smile on her face because her favourite soap opera was called *Search For Tomorrow.*

When her mother passed Becky's father, she gave him a squeeze on the arm and an odd look, then kept going.

"So what were you two whispering and laughing about?" her father asked.

"Nothing much, stuff, you know," Becky said, shrugging.

Her father was just looking at her, so why was she so nervous?

"Secrets. Are you and your mother keeping secrets from me?" he murmured.

There was no way she was going to say what she and her mother had been talking about and get her mother in trouble. Her father hated it when her mother or any of the relatives spoke about the past in Poland.

"So you're not going to tell me, huh?" her father said, rolling back and forth on his feet.

Becky shrugged. Her father should talk. He was the one with all the big secrets.

"So keep your secrets, then," he said.

Becky glanced over at him. His shadow on the blanket was as long as the longest string bean, making Becky think of how happy he'd been that time when he'd said they were both string beans.

"Daddy," she said, stretching her good arm toward him to give him a hug. Her father stepped onto the blanket and hugged her.

"That's my girl," he said as he pinched her cheek. "The one with secrets."

HUMEWOOD PUBLIC SCHOOL

"CLASSSSSSSSSS, YOUR ATTENTION IS WANDERING," Miss Payne-in-the-neck sputtered.

"Garter snake," Becky hissed to Linda, who was seated in the desk across from Becky's.

"Nah, python snake killer," Linda hissed back, slithering her left arm on her desk, as if it was a python, over to her right arm, and grabbing it at the wrist, pretending to strangle it to death.

Becky bit down on her bottom lip so she wouldn't laugh out loud. The what-was-worse game had begun again. All during class, ever since Becky and Linda had been put in Miss Payne's Grade Seven class three weeks ago, they'd been playing the what-was-worse game about Miss Payne.

Every day there were more and more different and worse things to choose between. Like if someone took a long time answering a question, Miss Payne would start tapping one of her long feet, and say, "We're all waiting. You don't want to keep the class waiting, do you?"

What was so wrong with thinking before you spoke? Finally, someone would answer. If it was the wrong answer, the second part of Miss Payne's Chinese water torture started. "Wrong! Wrong! Wrong!" she'd yell out and push her glasses up her wormy nose like she had to take a binocular look. "How is it you don't know? Is it perhaps because you don't apply yourself to your homework? Or is it perhaps because your comprehension skills are lacking?"

In other words, you were either a lazy dumbbell or a stupid dumbbell.

This was the first time Becky had ever been in a class where nobody's hand, not even those of the biggest browners, shot up to give the right answer, because everyone was either scared of or hated Miss Payne, or both together like Becky and Linda.

Slam-crack!

Becky twitched in her seat.

"It's back for a return engagement!" Linda whispered to Becky as Miss Payne slam-cracked the dreaded pointer against her huge wooden desk. That three-foot-long pointer had already been pointed into the chest of almost everybody in the class.

But today even the threat of the pointer didn't make the class settle down and listen. There was talking, chair scraping, laughing, and the whizzing of flying spitballs, pencils, and erasers.

"Classsssssss!" Miss Payne bellowed.

"Silent movie villainess," Linda hissed to Becky as she began to imitate Miss Payne. No two people could look more different than Linda and Miss Payne. Unlike Miss Payne's black helmet of hair, which stuck together on her head like it was too afraid to move and get mussed, Linda's short red curls flopped and bounced and never stayed in place even when they were clipped down with giant barrettes. Unlike Miss Payne, whose face was as skinny as her body, Linda had a face as round as an apple, and her arms and legs were all muscles from all the running and sports that Linda loved to do. Yet right now, with her mouth wide open like she was chewing air and finding it delicious, and her arms flinging around as frantically as a drowning swimmer, Linda looked *exactly* like her.

An explosion of laughter was coming. Becky could feel it bubbling up her chest and into her mouth. To stop it from bursting out, she stuck her right fist halfway into her mouth.

"What's the worst?" Linda whispered. "Miss Payne's shiny Viking helmet hair?"

Becky took her fist away from her mouth. "Nah, the icky red-and-white scales all over her elbows are worse."

"Nah, her shark teeth are worse!"

Even with her hand back against her mouth, Becky was laughing so much that she was shaking, and that made Linda start to laugh and shake too. They both tried to stop, but the minute they looked over at each other, they started all over again.

Thumpppp! Miss Payne dropped the giant Oxford Dictionary on the floor and suddenly the class went silent. Not just because of the loud boom, but because of the look on Miss Payne's face as she bent over and picked up the dictionary and held it in her hands like she was ready to hurl it at somebody's head. Her face was now as splotchy as her elbows and her mouth open so wide that Becky bet those seated at the front could count how many of her shark's teeth had fillings.

"Now that we have your undivided attention," Miss Payne said, "take out your copies of *The Day of the Triffids*. We will be reading it out loud." She didn't sound too pleased about it, but she had no choice since the principal, Mr. Lucas, had come into the class last week with a box of books and had taken away the book they'd been reading.

When Becky had started the new book, she was surprised by how much she liked it. In the book, after a mysterious shower of meteors, everyone in England who had looked at them went blind. Only a few people could still see, like William Masen, who had been in the hospital with bandages on his eyes. And if most everybody in England being blind wasn't terrible enough, then there were the triffids. The triffids were seven-foot plants that could walk, and they killed the blind people with their poisonous stingers, then ate them. Before almost everybody went blind, they'd controlled the triffids and used them to make gas for cars. Now the triffids were in control. When William Masen took the bandages off his eyes, he was horrified by what he saw. To survive, he joined up with a group of sighted and blind people who were trying to escape to the Isle of Wight where there were no triffids.

Becky mostly didn't like to read horror stories, because there were already too many ordinary things she was worried about, without adding killer plants and showers of blinding meteors to the list. But there was something about this story that made her read on and on, even though it was the scariest book she'd ever read.

Whizz, whack, stamp, stamp, stamp. Becky turned around. Perry Bernard and Joey Gottesman were pretending to be triffids again. Pudgy Perry looked like a snarling bulldog with a red brush cut, and Joey like a half-grown gorilla with a squashed nose and a swollen upper lip. They were just as bad as triffids, if not worse sometimes, punching and kicking kids during recess and playing dirty tricks in class, like the time they'd poured formaldehyde on Billy Watson's desk and when he'd put his arms on it, he'd got an awful skin rash.

To choose someone to read, Miss Payne searched the rows like a police officer checking out a lineup of criminals. "Linda Friedman, you can begin. Everyone turn to page 15 of Chapter One, 'The End Begins.'"

"The End Begins." Every time Becky read those words, she remembered the song her mother had heard the singers sing in the marketplace.

Linda stood up, her face the same colour as her hair. There was nothing Linda hated more than having to read out loud in class.

"Linda, Linda," Becky whispered, reminding Linda that she would whisper any of the words Linda couldn't read, the way she always did when Linda read out loud. The book shaking in her hands, Linda nodded but didn't look up.

"Linda, we are waiting," Miss Payne spat out.

Linda shifted the book onto the lower part of her right arm and began rubbing her eyes hard with her left hand, as if she was scrubbing a foggy mirror clean with Windex so she could see. After Linda finished rubbing, she started coughing. Any other teacher in the school would have told Linda to go out into the hall and take a sip of water from the water fountain, then have chosen someone else to read. But not Miss Payne. She just watched Linda cough and get red in the face and tremble.

"Linda, we are waiting!"

Linda nodded, cleared her throat and began. "'I certainly was getting the willies – and once you get 'em, they grow.'"

"Louder, Linda, we want the whole class to hear you, not just those sitting around you," Miss Payne said. "And pick up the pace, we haven't got all day!"

Leave her alone, you wicked old witch, Becky thought, as Linda bent her head even closer to the book, her body shaking like she was in the middle of a hurricane.

"'Already they were past the stage when you can shoo them away by whistling or singing to yourself. Was I more scared of enranging...enmagning...dangening...'" Linda stammered.

"'Endangering,'" Becky whispered.

"'Endangering...'" Linda's voice was getting softer word by word, "'...my sight by traking...'"

"'Taking,'" Becky whispered.

"'Taking....'" Linda stopped cold, and with her left fist, started rubbing her eyes hard again.

"'...off the bandages or staying in the dark with the willies growing every minute.'" Becky quickly whispered the rest of the sentence, knowing that Linda's eyes were throwing the letters up in the air and bringing them down in a different order. It was kind of like her eyes were playing a game of Scrabble with Linda, except in this game, the letters stayed scrambled and didn't come together to make words.

"'...off the bandages or staying in the dark with the willies growing every minute,'" Becky said again, this time forgetting to whisper.

"Are there two Linda Friedmans in this class?" Miss Payne snapped. "Becky Makowiecki, if we want you to read out loud, we will ask you. Who do you think you are, a ventriloquist?"

"And Linda's the dummy!" Perry yelled out.

"Linda's a dummy!"

"Linda's a dummy!"

Picking up the dreaded pointer, Miss Payne tapped it against the side of her desk. "What is the problem TODAY, Linda?"

"The problem is my eyes," Linda answered softly, her head bent so close to the book all you could see was her hair.

"Oh, your eyes. The problem TODAY is your eyes. That's one problem easily solved. Pack up your things. You're moving to the empty desk right at the front of the classroom."

"If I get a pair of glasses, can I stay here?" Linda pleaded.

"You're moving. It will improve your vision, and no doubt, your hearing too, once you start listening in class, and not chattering away with Becky."

As Linda packed up her books and pens, she kept peeking over at Becky. Each time her eyes met Linda's, Becky felt like she should do something. But what?

"The dummy's moving to the front of the class," Joey sang out.

Linda plodded down the aisle to the desk right in front of Miss Payne's desk. Perry and Joey and some other boys were hooting and whistling and doing some more triffid stamping and whizzing.

"Class, settle down!"

There was a sharp rap on the door, then it swung open. Standing in the open door was Mr. Lucas. "Is there a situation here?" he asked in a deep voice. For a short man, he had the giant voice of a hockey game announcer. He never shouted, he never had to, because there was something about the way he said things that told you he was in the punishment business.

"No, everything is in under control," Miss Payne said, flashing her shark's teeth at him in a smile. "We have been reading *The Day of the Triffids*."

"Good, good," Mr. Lucas said. "And has it been followed by the recommended discussion?"

"Right now," Miss Payne said breathlessly, as she rifled through the papers on her desk.

"Good, good," Mr. Lucas said. "And the drill exercises?"

"Following the discussion," Miss Payne said, waving the mimeographed paper she'd been searching for.

"Good, good," Mr. Lucas said. "We will be prepared." He looked around the classroom, then at Miss Payne, and left.

Prepared for what? Another boring school assembly?

"Now class," Miss Payne said. "Mr. Lucas has suggested some additions to our curriculum this fall. The handouts are being mimeographed and will be distributed tomorrow. We have a new discussion topic for current events. The Cold War. Who can tell us what the Cold War is?"

Louie Rosenblatt shot his arm up. In the two years they had been in the same class, Becky hadn't ever heard him give the right answer to any question.

"The cold war is a war that takes place in the Arctic."

The class started laughing.

"And a hot war takes place in the jungles at the equator," Joey added.

"Classssssss," Miss Payne sputtered, then picking up the pointer, jabbed it into the air. "Since the conclusion of World War II, the United States and the Soviet Union have been in conflict. This conflict is called the Cold War, even though there's no real war, because there is an atmosphere of warlike tension between the two countries. They are competing against each other in the arms race. Who can tell me what the arms race is?"

"Is it when you have a race walking on your arms?" Louie yelled out.

Everyone laughed even more, even Becky.

"That's enough from you, Louie! Do you understand?" Miss Payne said, thrusting out the pointer like a sword.

Louie understood. So did everybody else too, and most of the laughing ended.

"To prepare for the possibility of a war, the United States and Soviet Union are in a race to build the most missiles and bombs. The United States is winning so far, and has many more missiles than the Soviet Union, and this is called the missile gap because..." she said, looking down at the paper like she wasn't sure what it meant, "...there is a big gap in the number of missiles that the two countries have built. Are we clear?"

Clear? If Miss Payne wasn't clear on what she was reading from the mimeographed handout she'd gotten from Mr. Lucas, how could she expect the class to be clear? This was a teacher?

Becky got it because of her mother's stories about World War II. The German army had marched into Poland in September of 1939 and had won the war in less than three weeks, because they had so many more tanks, rifles, and guns than the Polish army. So, since the United States had more missiles than the Soviet Union, then there was nothing to worry about. But if there was nothing to worry about, Mr. Lucas wouldn't be telling Miss Payne to teach the class about the cold war. So what was there to worry about?

The fire alarm came on. But it sounded different. Rather than being a loud clanking that went on and on like when you rang a bell, it sounded like an ambulance siren. Everybody got to their feet, ready to file out of the door to stand on the school's front lawn like they always did during fire drills.

The class door opened and there was Mr. Lucas again. He stood there in the doorway, looking at Miss Payne as if he'd like to give her a long detention. "Miss Payne, the new drill procedures...."

"We were delayed," Miss Payne said, shouting over the drill siren.

He nodded, then turned and left.

"Now class, this new drill sound is to warn us about a missile and bomb attack."

"We can't hear you!" Louie yelled.

"We can't hear you!"

"We can't hear you!"

"Duck and cover, duck and cover!" Miss Payne shouted, then crouched down and went under her desk.

"Stay there!" Perry shouted, and Becky giggled.

Miss Payne crawled out and stood up again. Over the sound of the drill siren, she began shouting one instruction after another, just like the Air Canada stewardess had done over the sound of the engine during takeoff on the plane trip Becky and her family had taken to Montreal last year to go to the funeral of her mother's Uncle Benny.

Becky groaned. Miss Payne frantically shouting instructions and explanations as the siren was going felt exactly like some stewardess instructing the passengers how to use the oxygen mask and crouch in their seats for protection as the plane was crashing and everyone was too busy screaming to listen.

She tried to listen, because she always listened to safety instructions, because you never knew. But with the sound of the siren and the laughing, she could only catch bits and pieces of what Miss Payne was saying.

Still Becky tugged her ears forward to try to hear better as she ducked and crouched under her desk, holding *The Day of the Triffids* over her head. Gazing up at the ceiling, she shook her head. Like putting a book on the top of her head and hiding under her desk was going to save her and everybody else in the class. It wouldn't protect them from Miss Payne and her pointer, let alone a missile and bomb coming from the Soviet Union through the ceiling.

Some of the others, though, had had enough and stood back or sat back in their seats even after Miss Payne interrupted her shouting of safety instructions to shout at them for the regular stuff like making too much noise and not obeying her.

"You'll be sorry!"

Becky's knees were aching from crouching and she kept bumping her head on the top of the desk, trying to do everything Miss Payne was saying. Finally the drill siren stopped and Becky got up and sat back in her chair.

"It is you who would be sorry if that was a real drill," Miss Payne gasped as she pointed the pointer at the class. "Seventy thousand people died in Hiroshima, Japan, when the Americans in World War II dropped the first atomic bomb on the city on August the sixth, 1945."

Seventy thousand people. From just one bomb. And that was from a bomb made in 1945. Probably one of the newer models could kill a lot more people, Becky thought.

All during the rest of the afternoon, everything everybody said during the math lesson, during the geography lesson, and during social studies floated by Becky's ears like whooshing air. The only thing she heard loud and clear was the sound of the school bell ringing at three-thirty.

When Becky saw Linda putting on her raincoat in the cloakroom, she ran over to her, wanting to know what Linda thought about what Miss Payne had said, and the new drill. Did she think it was a real worry like being run over by a car if you crossed at a red light? Was it a "kind of" worry like having the dentist drill your tongue by accident instead of your tooth? Or was it just a *bubbe-tall-tale* worry like if you spilled salt, every grain of salt spilt brought a new and different trouble?

"Linda, Linda," Becky said, her voice squeaky.

Linda turned toward Becky. "Yeah," she muttered, as if she was too tired to even talk. Becky opened her mouth, then closed it. Linda already felt rotten enough. Besides, nobody else in the cloakroom seemed worried or was talking about it. The usual was going on. Perry and Louie were throwing raincoats on the floor and stepping on them, so that to get your raincoat you had to drag it out from under their feet. Elise Goodman and Rhonda Erwin were standing in front of the mirror on the wall, moving their rain hats back and forth on their heads like they were models. If everybody else could forget about the bombs and missiles, then so could she. Forget about it, she told her brain, hoping this time her brain would pay attention to her.

But most times it didn't, like right now as she and Linda were walking home. It was raining hard, the wind whipping the rain, making each drop sting like anything when it hit her face and hands. Good thing for raincoats with hoods, because a half block back when the wind had blown her umbrella inside out for the third time, Becky had just given up and closed it. Since her hood stuck out a foot from her face, Becky could only see straight ahead, and to look at Linda, she had to turn her head. Which she kept doing every minute or so, because so far Linda hadn't said a word. She just nodded her head yes or no to Becky's questions.

"You wanna go to Tom's? Maybe there's some new comics in. I got some money. We can get something to eat too."

"Nah," Linda mumbled.

So they walked side by side, Becky still trying to come up with something, anything, to make Linda forget faster. They stepped off the curb and into a deep puddle. Suddenly, Linda woke up. Pushing down her hood, she began kicking her legs, splashing herself and Becky.

"Linda, stop it!" Becky said, getting upset seeing Linda so upset. "Come on, let's go!"

Linda ignored her. "Linda!" Even with her thick raincoat zipped up right to her chin, Becky was feeling more and more cold and damp. What should she do? Tell Linda she shouldn't be upset? But she should be. So would Becky be if she was Linda. Then Linda unzipped her raincoat and flung it at Becky.

"Linda, Linda, come on! You're getting soaked. Linda, stop it!" Becky said, jumping into the puddle and shoving Linda's raincoat at her.

"Leave me alone!" Linda screamed, pushing Becky and the raincoat away. Shivering, Becky hopped back onto the curb and with a sick feeling in her stomach, watched Linda jumping around, getting wetter and wetter. All at once, Linda just stopped, like a car slamming on the brakes, and stood staring at Becky. Becky then helped her put her raincoat back on.

By the time they reached Arlington Avenue, Linda's teeth

were chopping as hard as castanets. When they got inside Linda's house, they hung up their coats in the front closet.

Mrs. Friedman was sitting on the living room couch with a magazine in her lap. Even when she was in the house alone, she dressed as if she was going out dining and dancing. Her blond hair was teased, her face was covered with makeup, and she was wearing a pink fluffy sweater and a black skirt. When she saw them, she stood up fast and came over to them.

"How'd you get so wet?" she asked, grabbing Linda by the shoulders.

"Hi, Mrs. Friedman," Becky mumbled, looking up and then away.

"Answer me, how did you get so wet?" Mrs. Friedman asked sharply.

"It's raining outside," Linda mumbled at the carpeting.

"Thank you for telling me that. I didn't know," Mrs. Friedman said, then stretched out Linda's sweater sleeve. "You're soaking! Why is Becky dry?"

Linda just hung her head down.

"Answer me right now! What did you do now?" Mrs. Friedman yelled.

"Mrs. Friedman, Mrs. Friedman," Becky said, panting as she spoke. "You see, we were walking and...a moving truck with twelve, no sixteen wheels drove past, splashing puddle water all over...Linda."

Still holding on tight to Linda, Mrs. Friedman glanced over at Becky. Becky made herself look back, because if she looked away Mrs. Friedman would know for sure that she was lying.

"So why are you dry, tell me that?"

"Because...Linda was beside the curb and so most of the water hit her and not me."

Shaking her head, Mrs. Friedman glared at Linda, then Becky. "Fine, see if I care if you get sick," she said, letting go of Linda. "Go, get out of here and get out of those wet clothes."

Linda dashed up the stairs and Becky followed behind her, thanking her lucky stars once again that Mrs. Friedman wasn't *her* mother. After Linda changed into pants and a sweatshirt, Becky hung around for a while. Lying on Linda's bed, they played Crazy Eights, but the games were pretty lousy. After each game, she wanted to ask Linda whether or not she believed the Cold War was a real worry, but just couldn't. It seemed like Linda wanted to talk about something too. She kept starting to talk, then stopped in the middle. Close to suppertime, Becky got up to leave.

"Thanks," Linda mumbled as Becky left. "For what you said to my mother."

"Sure," Becky said, feeling again like she should say something but didn't know what to say. So she just said goodbye to Linda and went home.

"So how was your day?" her mother asked as she helped Becky out of her raincoat and boots.

"Okay," Becky mumbled as she placed her wet boots on a plastic mat.

"An okay you give me? An okay is a description of a whole day?" Her mother had the famous long look on her face. Her eyes were open very wide, wrinkling up her forehead, and her nose was pointing down. Following that look, her mother always shook her head and said, "Such children? How did I get such children?" After hearing that for so many years, Becky usually said it before her mother had a chance, but not today, she wasn't in the mood.

"So...." her mother said, waving one arm like a maître d'.

"Such children? How did I get such children?" Becky mumbled.

"Mm," was all her mother said as she continued giving Becky the long look. Becky just shrugged and headed for the stairs to go up to her bedroom.

Her mother whistled. "Wait one minute. What happened today?"

Becky turned and looked at her mother, then looked down at the sleeves of her white blouse. "Nothing much."

Her mother walked toward her and put her hands on Becky's shoulders. "Nothing much? What do you mean by nothing much? Since when don't you talk like a machine?" She lifted one hand from Becky's shoulder and placed it on Becky's left cheek. "Always remember, it can be very lonely and very heavy to carry a story all by yourself. That's why I tell my story to you, so you can help me carry it."

Becky leaned her head against her mother's chest and nodded, deciding to tell her mother first about her real worry which was about Linda, and save her "kind of" worry about the Cold War for later. As they both went up the stairs to Becky's bedroom, she told her mother the story of what happened to Linda at school and at home. By the time Becky had finished, she and her mother were sitting on her bed, resting against the headboard.

"You know what this with Linda reminds me of? The story of Ruthie and Lucia in the school in Leninibat, the one I went to after the Siberian labour camp. Did I ever tell you that one?"

Yes? No? Becky tried to remember. Did it matter whether it was yes or no? "Tell me and let me see if I remember."

When her mother shifted closer to wrap one arm around her, Becky smiled as she smelt her familiar smell of Evening In Paris perfume and butterscotch candy breath.

"What are you smiling about? I haven't even begun yet. Though this is a funny one," her mother said, tickling Becky under the chin to make her smile wider.

"You smell of butterscotch candies," Becky said.

Her mother shrugged. "What the heck? So I get another lousy tooth. It won't feel alone in my mouth. It will have plenty of company. Speaking of teeth, you remember how everybody in my school in Leninibat called me 'Toothless' because I was missing one of my front teeth."

"Right, right," Becky said, the story coming back to her. "Except your very best friends Lucia and Ruthie. Whenever somebody started saying, 'Toothless! Hey Toothless!' Lucia would jump in and say, 'Guess who is going to be toothless too and very soon! You!'"

Her mother laughed. "Yes, you didn't mess with Lucia if you had any brains in your head. Every afternoon, because of the war, we had army drills where we learned to march and act like soldiers. For what, I don't know. Everybody was skinny and always hungry because nobody ever got enough to eat, and lots of us were getting sick or getting over getting sick because of the dirty water we drank from a big waterhole. The water was all brown, it had green worms in it, but we had no choice, we had to drink it or go thirsty. My mother boiled and boiled the water, then poured it through a piece of cloth before she let us drink it, but still she couldn't kill all the germs."

"You and your mother, you got cholera from the water," Becky said. "And you got so weak that you had to walk with a cane for months and months." She looked down at her mother's strong legs. To think that long ago her mother's legs were so weak she couldn't walk without a cane!

"Where was I? What was I trying to bring out with this story? Oh, okay, now Lucia and Ruthie were both trouble-makers at school," her mother said, with a big grin on her face as she was remembering. "Lucia, she made trouble at school the way you make trouble at school. Knew all the answers. Sometimes, no most times, faster than the teachers, especially in chemistry and algebra. For this, Lucia didn't win any popularity contests. The teachers, young Russian men, thought she was showing off. The students, they called her all kinds of names, like *Lokshen*, because she was as skinny as a spaghetti noodle, and ugly *Mieskeit*, because she was interesting looking like, you know, the actress Bette Davis."

"That's awful!" Becky said. "Was Lucia hurt?"

"Naturally, she was," her mother said. "But remember, Lucia was a tough customer. The point I was bringing out was.... You know, I jump like a cockroach from one part to another. With this going back and forth in my story, you don't get mixed up a little bit?"

Becky shook her head hard. "I like it that you do that," she said, squeezing her mother's forearm. "It makes your story like a big jigsaw puzzle with a million pieces."

"Like a jigsaw puzzle?" her mother said, sounding surprised.

She was quiet as she eyed Becky with the long look. She opened her mouth, but before she got one word out, Becky said this time with glee, "Such children! How did I get such children?"

Laughing, her mother knocked on Becky's head. "Such a head and a mouth on you, just like Lucia's. Okay, back to the Lucia piece. Every afternoon, we did the army drills with rifles with no bullets. Soon Lucia was spinning and pointing and pretending to fire the rifle as swift as an army sergeant. A boy started with the name-calling again during the drill. Before you can say *ready, aim, fire,* Lucia had the rifle deep in his stomach. From that second on, no more name-calling from nobody."

Becky sighed. That army drill was reminding her of the drill this afternoon and her "kind of" worries. "How come you had to do the drills? Was the German army nearby? Did they ever attack?"

"Nah, the German army was thousands and thousands of miles away, too busy fighting in Europe and in western Russia to bother with us, far, far away in Leninibat, Tajikistan. It was just because some big shot in the government made a rule about all the students in Russian schools had to be drilled like soldiers. If the German army had ever showed up, the twenty rifles with three boxes of bullets at our school would have

49

kept the German army away for maybe ten whole minutes, tops. Better they would have showed us how to fight against the real enemies in Leninibat – the mosquitoes and the germs in the dirty water, and the scorpions."

Becky smiled to herself, suddenly feeling relieved. Probably the drill at her school was just the same, just for show, just a rule the school had to follow. It was nothing to worry about.

"The scorpions, they're nothing to smile at, let me tell you from experience. When I got stung on the foot, it made my whole leg get as big as an elephant's and the poison, it gave me such a fever."

What her mother had gone through, it always amazed Becky. Her mother was a tough customer. Becky wished she was too, but she wasn't. Not at all.

"Do you want to hear the Ruthie piece now or another time?"

"Now, now!"

"So now it is. Ruthie was a troublemaker too, but in a funny way. A real comedian she was, that Ruthie. The faces that girl would make when the teacher was talking. She used to stretch her ears up high and wiggle them like a bunny rabbit. Once she put a pencil on her upper lip and held it there, making the same faces as the teacher, who had a moustache, did."

"That's just what Linda did today with Miss Payne," Becky said. To think that Linda today and Ruthie long ago had done the same thing in class!

"The moustache pencil," her mother said with a sigh. "That was the end of Ruthie and school. Mr. Moustache teacher, he caught her, gave it to her but good, and Ruthie refused to go back to school."

"Why didn't her parents make her go back?" Becky asked.

"Ruthie was already a teenager, and since she never did good at school, her parents were happy to have her go to work and earn some money. Now when I think about it, Ruthie never liked to learn. Maybe that was because learning was such a big headache for her. Like for Linda."

Maybe Ruthie's eyes had played the scramble game with her, just like Linda's did. Her mother's story was making Becky feel better. Funny how her mother's stories could do that. Why was that?

"What's cooking in there?" her mother said, tapping on Becky's forehead.

"Just some stuff," Becky said.

"Well, you know what's cooking in here?" her mother said, tapping on her own forehead.

"To be continued.... Right?" Becky said.

Her mother wagged an index finger at Becky. *"Er hot a kop oif di plaites."*

That was a compliment, to be told by her mother that Becky had a good head on her shoulders. "Like mother, like daughter?" Becky asked, grinning.

Her mother hooted. "I should hope so." As she got up from the bed, she turned toward Becky. "About Linda, let me think with my head on my shoulders to find a way to help Linda that I can tell to Miriam."

"You won't tell Mrs. Friedman what I said, will you?" Becky said.

"Of course not, don't you know me better than that? Aren't I a person of tact? I'll talk around and around, then before she knows what hit her, I'll put in my two cents about Linda."

"Mummy, thank you."

"Go away!" her mother said, waving one arm. "Nothing to thank me for."

There was lots, though, but Becky couldn't say them ever to her face because her mother got all squirmy when you gave her compliments – because it invited the attention of the evil eye, she said. When her mother had first said that a long time ago, Becky had imagined the evil eye was like the sun floating in the sky, travelling around the earth, beaming bad luck onto people the way sunbeams gave you bad sunburns. At least with the sun, you could put on suntan lotion to protect you. But against the evil eye, what could protect you?

23 ARLINGTON AVENUE

Lots of kids were away from school sick with the measles like Linda was. But she would bet a dollar, maybe more, that nobody else had been as glad to get sick and stay sick as Linda was, Becky thought as she rang the doorbell at the Friedmans'.

She'd been bugging and bugging her mother to let her go visit Linda. Why could Benny Alter, the rabbinical student her mother knew from the synagogue, whom she had arranged to tutor Linda, go over to see Linda three times last week, and Becky couldn't? Because, her mother had told her over and over, he'd had the measles as a boy, so he couldn't catch them from Linda like Becky could. Only today after Dr. Pearlstein had told the Friedmans that Linda was no longer contagious had her mother let Becky go visit Linda after school.

Mrs. Friedman opened the door, and before Becky could even say hello, she'd grabbed Becky by the arm like she couldn't wait to get her inside. That was weird. Usually she hardly noticed Becky, speaking to Linda, well mostly shouting at Linda, as if Becky wasn't there.

"You see, Mrs. Friedman, I was hoping that maybe Linda could go outside with me, since she's been inside for so long, and we could maybe play catch or something."

Mrs. Friedman didn't say boo. Becky cleared her throat. What should she do? Go straight upstairs to Linda or wait until Mrs. Friedman said something back?

"Good luck to you getting her out of that room!" Mrs. Friedman said. "She's grown roots in there like a weed."

That said, she slithered through the living room, a living room so clean, as Becky's mother said, you could eat off the carpet, which looked like the Friedmans didn't walk on it but flew over it to get to the kitchen. There wasn't one couch cushion out of place, and no mail or newspapers or toys or glasses or books on the coffee and end tables. That stuff, plus vases, pictures, and fruit bowls were all over the place in the Makowieckis' living room.

"Becky, where are you already?" Linda shouted.

"I'm coming. Wait a sec!"

Hiking up her schoolbag on one shoulder, Becky went up the stairs to Linda's bedroom. Still in her pajamas, Linda was standing at the top.

"Linda!" Becky said, happy to finally see Linda in person. She galloped up the rest of the way, and Linda stretched out her arms, yanking Becky and her schoolbag up the last two steps.

"So what's new?" Becky said.

"What can be new? An ache here, an ache there. Ech!"

Becky grinned. Linda did the best imitation of Mrs. Lepinsky.

"You think it's easy to be an old person. I wouldn't wish it on my worst enemy," they both said together, smiling.

"So how is Mrs. Lepinsky?" Linda asked, as they went into Linda's bedroom.

"An ache here, an ache there, ech!" Becky said. "Why don't you get dressed and we could go see her. Every time I visit her she keeps asking me, 'How's my girlfriend Linda doing? When am I going to see her? Give her my best.'"

"Maybe tomorrow," Linda said. "I still don't feel so good." She gave a few coughs. "Let's stay inside today."

Those coughs sounded like the fake ones Becky had been practising in the bathroom to get out of going to school, but she could be wrong.

"So maybe tomorrow we can play catch outside. It's still really nice," Becky said, sniffing. Linda's bedroom stank of air freshener. Why use air freshener when you could just open the window and get fresh air? Becky remembered what Mrs. Friedman had said about Linda growing roots in her bedroom. It was a nice bedroom to grow roots in, that was for sure. Linda had a white canopy bed and a white-and-gold-trimmed matching bedroom set. But in Becky's book, having to be trapped inside even the nicest bedroom, when it was sunny and breezy outside, was like being in prison. How come Linda didn't feel that way? Becky was already feeling that way and she'd been in Linda's bedroom only five minutes.

"Can I open the window, just a little bit?" Becky asked.

"Sure, if you want," Linda said, shrugging her shoulders, then flopping down on her bed. "What's in your schoolbag? That's not all homework for me, is it?"

"Sort of," Becky said, as she flopped down beside Linda after opening the window. As she began pulling notebooks and textbooks out of her bag for the Cold War presentation everyone had to do in pairs, she told Linda what had been going on in class. Now every day, Miss Payne kept talking and talking about missiles and bombs and the Cold War. It was like being at a military academy. Everybody was already getting sick and tired of it, and when the whispering got too loud when Miss Payne was talking, she'd take the pointer, slam it against the side of her desk, and say, "If you don't listen, you'll be sorry. You'll find out!"

"You'll find out, my pretty!" Linda cackled like the Wicked Witch of the West.

Becky laughed, but she was beginning to believe that for once Miss Payne was right. Why else would she keep talking about it and why else would the class have to keep doing the stupid duck and cover every time the new drill siren went on? Becky told Linda that she now knew the bottom of her desk as well as she knew the top. There were fourteen pieces of gum stuck under her desk and two carved-in names.

"We're supposed to do our presentation on the Diefenbunker," Becky said, pointing to the textbooks and newspaper clippings she'd piled on the bed.

"Diefenbunker?" Linda giggled. "What's that?"

The reason Becky had chosen the topic was because the word was so funny-sounding that she'd thought maybe it would be a fun topic. But it was just as gloomy as the rest of the topics.

"It's a four-storey underground shelter built for Prime

Minister Diefenbaker and the government to hide in if there's a nuclear war."

Linda just looked at her.

"It's not so bad," Becky said, trying to defend her choice. "We could have got stuck having to talk about atomic bombs."

If they had got stuck with that, after learning about it Linda would probably never leave her bedroom ever again, so maybe the Diefenbunker wasn't so bad. They worked on the project together for an hour, then went downstairs to watch their favourite cartoon show starring Bullwinkle J. Moose and Rocky J. Squirrel and their battles against those dirty trickster spies from Pottsylvania, Boris Badenov and his girlfriend Natasha Fatale.

It was so hilarious that Becky forgot about not leaning back against the couch cushions in case she messed them up and got it from Mrs. Friedman. Linda was laughing so much she started hiccuping. Becky stopped laughing, though, when Boris and Natasha stole a top secret plan about how to make an atomic bomb from an American scientist who was in love with Natasha.

The Cold War and bombs, it was everywhere. Even on her favourite cartoon. Couldn't she even enjoy Bullwinkle for a half-hour without having to think about the Cold War? After the show was finished, the one-minute test of the emergency broadcast system came on, the sound so high and piercing they both had to cover their ears with their hands. When it was over, Becky was so fed up that, if it been her house, she would have thrown the couch cushions at the television. Instead, she just messed them up more, not caring what Mrs. Friedman did to her.

"Some test, that is," Linda said with a groan. "We'll all be deaf by the time the bomb hits."

"Did you ask your mother what we're supposed to do, if it's real and not a test anymore?" Becky asked, the question slipping out without her even knowing.

"Yeah, my mother said if I ask her one more time, it's curtains for me!" Linda said, then made the motion of a knife slashing her throat.

In spite of herself, Becky giggled, but she shouldn't have, because you didn't know what Mrs. Friedman could do when she got really, really angry. More than once she'd seen Mrs. Friedman slap Linda so hard across the face that her cheek had glowed red for minutes, and every time the Friedmans and Makowieckis went out for dinner, Mrs. Friedman never stopped picking on Linda about everything and anything. Once Becky had asked her mother why Mrs. Friedman treated Linda like that. Her mother had just sighed and said that Linda was different than the kind of daughter Mrs. Friedman had expected.

Being different seemed to bother lots of people, and they always seemed to be trying to stomp it out, like they were squashing all different sizes and shapes of potatoes into a mush of all the same mashed potatoes.

Now, personally, Becky liked different. Different was interesting. But Linda's being different, just like Becky's being different, was nothing but trouble a lot of the time. It made people notice you, and once they noticed you were different, it was goodbye Charlie and hello woe is me!

"Give up asking your mother, I gave up asking mine," Becky said.

"Why?"

Becky just shrugged, not wanting to admit that when she'd asked her mother she'd gotten so jumpy that Becky had started talking about something else.

Becky asked Linda again if she would go outside for a short game of catch, but she wouldn't, so they watched more television. Becky kept peeking out the window and saw the blue sky lose its blueness and turn grey as if it had been washed too many times.

Mrs. Friedman came into the living room. "So girls, you had a good time together?" she asked as she came over and stood beside the couch.

"Yeah, a great time, Mom!" Linda said.

"Me too," Becky said, trying to figure out a way of looking at Mrs. Friedman while straightening the couch cushions at the same time.

"Good, so then you can go outside with Becky and play before supper," she said.

Linda coughed. "I still don't feel so hot."

Mrs. Friedman snorted. "That cough is as real as my hair colour. Tomorrow, you get out of those pyjamas and you go outside to play with Becky, do you hear me?"

Linda hung her head down and stared at the tiny roses on her pyjama bottoms.

"Supper will be served in half an hour," Mrs. Friedman said.

When Becky stood up, ready to go home, Mrs. Friedman

pressed a hand on Becky's shoulder. "I called your mother and said you're having supper here."

"Okay," Becky whispered, wishing she could go home.

Unlike the Makowieckis, who only stopped talking at dinner to swallow or chew, the only noises at the Friedmans' dinner table were chewing and slurping sounds. Did the Makowieckis also sound like vacuum cleaners when they ate? Becky hoped not.

It was dark by the time Becky got home. Her father opened the door for her. "Why the sour face?" he asked.

Becky shrugged.

"Okay, don't tell me, like you don't tell me anything," her father said, sounding hurt.

She didn't mean to hurt her father's feelings. It was just that her feelings were all mixed up right now. "All the Friedmans do is chew, chew, chew like cows at supper. Nobody talks!"

Her father smiled. "So you missed the Makowiecki mouths?"

Becky nodded. From the living room came the sound of the TV. "Jeffie there?"

"Where else, and on top of the television," her father said. "Jeffie, move away from the television, right now!"

"How do you know I'm near? You can't see me," Jeffie said back.

Her father stepped into the living room and Becky followed behind him. There was Jeffie, lying on his stomach with his nose practically on the television set. As usual.

"Now I see you. Was I wrong? Move, this second!"

Jeffie wiggled back a few inches.

"More!"

Jeffie wiggled back another few inches.

"Now stay there!" their father said, then left the living room.

Jeffie waited a minute, then wiggled all the way back until he was in front of the screen. Becky left him and went upstairs to put her school things away. When she came downstairs, as she entered the living room she heard a man with a deep voice announce, "There will be a one-minute test of the emergency broadcast system."

Not again. Wasn't having her eardrums attacked once enough for today?

"What's that again?" Jeffie asked, rolling over onto his side so he could look at Becky and the television at the same time.

"Don't know," she lied, looking away.

Then the lousy, piercing, high-pitched sound came on for a minute.

"That noise again! Dogs must be howling from here to Buffalo," her mother said as she came into the living room, wiping her hands on her apron. "You, Mister, you're close to the TV, shut it off before we start howling along with them."

Jeffie wiggled over and shut off the TV, then turned to face their mother. "What's the test for?"

"Mm," her mother said, then tugged on one earlobe. "If there's an emergency...."

Her mother caught Becky staring at her. "Why are you looking at me like that?" she said. "Don't look at me like that. This is nothing. Ignore it."

How could you ignore it?

"What kind of emergency, Mummy? Tell me, tell me?" Jeffie said, crawling over to their mother and grabbing hold of her ankles.

"If you want to know, Mister, let go of my feet," her mother said, staring hard at Jeffie until he let go. She then ran one hand through her hair. "Mm, the station...the station makes the noise when....when a tractor-trailer truck has an accident and flips over, blocking all the lanes on the Queen Elizabeth Highway and then no cars can travel between Buffalo and Toronto. Okay? Satisfied? The apple strudel is almost done. I can smell it. I have to turn off the oven."

Then she dashed out of the living room. Becky and Jeffie looked at each other. "Mummy must know," she said, wanting Jeffie to believe that was the reason.

"You think so?" Jeffie asked.

"Of course," Becky said. "Let's watch, okay?"

Jeffie turned on the TV again and went back to his favourite position inches away from the screen as they watched *The Dick Van Dyke Show*. Becky continued to watch after her mother took Jeffie upstairs to have his bath. Nothing good was on, so she kept getting up and switching channels, until the channel switcher dial fell off. This wasn't her day. She pulled out the television plug and tried and tried to put the dial back on but couldn't, and just left it on the top of the television for her father to fix.

She went upstairs. From the bathroom came the sounds of splashing water, Jeffie's giggling, and then her mother. "Mister, I'm not taking a bath. You are. Splash me one more time, and you're out of that bathtub, one, two, three."

Becky stood in the doorway of the bathroom. Her mother was kneeling by the bathtub, shampooing Jeffie's hair.

"Let me finish here with Jeffie, and then come downstairs with me and keep me company while I iron. I want to hear how Linda's doing," her mother said.

While her mother dried Jeffie and got him ready for bed, Becky went downstairs to the basement. Her father was saving up money to turn it into a rec room with a tiled floor and wood panels on the walls. Right now, unfinished, it was a good setting for a horror movie. There were no light fixtures, only three bare bulbs with metal chains that you had to yank to turn them on and off. The stairs didn't have a railing; the floor was concrete and so were the walls. The furnace chugged away in one corner and in another corner there was a wringer washing machine and a big sink. In the wintertime, her mother strung a clothesline from one wall to the other, where she hung the clothes to dry. When Becky had been little, she'd never gone downstairs alone, and even now, in the second before she leapt up to yank on the light bulb chain hanging above the second step, she felt that old rush of shivering fear as if there was a monster or a mad killer hiding in the dark.

The light showed that all there was, was clothes on the line, which Becky took down and placed in the basket for ironing. By the time her mother came downstairs, Becky had set up the ironing board and was ironing the pillowcases – her mother only let her iron the bedding; the rest, she did herself.

"So how come Linda doesn't want to go outside?" Becky blurted out.

"Hold your horses. Some people, they think better on their feet. This tired person thinks better sitting down, feet up." Her mother opened up one of the folding chairs stored in the basement and sat down, resting her feet on the laundry basket.

"Now, how to say this? Every person escapes trouble in a something. My family, we escaped in wagons, trains, boats, and more than a few sometimes, in just a pair of worn-out shoes. You, my darling daughter, escape trouble by travelling in all the dreams you have in your head. Am I right? Somebody's blushing, I just know it," her mother teased.

Becky was too embarrassed to look up at her mother.

"Do you think I tell you this to shame you? You think you're the only person on earth who escapes into their imagination? If people didn't escape their troubles by making up things, we wouldn't have books, plays, and movies, and there would be even more unhappy people. The imagination can be a very nice place to escape to. You think all the times me and my family were escaping on boats that made me seasick, on wagons so bumpy that my *kiskehs* felt like chopped liver, I wasn't doing my own escaping in my head? When we were in the Siberian Labour Camp with snow and ice everywhere, you think every day I wasn't escaping to a warm place with lots of flowers and trees?"

Becky raised her head from the ironing board and glanced at her mother. "Tell me the Siberia story."

"What about the Linda question, you want it answered now or after the Siberia story?" her mother asked.

Before Becky could answer, her mother said, "It just came

to me. The Linda question, it can be answered by the Siberia story."

"Really?" Becky asked, squinting at her mother. "How?"

"How? You'll see how, how's that?" Eyeing the ironing board, her mother said, "That pillowcase, it looks finished to me. Maybe next, a sheet."

Folding up the pillowcase, Becky placed it on the end of the board, took a sheet from the basket, and arranged it on the board for ironing. "Can we begin the Siberia story after you had to leave Krasnobrod because the German army had burnt it to the ground?"

Her mother nodded. "A beginning's a beginning. I can begin my story at any place in my story. Except the ending, of course. So since you chose the beginning, you begin."

Becky sat the iron up, then began. "After the German army beat the Polish army, they took control of the country. They divided it in half, taking half for themselves and giving half to Russia, because Russia was then fighting on Germany's side against England, France, and the rest of the armies from all the Allied countries. Zaide, he didn't want to live under the rule of the Germans, so he decided you should all go live in the Russian-ruled side of Poland. When you got to a town there, it was terrible. There was no place to sleep. And everybody hated you and called you names. Zaide and Bubbe met up with three other families from Krasnobrod, and all of you together broke into a synagogue and hid in the basement. Then...then...."

Becky paused. She didn't want to make a mistake. If she made a mistake, it was like saying to her mother that she

65

hadn't been listening carefully enough to her mother's story. But this part was kind of confusing.

"You look like you need a little help. Maybe I should tell this part, and you can listen and iron," she said.

"Thanks, Mummy. I can tell more later, okay?"

"And why not? You're the expert on my story," her mother said, smiling.

The expert! Feeling proud, Becky smiled, and started ironing a bedsheet.

"Okay, so where were we?" her mother asked.

"The synagogue," Becky answered.

"Right, right. It was so bad, imagine, that Zaide had enough and wanted to go back, even though our village was gone, burnt to the ground, and with the Germans ruling. He was homesick. One day, on the main street, a Polish army officer riding on a horse was shouting out that any Polish citizens who didn't want to live in the Russian-ruled side of Poland could return to the German-ruled side of Poland. All they had to do to return home was to sign some papers. So Zaide and Bubbe signed the papers. And that very evening, on the Sabbath, Russian soldiers came to the synagogue and arrested us and everybody else in town who had signed the papers. They said we were German spies."

"German spies?" Becky said, surprised as always. How could anyone think that the Simkovskys were German spies?

Her mother shook her head. "Us spies? So our family and the rest of the *big German spies,* poor families with small children and babies, with no homes, no food, no nothing, we were arrested for being German spies, and for punishment, a

Russian judge, he sentenced us all to hard labour and put us on wagons and sent us off to a Siberian labour camp north of Novosibirsk."

The second her mother said the word Siberia, Becky saw a land that went on for miles and miles and miles, covered in deep, deep snow. Siberia was a northern region of Russia and the Russians built lots of prison camps there. And why not? As her mother always said, even if a prisoner escaped, where could he or she go? If a prisoner escaped in the winter, he or she got frozen in the snow, and if he or she escaped in the summer, he or she either got lost in the swamps and got bitten by millions of bugs, or got swallowed up by giant pools of mud, mud so thick and sticky that if you were lucky it only sucked off your boots and shoes and not your whole foot.

"Can I tell this part? I remember it good," Becky said, standing the iron up.

"Of course you can tell it, so what's next?" her mother said.

"So after weeks and weeks on trains and boat barges and trucks, you reached the Siberian labour camp."

"Such a wilderness. I didn't know there was such a wilderness in the world," her mother added.

"You lived in a wooden barrack with ten other families. Each family was assigned a tiny little kiosk with wooden bunk beds. Zaide, Chaim and Rivem worked building more barracks, and Bubbe did sewing. You did the cooking on a stove where you had to wait and wait your turn before you could use it, because there was only one stove for all the families. And one night you couldn't sleep and looked out the window. And who looked back but a huge brown bear, and boy did you ever scream loud!"

Her mother grinned. "That was some huge brown bear. I had a right to be scared. A bear had just killed a man who was working building a barrack. So after the bear, then what?"

Becky tapped her finger against her bottom lip. "It's *your* story. You know."

Her mother pointed at her. "I gave it to you. So it's your story now too. So you tell for a while, because my poor tired jaws, my poor tired voice, they need a little rest from talking the whole day long."

Becky scratched her head. After the bear at the window, what came next? She thought and thought, trying her best to put her mother's story in the right order.

"Your family was in the Siberian labour camp prison for more than a year."

Her mother nodded.

"In 1941, the English told the Russians, who were now on the side of the allied countries fighting against Germany, to free all the Polish citizens they had put in labour camps in Siberia. And Stalin, the Russian leader, did."

Becky never understood this part very well. From what her mother had said, Joseph Stalin, the Russian leader with the big moustache, was evil too, just like Adolf Hitler, the German leader with the little moustache.

"Why did Stalin agree to let the Polish citizens out of the camps?" Becky asked.

"You see, Russia now was at war with Germany and losing badly, and to continue fighting, they needed help from

England and the allies. So Stalin let the Polish citizens out of the camps, but there were still lots and lots of poor Russians in the camps during and after the war."

Sighing, her mother stretched out her hand and took Becky's right hand in her left and squeezed it. "You thought I forgot about Linda?"

Becky's face got all hot again, because she had gotten so wrapped in her mother's story that she'd forgotten about Linda herself.

"Now how does Linda and the Siberian labour camp part of my story fit together, you are asking yourself right now," her mother said. "Remember how before, when we were talking about Linda, we talked about how different people escape trouble in different ways?" her mother asked.

"Some people escape in trains and boats, and others, they escape trouble in their imaginations," Becky said.

"Linda got sick, and think how unhappy Linda was at school, so that as awful as the measles are, those pains were less painful than the pains she suffered at school."

"Yeah," Becky said, remembering the horrible day at school when Miss Payne and some kids had been so mean to Linda when she'd read out loud. "Okay, Linda doesn't want to go back to school, who would? But why doesn't she even want to go outside?"

"Why?" her mother asked, pushing her hair off her forehead with one wrist. "Let me travel back to Siberia to explain why. What a person can get used to! In Siberia, you got used to the bitter, bitter cold, and you got used to the hard, hard work, and you got used to the bread that tasted like paper, and the soup that tasted like heated-up dirty water with a few grains of rice in it, and you even got used to those bedbugs that bit you all over all night long.

"So when the guards came to us all in the barracks and said, you are free to go, you are no longer prisoners, my family was glad, but still, this place was a terrible we knew, we were used to it, and what kind of terrible was waiting for us, outside the labour camp, this we didn't know. But Zaide and Bubbe, they were brave and tough, especially Bubbe, and she said, we made it so far, we'll make it a little farther. So let's pack and go. But two of the families in our barrack, they didn't want to leave, they were afraid to leave.

"You see, Linda, she leaves her bedroom, and she doesn't know what's coming up...like the trouble at school, whether it's disappeared or waiting for her. So she stays in her bedroom.

"The same with the two families that chose to stay in the Siberian labour camp. The camp was a terrible prison, but they knew its terribleness, inside and out, and to them, that made it safe. They thought they could last out the war in the camp. Maybe they did, maybe they didn't, who knows? We thought the conditions in the camp were so terrible that we would not survive the war there, so we escaped. But where to go? Where to escape to so we could all be safe? It wasn't safe to go back to Poland, with all the fighting and killing going on. And a blessing from God that we didn't. The camps there...."

Every time her mother mentioned the camps in Poland, she wouldn't say anymore about them. Becky had tried and tried to get her mother to tell her about the camps in Poland. But so far, even after so many tellings of her story, her mother had not told her what the difference was between the Siberian labour camps and the camps in Poland. The Siberian labour camps sounded pretty horrible to Becky. Were the camps in Poland even worse? But how? "The Jews in the camps in Poland, they were working hard like you did in the labour camp?" Becky asked.

A strange expression came over her mother's face. Becky was sorry right then and there that she'd asked her mother again.

Her mother hunched forward and hugged herself. "Not exactly. It's not to tell now. Later when you are older. No more questions about the camps in Poland. Promise me?"

"I promise," Becky said, storing away the camp question with all the other questions her mother wouldn't answer just yet. But still, what did her mother mean by not exactly?

Her mother stretched her arms in the air and as she brought them down, she looked at her wristwatch. *"G'vald,* look at the time!"

"It's 'to be continued' time," Becky said, folding up the bedsheet that she'd mostly ironed out and switching off the iron. That was good enough, it only got wrinkled up in five minutes once you lay on top of it in bed, anyhow. "But this part hasn't ended yet?"

"The ending to this part. Okay, Goodbye cold, goodbye brown bears, and good riddance Siberia, I said to myself when my family got on a truck to leave. We travelled and travelled deeper south in Russia on barges, boats, trains, and sore feet until we got to Leninibat, a tiny town in Tajikistan, a Russian republic bordered by China on one side and Afghanistan on the other. To be continued."

Her mother stood up and they climbed the stairs out of the basement. "Mummy, how long will it take for Linda to feel better and want to leave her bedroom? A couple of days? Longer?"

As Becky got to the top of the stairs and entered the kitchen, her mother, who was behind her, reached up and pulled the light bulb chain off. "A person's time to feel better cannot be timed like baking a cake. Before you know it, Linda will be back with you at school and telling you to hurry up and eat your Mister Softee ice cream cone before it drips even more over your blouse."

Becky gave her mother a tired smile. Linda liked to gulp down her ice cream like a sword swallower, while Becky licked hers slowly to make the pleasure last and last.

They walked through the kitchen and living room and up the stairs to the bedrooms.

"Now, go to sleep," her mother said, after she'd kissed Becky good night. "And don't go over to the window to wait for...? Who was supposed to come to take you away...? Ah, I remember, Tinkerbell," her mother kidded.

"Mummy, I haven't done that for *years,*" Becky mumbled.

"Good, so I'll see you tomorrow morning, then," her mother said, as she went down the hallway.

RUSHTON ROAD

To TELL JEFFIE THE REAL TRUTH OR TO TELL HIM HARDLY any truth, what should Becky do? Should she warn him, just like her mother always warned her, that it was dangerous out there on the streets? Knowing *that,* did it keep her safe or did it just make her neck hurt from always twisting her head around to look over her shoulder for danger? *That* was on her mind like a too tight hat today because there was no way around it, she and Jeffie had to go down Rushton Road to get to Abie's butcher shop so they could buy the chicken necks and brown eggs her mother needed for supper.

Today, like every day, as Becky was getting ready to leave for the butcher, her mother, along with the six dollars she gave Becky to pay the butcher, gave her *the daily warning.* A week ago, it was "the sidewalk's slippery from rain, so don't run because you will fall and break a leg!" Two days ago, it was "the traffic lights are out at Vaughan and St. Clair, so don't cross the street there, or you'll be hit by a car!" Today, it was "those no-goodnik Gottesman brothers! Watch out for them and hold on tight to Jeffie."

Becky would, once Jeffie was done retying the laces on his sneakers for the sixth time, because they were almost at Rushton Road. Every three houses, they'd had to stop when Jeffie saw that the laces on his sneakers were loose again.

"Let me do it myself!" Jeffie said, each time Becky asked if she could tie them up so tight, once and for all, that he'd have to use scissors to cut them off his feet. Since it was important for Jeffie to learn how to do it all by himself, Becky let him, but that didn't mean she was happy about it.

To teach him the right way to tie up laces, Becky was untying her sneaker laces and tying them back up at the same time he was tying up his. But Jeffie liked his way better than the right way, so it meant it was going to take *hours* to get to Abie's shop.

"Finished?" Becky clutched her hands behind her back so that they wouldn't swoop down on Jeffie's laces and give them a tie they'd never forget.

"In a sec," Jeffie puffed.

Whenever she stepped onto Rushton Road with Jeffie, she held his hand as tight as a handcuff as they got nearer and nearer to the Gottesman brothers' house. The three brothers, Fred, Leonard, and Joey all looked and acted like ape men. They ruled over Rushton Road like trolls. They threw rocks and garbage at kids. And they chased after them, and if they caught them, beat them up. Just last week, they'd given Frankie Mankiewicz a black eye, and the week before, they'd given Mark Goldblatt a bloody nose. And the great mystery was, when they'd never, ever, lost a fight with any kid, how come all of three of them always looked so beat up themselves? Joey was never without bruises on his face and welts on his arms, and he'd had a couple broken fingers last year. Becky figured that the brothers must be practising fighting on each other at home.

When Jeffie stood back up, Becky tightly clutched hold of his right hand and began to drag him along.

"You're hurting me! Don't pull me so fast!" Jeffie wheezed, as Becky tugged him so fast that he was practically flying behind her like a kite.

"So move faster, then I won't have to pull you, okay?" she said, slightly out of breath from having to tug Jeffie and from being on the lookout.

"I can't, I can't, I can't," Jeffie said, sticking out his bottom lip – the surefire sign he was getting ready to cry.

"Okay, okay," Becky said, trying to walk slower as she looked right, left, then behind her for any sign of them. When they finally reached Abie's Butcher shop, Becky knocked three times on the wood frame of the door. They'd done it! They'd made it down Rushton Road without running into and having to run away from the Gottesmans.

"Why do you always run on this street?" Jeffie panted.

So Jeffie had noticed. What should she say? He'd only really noticed the Gottesman brothers the one time when their father had been hitting them as he'd ordered them into their station wagon. "Look at that mean Daddy!" he'd said, pointing to Mr. Gottesman. Even though she hated them, it had been pretty horrible to watch their father punch at them like a psycho boxer.

"We weren't running, we were just moving fast to get to Abie's before he runs out of chicken necks," she said, knocking three times again on the door frame. "Your laces. They've come undone AGAIN!"

As Jeffie knelt down to retie them, Becky opened and closed her mouth, almost ready to tell Jeffie the real truth about the Gottesmans and to warn him to run for his life if he ever saw them coming for him. Yes, no, yes, no. No. No. NO. No, she wouldn't scare Jeffie with the real truth and real warnings. What was the point? Bad things always found new and unexpected ways to get to you anyhow. And besides, she didn't much like always feeling like Chicken Little, worrying and waiting for the sky to fall on top of her, and she didn't want Jeffie to feel that way too. No, she wasn't going to warn Jeffie about them. Or anything else. She would just keep on hoping – she knocked three more times on the wood frame – that if something bad should happen, she would be able to run away fast enough, dragging Jeffie along with her.

HIROSHIMA, JAPAN

"YOU SEE, INSIDE THE ATOMIC BOMB IS SOMETHING LIKE a gun barrel, and when you set off the bomb trigger, it shoots these tiny particles called neutrons at the stuff that makes the bomb explode – the atoms inside uranium and plutonium. One uranium atom hits the next uranium atom in a chain reaction...until kaboom!"

Perry stopped in the middle of his presentation on the atomic bomb to glare at his partner Marty Rappaport, who looked like he'd fallen asleep on his feet. Marty's long brown bangs were over his eyes, his square chin touching his chest, his long, skinny arms hanging loose.

Becky sighed. Only Marty Rappaport – the sleeping pretzel as he was called in class, because he could fall asleep anywhere in any position – could fall asleep in the middle of Perry giving the class the willies in the worst way. Perry had the same thrilled-to-be-rotten expression on his face he always had when he was telling some kid he was going to get him during recess or after school. No wonder he was so thrilled now; instead of giving just one or two kids the willies, he got to do it to thirty kids at once. Becky had always thought nothing could be worse than having Miss Payne at the front of the class, but Perry was worse. Much, much worse!

"KABOOM!" Perry shouted, and Marty jerked, as if he just woke up. He bent over and started going through the cardboard box at his feet. Since Marty stuttered, Perry was doing the talking during the presentation and Marty was holding up pictures and diagrams. When Marty found the picture he was searching for, he held it up.

"You see...." Perry glared again at Marty who was holding the picture too low for anyone to see except the kids stuck at the front of class. Like Linda. Becky strained her neck to the right to try to see how Linda was doing. She'd bet ten dollars that Linda was sorry she'd ever left her bedroom to come back to school for this. She probably wasn't the only one sorry they hadn't stayed in bed this morning. With the blankets over their heads. Becky was too.

Even with her glasses on, all she could see was Linda's hunched back. If only Linda would turn her head so Becky could see her face, but she didn't. When she looked away from Linda and back to the front of the class, Marty was holding a picture of an atomic bomb explosion over his head.

"You see..." Perry went over to Marty and, using his ruler like Miss Payne used her pointer, pointed to a gigantic flash of light as brilliant as the sun. "...when the bomb explodes, it first turns into a HUGE FIREBALL. The fireball is millions of degrees hot and is thirty times brighter than the sun. It's so hot and so bright that when you look at it, it burns your eye-balls out!" he said, his voice breaking with excitement.

That must have been what happened to the people who watched the meteor shower and then went blind in *The Day of the Triffids,* Becky thought. It was probably a new kind of sneak attack atomic bomb that when it exploded looked like a meteor shower to fool people. So *that's why* Mr. Lucas had put the book on the new curriculum because it was about...his favourite subject, the Cold War.

She had never seen Perry ever work so hard on a class presentation. Usually he copied it straight from the World Book encyclopaedia – she knew because she had the same encyclopaedia at home. This time he had so much information he and Marty must have copied stuff from a couple of encyclopaedias.

Usually during a presentation, there was chair scraping, whispering, and laughing. Not today. There was only the sound of Perry's telling more and more gory stuff about the atomic bomb.

Nuclear war with nuclear bombs. Becky's ideas about war came from her mother's stories of what the war had been like in Poland. The bombs used in World War II were made of ammunition just like bullets in a gun were. When the pilots dropped the bombs out of the plane, the bombs destroyed whatever they hit, and the worse was over. But from what Perry was saying, the worse just began after a nuclear bomb exploded. Unlike the old-type bombs, which turned buildings into stone and rubble as if they'd been hit by a giant hammer from the top, the uranium and plutonium atoms in a nuclear bomb worked like a chemistry experiment by a mad magician. The atoms sizzled together, and when the fireball hit, buildings just disappeared. They turned into vapour and dust and rose in the air, becoming a cloud in the shape of a mushroom.

"You see...." Perry said, now tapping his ruler on a picture of Hiroshima, Japan, after the first atomic bomb was dropped on it by the US Army Air Force B-29 bomber. Over the five square miles where the bomb had exploded, it looked like part of the city was missing. What was left looked like a rocky desert.

"And if you think that's bad, wait till you see what the bomb did to the people," Perry said. Marty bent over and started going through the box. "The bomb, it makes radiation. You know, like in an X-ray machine. All the stuff – the parts of the buildings, the earth, the dust that got sucked up by the fireball – it falls back on the earth. That's why it's called fallout. The fallout looks like a do-nothing snowflake or piece of dust, but it acts like an X-ray machine that zap, zap, zaps you with radiation. And these radiation zaps, they're real killers. They make you barf, your hair falls out, you get a high fever, bad stomach pains, and then, after a few days, you die! It's called radiation sickness!" Perry said, smirking.

"Perry, that's enough!" Miss Payne said gruffly. She was leaning against the door. If she wasn't a teacher and had to be in the room, Becky bet Miss Payne would have pushed that door open and run down the hallway and everyone in the class would have followed quickly behind her.

"I'm almost finished," Perry said.

"Finish up, and fast!" Miss Payne said.

"Marty, you found that picture yet?" Perry snapped.

The class watched Marty root through the box. It was no wonder he was having trouble finding it. From what Becky could glimpse under his bangs, his eyes seemed to be squeezed into tight slits. When he found the picture he was searching for, he closed his eyes and held it up. It was the most horrible picture Becky had ever seen in her whole life. It showed a photograph of people in Hiroshima with radiation sickness. Becky whipped her glasses off her face, sorry like anything that she'd put them on to see the presentation.

"That's more than enough from you, Mister Perry Bernard!" Miss Payne screeched. "Put that picture back in the box immediately, Marty!"

Marty did, dropping it as swiftly as if it was a match burning his fingers.

Perry strutted down the aisle to his desk like he was a prize fighter who'd just won a championship, while Marty skulked behind him, his head bent so he didn't have to look anybody in the eye. He didn't have worry about that. Everybody in class was hunched over their desks, like passengers crouching down during an airplane crash.

Becky's head started spinning. That Perry! He was even worse than Becky's Aunt Frightful. Practically every time Becky and her mother had the bad luck to meet the Frightful on the street or in some store, the first thing she said after hello was, "Guess who died?" Neither Becky nor her mother ever wanted to know, but did that ever stop the Frightful from telling them?

The drill siren went off. And for the first time Miss Payne didn't have to shout, "Duck and cover! Duck and cover!" Without any complaints, everybody quietly and very quickly got under their desks.

17 ARLINGTON AVENUE

"You know, this isn't five-pin bowling," Linda said, laughing.

Becky watched the white blur of the softball whiz past her catcher's mitt and strike down the three empty milk bottles her mother had left standing next to the milk box at the side of their house. She dashed over to straighten them up, then tried to stuff them on top of the three other empty milk bottles already in the box, but of course it didn't work because if it had, her mother would have put all the bottles inside.

So Becky just left them standing there, and picking up the softball, dashed over to the driveway where Linda was waiting for her to throw it back.

"Maybe you should put on your glasses," Linda said when Becky got back into position on the driveway.

Becky took off her mitt and went through her jacket pockets looking for her glasses. Like they would help. The problem wasn't just seeing the ball, the problem was catching it, and for that she didn't just need glasses, she needed another arm that could catch balls instead of waving hello and goodbye to them as they whooshed by.

Winding up her arm the way she'd watched real baseball players do when she, Linda, and Jeffie had gone to see a couple of minor league baseball games at Christie Pits in the summertime, she threw the ball to Linda, who had no trouble catching it.

"Ready?" Linda asked, as she raised her arm to throw it back.

"Ready," Becky said, pushing her glasses up her nose with her catcher's mitt, then holding the mitt up in the air. As she saw the ball come toward her, Becky leapt up, her glasses slamming down onto the bridge of her nose. She saw the ball all too clearly graze the top of her mitt and head like a missile right for the milk bottles, striking them all down again.

"Beck-ee!" Linda said, now laughing so hard she had to sit down on the curb. "You've never been this bad before! What's wrong with you?"

What *was* wrong with her? More than the fact that she was crummy at catch, and worse than usual, thanks to the fact that every time she saw the ball whiz past it made her think of missiles. Which made her think of Perry's presentation about atomic bombs and radiation sickness. When she got a worry into her head, it stuck like it was glued to her, even though she tried her best to do what Mrs. Lepinsky always told her to do. Let it go, Mrs. Lepinsky told her. If she didn't let go of her worry, it wouldn't let go of her. That was hard enough to do when it was just a worry that Becky had alone, but when it was a worry – like the worry about a possible nuclear war – that her whole class, Miss Payne, and even

Mr. Lucas shared, it wasn't so easy to do.

"Let it go, let it go!" she whispered to herself as she walked over to Linda and sat down beside her on the curb.

"Let it go? That's what you say to yourself when you're supposed to be catching a ball? You're supposed to say, come to me, come straight to me!"

"I could yell that at the top of my lungs and the ball would still go right past me," Becky said glumly.

"Probably!" Linda said, still laughing.

"Thanks," Becky said, lightly punching Linda on the shoulder.

"Caught a fly?" Linda said, pointing to Becky's mouth, which was open because she mostly breathed through her mouth and not her nose.

Becky closed her mouth and just as she was about to pretend she was spitting out a disgusting fly, she froze. Coming toward them on his bike was Joey Gottesman. He squealed to a halt in front of them. Most times Becky was never near enough to him to see his face close up like now. He looked like the Frankenstein monster. Big, ugly red stitches were slashed across one of his cheeks, and there was dried-up blood at the bottom of his nose like he'd been punched there.

"Still got the cooties, Friedman?" Coughing and sneezing on purpose, he said, "Oh Miss Payne, I can't read because I'm a dummy. I'm a big dummy!"

"Get lost!" Becky said softly, edging closer to Linda, who had turned a bright red.

"What'd you say? Can't hear you?" he said, sticking his Frankenstein face right against Becky's.

"GET LOST!" she shouted and, surprising herself, shoved him away so hard that he fell back onto the road.

As Joey got up, he grumbled something that sounded mean. Becky's knees started to knock. Was this the end? Was Joey going to strangle her to death in broad daylight? Praying that her legs would hold her, Becky stood up. "Shoo, shoo!" she said, fluttering her arms like Mrs. Lepinsky did whenever a bee came near her.

"Shoo, shoo!" Linda said, standing up fast and fluttering her arms too.

Squinting, Joey stared at them like he didn't know what to do.

"Is this boy bothering you?" her father asked, suddenly standing behind them. They both turned around to look at him. He was still in his work clothes, a grey cotton shirt and pants streaked with grease and dirt from twisting wires to make springs for mattresses.

He wrapped his arms around them and just stared long and hard at Joey, like the actor John Wayne had at that slimy killer Liberty Valance in *The Man Who Shot Liberty Valance*. Her father had taken her and Linda to see it at the St. Clair theatre.

Joey shifted from foot to foot, like he was nervous about exactly what Becky's father was going to do next. Grab him by the collar and shake him? Yell at him? Threaten him? That was her father's greatest power, you could never tell what he was going to do.

"Was this boy bothering you?" he asked again, in a low voice.

Becky and Linda exchanged glances. Should she tell her

father the real truth? If she did, would Joey get back at them with his brothers along to help him finish the job, or would her father scare Joey off once and for all?

"A little," Becky whispered, deciding that the "kind of" truth might be safer in the long run. You never knew just how rotten bad mean those Gottesmans could be.

"Get going!" her father said in a voice that said loud and clear that if Joey didn't, her father was going to do something...that would make him very sorry he hadn't.

They all watched as Joey scrambled onto his bike and rode fast down the street like one of the Wicked Witch of the West's flying monkeys.

"Thanks, Pilgrim," Linda said in her John Wayne voice, as she smiled widely at Becky's father. Every since they'd seen the western, Linda had been calling Becky's father "Pilgrim," just like John Wayne called the other hero in the movie – Ransom Stoddard, played by James Stewart.

Her father winked at Linda and pretended to tip a ten-gallon cowboy hat at her. "No thanks needed, little lady!"

Linda giggled, then blushed red again, this time, though, because she was happy. Linda got along better with Becky's father than practically anyone else did. They were always kidding around.

"Thanks a lot, Daddy!" Becky said.

"That boy, he won't bother you again!" he said.

Becky hoped like anything her father was right.

CARP, ONTARIO

FOR ONCE, EVEN MISS PAYNE WAS IMPRESSED BY SOMETHING Linda had done. Linda had chalked a diagram of the Diefenbunker's four stories under the ground in a farmer's field in Carp, Ontario, that was as detailed as an architect's building plan.

Becky and Linda took turns explaining what was on each floor and why. You entered the Diefenbunker through a long blast tunnel, then went inside it through steel doors. Right there were decontamination rooms where everyone who came in had a kind of Geiger counter run over them to see if they had radiation on them. If they did, they had to take a special shower and their clothes were put in lead-lined hampers so the radiation couldn't leak out. Once they were clean of radiation, they stepped into the main part of the Diefenbunker, which was a combination hotel, government building, and military headquarters all in one. Inside it were bedrooms, bathrooms, kitchens, food storage rooms, dining rooms, conference rooms, offices, a computer room, a CBC radio studio, and a weather station with equipment to measure the amount of radiation in the air. There was a hospital and even a morgue, in case anybody died when they were hiding inside to avoid dying outside from the radiation.

"How's it decorated? Like the Prime Minister's house at 24 Sussex Drive?" asked Rhonda.

"Did they bring in antique furniture and an oil painting of Queen Elizabeth?" asked Elise.

"How's it decorated? Did they hang a picture of the Queen? What kind of stupid questions are those?" Judy Levin asked, with a big groan. "What do you think the Diefenbunker is? A big Barbie's dreamhouse? When you're lucky to be alive inside, do you care that you're sleeping on a cot and not on a four-poster antique bed?"

Perry and Joey whistled and stamped their feet. Before Miss Payne could tell them to pipe down, Judy turned around and spat out "IDIOTS!" shutting them up faster than Miss Payne ever had.

Becky had to look down at the floor, because she knew if she looked over at Linda, they'd both start laughing. That Judy Levin had guts! She sat a couple seats ahead of Becky in the next row. Judy's family had just moved to the neighbourhood, and this was only Judy's first month in the class, but you wouldn't have known it from the way Judy acted. Even though she was even shorter and skinnier than Becky, she talked and walked like a tall, tough person.

Becky liked her. When Linda had been home sick, Miss Payne had made her and Judy partners for three chemistry experiments. And for once, Becky was glad about something

Miss Payne had done. Judy had told Becky that her father was a lawyer and his motto was, "I give guff, I don't take guff!" And that was Judy's motto too. Even with Miss Payne.

"So who gets to go inside there after a b-bomb explodes?" Marty Rappaport stuttered.

Poor Marty! Doing that presentation with Perry on the bomb and having to look at those pictures had really scared him, and why not? He must have seen those pictures once or twice, even though he'd held them up with his eyes closed shut.

"It's big enough to hold five hundred people," Linda said, stepping away from the blackboard and toward the teacher's desk. "It's for government and military leaders...and of course for Prime Minister Diefenbaker."

"But what about...everybody...else?" Marty Rappaport stuttered out.

He wasn't only the only one thinking that, Becky thought as she looked around the classroom and over at Linda.

THE HOSPITAL FOR SICK CHILDREN

As BECKY WAS GOING OUT THE DOOR, HER MOTHER YELLED from somewhere in the house, "Take Jeffie with you, will you. He's inside too much!"

"Okay, okay, okay," Becky muttered, even though she wasn't in the mood this afternoon to be stuck after school with Jeffie. But why not? Nobody else was around. She'd called Linda, who was in the middle of a tutoring lesson with Benny Alter. She'd called Mrs. Lepinsky, who was in the middle of a canasta game, and she'd even gotten up the nerve to call Judy Levin, who had to be in the middle of something too, because nobody had answered at her house.

"Jeffie, come outside with me!" Becky said, going into the living room. He was racing his Dinky cars up and down the couch.

"Okay," he said, stopping playing right away. He must be really bored if he was coming without a "long discussion" as her mother called it.

"Where are we going?" Jeffie asked as he went over to the

closet to put on a jacket.

"Don't need a jacket. It's warm outside," Becky said. It was the second week of October, but it felt as warm as May.

"You taking Jeffie?" her mother yelled out.

"I'm TAKING Jeffie, okay!"

"Make sure to take care of him. He's the only brother you've got," her mother yelled.

"Don't I always?" Becky yelled back.

"Okay, okay, don't get so hot. In case you forgot, I thought I would give you a little reminder," her mother yelled.

"How could I forget! You tell me the same thing every time I go somewhere with Jeffie!" Becky yelled back.

"Let's go already," Jeffie said, tugging impatiently on Becky's sleeve. "Bye Mummy, I'm going with Becky. NOW!"

"So who's stopping you? Go already. Have a good time," her mother yelled out.

"We're going!" Becky yelled back.

"How long will we be going for? Let's GO!" Jeffie said, no longer tugging but yanking Becky toward the door.

Becky opened the door to go out, then paused. "If Linda calls, tell her I'm outside with Jeffie and to look for us. No, better call me and I'll talk to her."

"If Linda calls, you will know. I will stop traffic all the way to St. Clair Avenue because I will shout so loud. Happy now?" her mother yelled out.

"Very happy," Becky yelled back.

"Let's goooooooooo!" Jeffie screeched.

So finally they went. Outside on the street, Becky stood

in front of her house, trying to make up her mind what to do. Not that there was a lot to choose from. There was just Eddie Gelbert and some other kids who were playing hide-and-seek across the street.

"Can we play hide-and-seek with Eddie and them, over there?" Jeffie said, pointing. "Can we? Can we?"

She squinted to see if there were any kids Jeffie's age playing. She couldn't see any. They were mostly older. Even if she could get them to include her and Jeffie, it wasn't hard to guess how the game would go. Jeffie wasn't so good at hide-and-seek. He always seemed to choose a bad hiding place, like a hedge that was too short, so you could see the top of his head over it. If there were some other kids Jeffie's age playing, it wouldn't matter so much, because most of them were as bad as Jeffie. But the older kids would get tired fast of finding him so easily and then just ignore him, leaving Jeffie just sitting there.

"Puh-leeze, puh-leeze, Becky," Jeffie said in a tiny voice. "Just one game!"

"All right!" Becky said, sighing.

"We're playing, we're playing too!" Jeffie said as he ran on his short chubby legs toward Eddie.

Kicking her feet in the dirt, Becky followed behind, hoping the game would be over fast. It was. But one game became two games became three games, and Becky had had enough. It was sunny and warm and she didn't want to have to hide in another damp, dark place. Besides, hiding was reminding her of having to hide under her desk every day in class, and that was reminding her of why they had to hide, and that was reminding her of what Marty had said after she and Linda had given their presentation on the Diefenbunker.

She went over to look for Jeffie and found him hiding behind a hedge that was missing so many branches and so many leaves that you could see his blue sweatshirt through the holes. Crouching down by one of the bigger holes in the hedge, she stuck her arm through and wiggled her fingers at Jeffie. "Let's do something else!"

"No, I wanna hide still!" he said.

Becky didn't call sitting behind a hedge filled with holes that you could stick arms through hiding, so she made a snorting sound.

"Let's go!"

"No, I wanna hide still. Go. I'm not a baby!" he said.

"Yes, you are so!" Becky snapped.

"AM NOT!" Jeffie hollered.

"Are so!" Becky hollered, then stood up and went around the hedge and tried to grab hold of Jeffie's arms.

"No!" He hit her arms. "I want to play more!"

"You played enough, let's go!" Becky said, getting mad as Jeffie continued to hit her. Not that it hurt much, but still.

"Leave me alone! Go away!"

Becky stood up. "I'm going!" She ran across the street, flung open the screen door, and knocked hard on the front door.

"Why are you knocking on the door like a crazy person? I left it open for you two!" her mother yelled from someplace in the house. "So lock it behind you, now!" So Becky did and stomped into the living room. "Did anyone call for me?" she yelled.

"Who are you expecting to call? Hollywood? They didn't call!"

It was times like this that if Becky didn't like her hair so much she would have ripped it out, she was so mad! Why shouldn't she knock on the door like a crazy person and yell like a crazy person and be as mad as a crazy person, when everybody and everything was driving her crazy! She flung herself onto the couch, and lay there for a minute, then sat up, and kicked her feet against the bottom of the couch.

She jumped up and went over to the phone and dialled Linda's number. When Mrs. Friedman answered, she hung up fast. Then she dialled Mrs. Lepinsky's number. When one of Mrs. Lepinsky's canasta ladies answered the phone, she hung up fast. She glanced over at the television. She could watch something on television, but then there was a chance, more than a chance, that she'd have to listen to another test of the emergency broadcast system, and if she heard that she might do something really crazy like....

What could she do? She could do the homework that her Hebrew school teacher, Mr. Elkin, had assigned. No, she definitely wasn't in the mood for that, not that she ever was. How many years of Hebrew school had she had, and while she sort of could read Hebrew, could kind of write it, she still couldn't string a sentence together to speak it. Unlike either of her parents, when it came to languages, she was no fast learner. Just the opposite. Of course, her parents had wanted to learn English, and Hebrew school was nearly always the last place on earth Becky ever wanted to be trapped in. Cross out Hebrew school homework! So what was there to do?

While she was deciding, she heard a light thumping on the front door. Probably it was Linda. She must have finished her lesson early. Becky raced to the door, flung it open, and there was Jeffie standing there sobbing, dressed only in his pants and sneakers, his sweatshirt gone.

She stepped onto the porch, stumbled and almost fell on top of Jeffie, clutching onto his shoulders to catch her balance. When she took her hands away, they were bloody.

"I just knew that rotten Rufus was going to bite somebody sooner or later," Becky gasped out, practically feeling like fainting as she pictured Mr. Rutland's German Shepherd leaping up onto Jeffic and biting him on the shoulders.

"It wasn't him, it was the Gottesmans. They bit me," he wept, turning around to show her his back. His back was covered with bloody teeth marks.

"Bobby and me were hiding, and they found us. They chased us, but Bobby got away."

She stretched out her arms and held Jeffie against her. "Mummy! Mummy! MUMMY COME!" Becky howled.

"So what's now?" their mother said as she came onto the veranda. "Blood, where's all the blood coming from?"

"The Gottesmans, they bit Jeffie on his shoulders and back. Look, Mummy, look!" Becky said, her heart pounding like it was going to explode in her chest, as she spun Jeffie around. Jeffie had stopped crying and his face was as white as snow. When their mother saw all the bites, she got as white as Jeffie. She knelt down, lifted him up and cradled his head against her shoulder.

"What are we going to do Mummy?" Becky asked, holding onto the material of her mother's blouse as they went inside.

"Becky, run upstairs, get Jeffie a shirt, and bring me down a bottle of iodine, two facecloths – make them wet and soapy – and a dry bath towel. I'm going to call Daddy at work, then a taxi, and we're going to take Jeffie to the hospital."

"The hospital?"

"The bites – Jeffie – he could get an infection," her mother said. "Now go quick!"

With a last glance at Jeffie, who was so still in their mother's arms that Becky was getting more frightened by the second, she dashed upstairs. In the bathroom, she soaked two facecloths in the sink, squeezed the water out of them and soaped them up, grabbed a towel off the rack and a bottle of iodine from the medicine cabinet. In Jeffie's room, she chose his biggest, loosest shirt and a windbreaker, then ran back downstairs.

Her mother took everything from Becky. Jeffie was sitting on the edge of the couch, as stiff as a mannequin in a store window. Her mother went over to him and cleaned his bites with the wet cloths, then patted them dry and applied iodine. Knowing how much iodine stung, Becky flinched each time her mother swabbed the iodine on the bites, but Jeffie didn't move an inch. Why wasn't he crying? His quiet was worse, much worse. After he was dressed, they all put their jackets on and waited outside for the taxi.

Five minutes later the taxi arrived. Her mother told the driver to take them fast to The Hospital for Sick Children. Jeffie was so still that Becky kept reaching over and putting her hand on his back to make sure he was breathing. She shouldn't have gotten mad at Jeffie. She shouldn't have left him alone. She shouldn't have shoved Joey onto the road. And she shouldn't have told her father the "kind of" truth about it. She should have told him hardly any truth. The less you had to do with the Gottesmans the better, and between her shoving and her father giving Joey a look that said, you'd better watch it or...else, all that was like waving a red flag in front of a bull in a bullfight. What else would Joey do but get back at them by siccing his brothers on Jeffie.

"Mummy," she whispered, looking down at the cigarette butts on the floor. "I'm sorry. I shouldn't have left Jeffie alone."

"No," her mother said. "You shouldn't have. But what's done is done. But promise me, never again. He's the only brother you have. You're the only sister he has."

"I promise," Becky said, forcing herself to look her mother in the face. She would make it up to Jeffie, she would.

The driver let them out at the emergency entrance. Inside the hospital, a nurse took Jeffie out of their mother's arms and put him in a wheelchair, and they went with her down a long corridor. The nurse reached a small room and placed Jeffie on one of the beds in it. Before the doctor came to check Jeffie over, the nurse cleaned up the bites again with a germ killer. When she was almost through, the doctor came in. He examined Jeffie, and when he was done, he came over to Becky and her mother who were leaning against the other bed.

"Your boy will be fine. I'm going to give him a tetanus shot, and put some gauze over some of the larger bites on his back."

"Thank you," her mother said.

On the way back home in another taxi, Jeffie slept in their mother's lap. Each time Becky looked over at him, tears gushed out of her eyes. This was all her fault.

Their father was pacing on the veranda when the taxi pulled into the driveway. He hurried down the stairs, opened the taxi door, and carried Jeffie into the house and up the stairs. As Becky and her mother went through the door, her mother put her hand on Becky's head. "I'm going to make a fast supper. When Daddy comes back downstairs, keep him company, okay, do that for me?"

"Okay, Mummy," she mumbled. "Daddy? Is...is he mad at me? Will he...give it to me?"

"No, your father is not mad at you," her mother said, sighing. "Your daddy, just like me, knows too well what it is like to want the best for people and still not be able to help them."

What did her mother mean by that? Before she could ask, her mother had left the living room. Becky sat down on the couch, but then got up. The clock chimed seven times. It was only seven o'clock, but it felt like three days had passed. Becky didn't know what to do with herself. She went over to the circus puzzle that she and Jeffie had been doing on the coffee table, flipped through the box, searching for the pieces for the lady on the flying trapeze, found a couple, put them in place, then jumped up when she heard the sound of her father's footsteps on the stairs.

He walked in, dragging his legs like he could barely lift them to take a step. His eyes were all puffy and his face splotchy. Should she go over to him or not? Then he raised his arms and Becky rushed over to him and hugged him, and he hugged her back. "I'm sorry, Daddy, it's all my fault," she said, feeling tears again gushing down her face.

""Don't talk to me about this is your fault. The animals that bit Jeffie, it's their fault, nobody else's," he spat out. "What a day! What a day!" He let her go and they sat down on the couch. He picked up the *Toronto Daily Star* newspaper from the end table, rifled through it until he found the section with the comics. Handing them to her, he began reading the front section.

Becky tried to read but couldn't; she peeked over at her father. His hands were shaking, making the newspaper rattle. From the way he was quickly turning from page to page, it seemed like he was having trouble reading too. After going through two sections, he tossed the paper onto the puzzle on the coffee table.

"So Becky," he said, clearing his throat.

Putting the comics down in her lap, Becky looked over at him. Had he changed his mind after thinking about it and was going to give it to her now?

"Daddy?"

"Becky?"

They both spoke at once, then stopped.

"You go first," her father said, rubbing the beard stubble on his cheeks.

"No, you go first," she said.

"These boys, these boys that bit Jeffie, you know them," he said.

"Yeah, remember the boy on the bike that you said

wouldn't bother me and Linda anymore, it was him," Becky paused, suddenly realizing what she'd just said sounded like she was kind of saying to her father that he couldn't protect them.

"I remember," he said, in a low voice. "Tell me about them. I promise you, they won't bother you ever again."

As Becky was in the middle of telling her father every mean, rotten thing the Gottesmans had done to kids at school and in the neighbourhood, her mother called them into the kitchen for dinner.

"Thank you, Becky, this is good to know," her father said when Becky ran out of Gottesman stories as they were finishing eating supper.

"You know this mark on the side of my forehead," her father said, pointing to a dark spot on his left temple.

Becky nodded.

"I got it from a bully. When I was maybe a year older than you," he said, with a sigh. "Right before the war started."

Startled, Becky looked over at him. Her father was talking about his past? Did her father want to begin talking about his past or had it just slipped out like secrets sometimes did?

"What happened?" she asked.

"My big brother, Hershel, he had to stay late at school. So that day, I walked home alone. Boys from school, they followed me, calling me 'dirty Jew' and...the rest not to repeat. With my big brother, we would fight back when we were called names. Alone, three against one, it's not such a good idea. So first I walked fast, then I ran, but they caught up to me anyway and threw snowballs with rocks in them at me.

One hit me, where the spot stays. Stitches I had to have."

Becky waited for her father to say more. But he didn't. Was he silent because he was remembering or because he was trying to forget? Maybe she should ask another little question about his past "Daddy..."

Her mother put her index finger over her mouth and shook her head at Becky.

"I have a bully story too, and I have a mark too, from some bullies. On my right knee," her mother said, stretching out her leg and pointing to her knee. "I was going home from school too, and some bullies, they started picking on me. So I threw stones and twigs, whatever I could find loose on the road at them...."

"That's my Hannah all over," her father said with a smile. "Excuse me for interrupting."

"Not so smart when there's many of them, and only one of you. They chased after me. Then, no more big hero. I ran. You know, in small villages like Krasnobrod, the roads were made of cobblestones. Near a house, I fell down and ripped off all the skin on my knee. I'm a goner, I said to myself as the bullies surrounded me. Who should come out of the house but an old lady with a big broom. She beat the boys with the broom, yelling *Gai avek, mamzers! A finister yor!*"

"What does that mean?" Becky asked.

"Go away, monsters, and your future should be cursed," her mother said.

"Like a witch would say?"

Her mother nodded. "The old lady, she looked like a witch. She had tangled grey hair, not many teeth, such a pointy chin. She looked like a witch so the *mamzers,* they ran away."

"But she wasn't a witch," Becky said. "She was a brave and kind old lady."

"Exactly," her mother said. "She took me into her house, washed up my knee, wrapped it with a piece of cloth, and gave me a piece of strudel."

Becky looked at her father, then back at her mother. So many things had happened to them in their lives, and while she knew lots about her mother's story, she knew next to nothing about her father's. Would she ever know?

Her father stood up from the table. "I'm going over now to speak to Mr. Gottesman. Sixty-six Rushton Road, that's the house?"

Becky nodded.

Her mother said something to Becky's father in Polish, and he said something back in Polish. Whenever her parents didn't want her or Jeffie to understand what they were saying, they spoke in Polish, so Becky called Polish "the big secrets language."

"You and Jeffie will have nothing to fear no more from them. I will make sure," her father said, coming over to Becky and kissing her on the cheek. "I will take care of this," he said, then left.

"I wash, you dry?" her mother said, getting up and going over to the kitchen sink.

"Okay," Becky said, getting up too.

"You know when I had you, and then I had Jeffie, I said to myself, what more could a mother wish for? A happy, healthy girl, and now a happy, healthy boy. But there was one more thing I wished for...."

"What was that?" Becky asked as she twisted up the towel to stick inside the glasses she was about to dry next.

"I wished for something I never had. I wished that you and Jeffie would always love each other, take care of each other, and be friends. This I never had, ever, from my brothers," her mother said, her head bent over the sink as she scrubbed a pot.

Becky knew her mother and her two brothers, Chaim and Rivem, didn't get along so good. But she didn't know it was that bad.

"Did I ever tell you about Rivem and the chocolate bars? No, I never told you," her mother said, answering her own question. "This was in Germany. After the war, in Pocking, the displaced person's camp. A soul I didn't know. So Bubbe, she would tell Rivem, when you go out, take your sister with you. He would take me all right, and when we left the camp, he would run like a racer because he didn't want me with him, and I would run behind him trying to catch up. Most times, I couldn't, and I would be left alone on the streets, and I had to go back to the camp, because a girl wasn't safe alone."

"That's so mean!" Becky said.

"Rivem was full of mean tricks," her mother said. "In charge of the camp were American and British soldiers. Once a week, for a treat, the soldiers would give each of the children and teenagers in the camp a carton of milk and a chocolate bar so thick you couldn't cut it with a saw. Such a treat it was to drink the milk and scrape off pieces of chocolate and have them melt in my mouth. Did I ever look forward to that chocolate! But that chocolate came to me with a fight to the finish with Rivem. Once he saw the soldiers leave, he would come over to me and punch me to get my chocolate bar. I wouldn't give it up, but he was bigger and stronger than me, and lots of times, after a big fight, he would take it away from me."

"That's horrible!" Becky said, shocked. No wonder her mother still didn't like Uncle Rivem. Who would?

"I tell you this just so you will know why I want you and Jeffie always to be close to each other, and good to each other, that's all," her mother said, handing the pot over to Becky to dry. "Finished! I'm going to check on Jeffie. You wait for me in the living room and I will tell you the story of my mother and the German soldier. It's time you knew."

In the living room, Becky went back to working on the circus puzzle. Finding the right pieces for the right spots was taking longer than most times, because she kept thinking about the new stories from her mother...and her father too. Lately, all the new parts in her mother's story were sad, like the part about the singers in the marketplace singing about the end of the world coming and the story about how mean Uncle Rivem was. It used to be that her mother's story was mostly an adventure story. But not anymore.

"Jeffie, he's sleeping deep," her mother said as she came into the room and sat down on the couch beside Becky.

"So where was I? I remember, the German soldier and Bubbe," her mother said. Then she was quiet for the longest time, and from the way her face kept changing every minute, Becky could see that her mother was remembering things,

things she probably wouldn't be telling her, even if Becky asked a thousand and one questions.

"Mummy, tell me again what happened when you all hid in the forest?" she asked.

Her mother sat up very straight, then began. "The battle between the German army and the Polish army near Krasnobrod was over one, two, three. The German soldiers who were mostly in tanks shot down with machine guns the Polish soldiers who were mostly on foot, until there were no Polish soldiers left, only bodies all over the ground. Remember, most of the houses in Krasnobrod were made of wood and straw. So when the Germans finished killing the soldiers, they began firing at the barns and houses. They fired at a barn, poof, it went on fire, then the farm next to it went on fire, and the house next to it went on fire, and before you knew it, all that was left were some brick houses and stores which didn't burn. There we were in the forest, watching our village burn to the ground, right before our eyes."

Since then, her mother was afraid of fire. Her hands would shake every time she had to strike a match to light the Sabbath candles.

"And then what, Mummy?" Becky asked.

Her mother looked down at her wedding band which she began to twist around and around.

"Before the German army had come to our village, Bubbe had put our best things in bundles and stored them in the basement of one of the brick stores near the marketplace. After the fires went out, Bubbe and me, we came out of the forest and went into Krasnobrod to see if the store was standing. It was," her mother murmured.

Becky's heart began to beat very fast. She peeked at her mother, who was still twisting her wedding band round and round her finger. Was her mother's heart beating fasting too? To find out, she placed her hand on the left side of her mother's chest.

"What are you doing?"

"Nothing," Becky mumbled, snatching her hand away quickly. Her mother's heart seemed to be beating the same as always.

"Well, are you going to tell me or not?" her mother asked again, louder this time.

"Hmm," Becky mumbled.

"Aha, aha!" her mother said, suddenly grinning as she thumped her chest like Tarzan. "It's still ticking. Better than a Timex watch. It took a licking, but it keeps on ticking. So I should go on?"

Becky shook her head, yes. Nothing much ever got past her mother. Then when her mother wasn't looking, Becky placed her hand back on her own heart. It was beating like a tom-tom.

"So you and Bubbe went to the store to get your bundles back, then what?" Becky asked.

Her mother gave Becky's arm a squeeze. "You're not going to get upset, are you? If you're going to get upset, maybe this part should wait for later."

"No, no, please tell me now. I won't get upset," Becky said, then she almost changed her mind. But if she did, then she would never hear the whole, complete story of her mother's life and then how could she be the expert on her mother's story?

"By the time Bubbe and I reached the store, there were lots of people there. There were German soldiers who were taking the bundles from the store's cellar and throwing them onto the muddy cobblestones. There were Jewish families who had come to pick up their bundles, and some Polish people from our village and from some other villages. Laughing the whole time, the German soldiers threw the bundles one by one into the mud. Plop! Plop! Plop! Then after all of the bundles were out of the cellar, when some Jewish people tried to get their bundles, the German soldiers snapped their whips, and said, 'Get away, you vermin *Yids!*' and called over the Polish villagers to take whatever *Yid* bundles they wanted."

Picturing the scene, Becky saw the Jewish people all huddled together, some crying, some yelling and cursing, as they watched their bundles being thrown on the street. She saw the Polish people all huddled together on the other side, some of them grabbing the bundles, some of them not knowing what to do, and others just walking away. Standing in the middle of the Jewish people was her Bubbe, her hair still black, her face not wrinkled yet, and her mother, as small as Becky, her long sandy hair tied up in one long braid.

"Bubbe was very brave," her mother said slowly. "When she saw her two bundles in the pile, she wanted them back. In the bundles were her best dress – a beautiful brown velvet dress with a pink velvet bow – and Zaide's only good suit. They were presents from Canada, from Zaide's brother

Benny. When Bubbe saw one of the soldiers spear one of her bundles with his rifle, hold it up and shout, 'Who wants this *Yid* bundle?' Bubbe shouted back, 'It's mine, give it back to me!' Then in a second, Bubbe was running over to the soldier to snatch her bundle off the end of his rifle."

What a brave but dangerous thing that was for Bubbe to do, Becky thought.

"Bubbe tried to snatch the bundle off his rifle. Then the German soldier, he whipped his horse and the horse stood up on its hind legs. Did I get a fright! It looked like the soldier was going to hit Bubbe, maybe kill her even with his rifle, so I ran fast over to help her. When I got close to the soldier, he kicked me in the face, knocking out my front tooth and breaking my nose. Bubbe picked me up and carried me back to the forest. She took me to a cold stream where she ripped off the sleeve of her dress, made it cold with the water and put it on my nose to stop the bleeding and swelling.

After that, I had trouble breathing through my nose. During the war, wherever we went, people made fun of me and called me 'Toothless' – remember this I told you already. To hide it, I got into the bad habit of covering up my mouth when I talked. I can't remember when and where I got the new gold front tooth. But the nose, I remember. After the war, I was sent to a hospital run by nuns, and a doctor fixed my nose, so I got a new nose to go along with my new tooth."

Her mother paused, then leaned back against the couch, closing her eyes. "Give me a minute to rest, okay?"

"You mean a Makowiecki minute or a real minute?" Becky teased, because when any of the Makowieckis said a minute, what they meant was a minute that could be as long as ten minutes.

Her mother wrinkled her nose. "A Makowiecki minute, what else?"

A long time ago, when Becky's mother had started to tell Becky her story, Becky had kept interrupting her mother with a million and one whys. Why was there a war? she'd asked. Because Adolf Hitler, the ruler of Germany wanted to gobble up and rule all the countries in Europe, so that in time he could rule the whole wide world, like the devil ruled hell, her mother had answered.

Why did nobody in Krasnobrod fight back when the German army came to the village? Why did everybody hide? she'd asked. Many Polish boys and men had joined the Polish army, just like they did in all the countries in Europe and in England to fight back against Hitler, her mother had answered. But for some people, like the Jews whom Hitler especially hated, often the very best and only way to fight for their lives was to hide and escape, her mother had added.

Wasn't it important to fight back? Becky had asked. Yes, her mother had answered, but it's important to pick your fights. You should fight the fights you could fight, like when some-body wanted to do something you knew was wrong – then you fought back. But sometimes, you fought best by hiding. Like when Hurricane Hazel had come to Toronto. If you had fought the hurricane with galoshes and an umbrella, you could have been very hurt by the strong winds and the flood waters. But if you hid in the basement, you saved your life.

"So where was I?" her mother said, opening her eyes and

shaking her head from side to side like she'd just woken up from a nap.

"Bubbe ripped off her sleeve to use as a facecloth on your nose," Becky said.

"Right, right."

"Mummy, why did Bubbe fight the Germans for the bundle?"

"Bubbe fought back because she believed that it was wrong for the Germans to take things that people worked very hard for and loved, and just throw them in the mud like garbage or give them away to other people, and...well, that's enough for you to know for now, Beckelah," her mother said, rubbing her temples as if she had a headache.

Though Becky knew why her mother had run over to Bubbe – because she loved Bubbe and wanted to save her, there were still many whys that her mother had never answered...yet. Like why had Hitler hated the Jewish people so much he wanted to kill them? And why hadn't God done anything to stop him? Every time Becky had asked those whys, her mother had just said, she would say why when Becky was old enough.

Was she old enough today? She glanced over at her mother, who looked so sad. No, she wasn't old enough...yet.

Her mother sighed loudly. "What we went through! But not so bad when you think about what many others went through. We survived, the whole family," her mother said.

The front door squeaked open, and Becky and her mother looked at each other. Her father was back from the Gottesmans. He shuffled into the living room, looking awful, like he was going to faint or something. His face was sweaty and around his lips there were traces of what seemed like barf.

"Daddy, what happened?" Becky raced over to him. Close up to him, she saw she was right. Her father had thrown up. She could smell it on his breath. Just what had happened over there?

"Ira," her mother came over, and helped Becky's father off with his jacket. "You threw up?" she asked with concern.

Nodding, he rubbed the back of his neck.

"Let me bring you some ginger ale to settle your stomach," she said, and went to the kitchen.

"Daddy, you okay?" Becky said, patting her father's right arm. Had her father gotten into a fist fight with Mr. Gottesman? She studied him carefully. No, it didn't seem like it. He didn't have bruises on his face, and his clothing was all neat – which it wouldn't have been if Mr. Gottesman had done to her father what she and Jeffie had seen him do to his sons outside their station wagon.

Her mother returned with a tumbler of ginger ale that her father gulped down in one swallow.

"So, Ira?" she asked, in a very worried voice.

Her father answered in Polish. While he talked, her mother nodded, adding a few Polish words here and there, and then to Becky's shock, tears trickled out of her eyes.

Maybe her father had gotten into a terrible fight with Mr. Gottesman. Or worse.

"You have to tell her," her mother insisted.

Usually when her mother told her father that he had to

tell something or other, mostly he didn't. He just clammed up worse.

"Becky, sit down with me on the couch," her father said in a voice that sounded like he was struggling not to cry. What had happened? He was scaring her.

Her father sank down onto the couch and Becky sat beside him, and her mother went to the kitchen to refill the tumbler with ginger ale.

"The boy in your class...."

"Joey," she said.

"This Joey, he comes to school lots of times, looking like he was in a fight?"

Becky nodded. "He always has bruises on his face and his arms. Now he's got stitches across his face like the Frankenstein monster. Why?"

Sighing loudly, he shook his head. "What the boys did to Jeffie – terrible, just terrible. But you go into that house, and in a minute, you see why the boys are wild animals, with a father like that.

"I told the father what the boys did to Jeffie, and one by one he ordered them to come to the living room. The oldest, he came first and the father, he picked him up by the shirt collar, strangling him almost, and asked him if he did what I said he did, screaming 'No lies this time or you'll really be sorry.' The oldest then admitted what he did to Jeffie, and the father slugged him, he fell to the ground, and the father kicked and kicked him, didn't stop for a second, and the boy crawled out of the living room. I was sick watching, just sick.

"He called in the middle one, took the belt off his pants

and whipped him everywhere, the face, the arms, the back. The boy howled and howled. The boys deserve punishment, but this, never this." Her father stopped, and rubbed an index finger under his right eye, then his left, like he was drying tears.

Becky inched closer and put an arm around him, and he leaned against her.

"You get the picture," he said, in a tired-out voice.

Becky did, feeling sick just as her father was. It was no wonder that the Gottesmans were bullies and worse if that was the way they were treated by their father. How could she feel sorry for them after what they'd done to Jeffie and so many other kids for so many years, but she suddenly did.

Her mother came back with more ginger ale which her father again gulped down. "Ira, why don't I make a nice hot bath for you to soak in?"

"Okay," he said, then turned to face Becky. "Becky, don't look so worried. It's just everything all together today, it got to me, but I'm okay. And the Gottesman boys, from today forward, they will stay away from you and Jeffie and Linda."

"Thanks, Daddy," she murmured.

Wearily, he waved his hand. "Let's not talk about it any more. Jeffie, how is he?"

"Sleeping," her mother said.

"Good, good, by tomorrow or the next day, he will forget," her father said.

Becky didn't think so. It was hard enough to forget mean little things like being called names or being picked last for a team, let alone forgetting being bitten all over by three

Gottesmans. No, she didn't think Jeffie would forget that any time soon, or that the rest of the Makowieckis were going to able to forget this day for a very long time.

BUCKINGHAM PALACE
& SCHWAB'S DRUGSTORE

THE NEXT MORNING, INSTEAD OF JEFFIE DRAGGING BECKY out the door like always, it was Becky who had to drag Jeffie out. By the time she half-carried, half-pulled him down the stairs, she was breathing as hard as Mrs. Lepinsky sometimes did when they went for walks together and Becky had forgotten she had to slow down so Mrs. Lepinsky could keep up. Most times, Jeffie ran ahead of Becky, and she was running after him, shouting for him to slow down! Not this Saturday morning. If Jeffie got any closer to her, he'd be her Siamese twin.

"Want to play some soccer?" Becky asked because it was one of his favourite games.

"What?" Jeffie asked, looking as if he thought the Gottesmans were going to pop out like an evil jack-in-the-box any minute. She remembered her father had said the Gottesmans would leave them alone from now on. Becky wanted to believe him, but she wasn't so sure. Would they stay away because of what their father had done to them or would they want to pay her and Jeffie back, but good?

"First, blow the whistle to see if it works good," Becky said, as she stood with Jeffie on the sidewalk in front of their house. He was wearing a whistle around his neck on a shoelace, so he could whistle for help if he ever needed it fast.

He blew the whistle, and several dogs barked back, but thank goodness one of them wasn't Rufus. That's all she needed today, Rufus snarling and sniffing around her.

"Pretty good, huh?" Jeffie said.

"Too good!" Becky said, rubbing her ears. "Now we are going on a special tour of the street. The super-duper-hiding-place tour."

Like a real estate agent selling hiding places, Becky pointed out all the possible hiding places on their street. She pointed to the crawl spaces under verandas, garage sheds at the back of driveways, and if worst came to worst, empty garbage cans.

"There too?" he said, pointing to the tiny crawl space under their own veranda as they returned to their house.

"Yup, there too!" Becky said. "Just big enough for the two of us!"

"Just us!" he said.

"So how about some soccer?"

Dashing up the porch stairs, she picked up the soccer ball. As they played on the lawn, Jeffie kept kicking her ankles even more than normal and he clutched the whistle every time he heard a noise that could be a Gottesman brothers' noise, like bike tires squealing or kids squealing at the sight of them.

Was Becky ever relieved when the Mister Softee ice cream

truck came rolling down the street. One more game with Jeffie and she'd need crutches to walk. She bought two vanilla swirl cones and as they stood there slowly licking them, she saw Joey and Fred on their bikes heading down the street.

What should she do? Did she want to find out now if what her father had said about the Gottesmans leaving them alone was the real truth? Not that she didn't believe her father, but right now didn't seem to the time and place to test it out. She could see what's what with Joey in school on Monday. Quickly, she snatched hold of Jeffie's hand and pulled him toward the crawl space under their porch.

"What are ya doing?" he said. He hated to be interrupted in the middle of eating something.

"It's...it's.... I'm hot, the ice cream is melting all over me, and I want to sit in the shade under the porch. We can make up stories. We'll start with a story about you this time, okay?"

"I dunno," he said.

What kind of story would he like to hear so she could get him under the porch fast? A royal story! Thank goodness for brains that worked!

"In the story, you'll be Prince Jeffrey," she said, crouching down and yanking Jeffie under the porch.

"Prince Jeffrey," he said, smiling. "The lady at Dominion's always says I look just like Prince Charles."

"That's right, that's why you're Prince Jeffrey, Your Majesty," Becky said, bowing her head at Jeffie who was now sitting cross-legged next to her. Dolores, the nicest of the cashiers at Dominion supermarket, always told them, when their mother was paying for their groceries, that Jeffie was the spitting image of Prince Charles, the eldest son of Queen Elizabeth II. And he was...well, kind of.

"So what's my story?"

Out of the corner of her eyes, Becky watched the Gottesmans' bike tires whiz pass. Go, go, go, she said to herself, don't stop, don't stop.

"Where's my story?" Jeffie said, knocking on Becky's knee.

"It's coming," Becky said, letting a big breath out. "You think a story comes to me, one, two, three. It takes thinking time. One more minute and it's ready, Your Majesty."

"A real minute or a Makowiecki minute?" Jeffie asked.

"Ha, ha, ha!"

Chewing on the tip of one braid, Becky thought and thought until she had cooked up a royal story that seemed pretty good, if she had to say so herself.

"Okay, listen, this is it. You are the youngest son of Queen Elizabeth. When you were born, you had to stay in the hospital in an incubator because you were a little sick. So the queen hired a nanny specially for you. But she didn't know this was a bad nanny who wanted a baby all for herself. The nanny saw you in the crib, and you were so cute, she couldn't resist you, she had to have you all for herself. So early one morning, she came to the hospital with a big purse, put you in, and stole you. Since Queen Elizabeth already had a couple children and so many Corgi dogs, the nanny figured the Queen wouldn't miss her newborn son...for very long."

Jeffie was leaning forward to listen. "Then what?"

"The nanny couldn't stay in England because you were

famous, and sooner rather than later, somebody would figure out who you were, so she took a boat to Canada. On the boat, the nanny who wasn't really bad, just a lady who wanted a baby of her own to love, started to go crazy, feeling terrible for what she'd done, but she had to have you."

"Because I was so cute," Jeffie added.

"Exactly. Who could resist such a baby boy with such blue eyes and such dimples, and such pudgy cheeks?" Becky asked, reaching over to pinch one of Jeffie's cheeks.

"Stop it! Then what?"

"By the time the boat docked in Toronto, the nanny was completely cuckoo. Talking to herself, muttering all the time, and didn't know where she was. So the boat's captain called the Toronto police and they came on board and took you to Mount Sinai Hospital, and the nanny to the crazy hospital at 999 Queen Street West. Who was in Mount Sinai hospital then, but our, excuse me Your Majesty, *my* mother, who had just had a baby boy. They put you in the nursery and attached a sign, 'Mystery Baby Boy,' to the front of your crib. You were right next to the crib with the sign, 'Makowiecki Baby Boy.' A cleaner was dusting, and by accident she mixed up the signs, and so you became the Makowiecki baby boy and came to live with us."

"The Queen, didn't she miss her baby?" Jeffie asked.

"Of course, she's a mother. She went on television, begging for the return of her baby to her. She described how you looked. But who was to know you were royalty and not a Makowiecki? So one year passed, and another, and another. Then one day, your loving sister, me, noticed a purple birthmark in the shape of a crown on your leg. Was that the same birthmark that all the royal children had, and could it be that you were the missing prince?"

"I was," Jeffie said happily.

"But who could be sure? So when I heard the Queen was coming to Toronto for a visit and there was going to be a parade in her honour, I took you to the parade, and told you to jump up and down when the Queen's convertible was driving by so she could see you. You jumped up and down, and what do you think happened? Her motherly eye landed on you, and in a flash she recognized you. She ordered the driver to step on the brakes. She rushed into the crowd, swept you into her arms, and before she whisked you back to Buckingham Palace, she thanked my parents for taking such good care of you. Everybody was crying when you were leaving. You cried and said you would really miss us, but you had to go, because royal duty was royal duty, but the Queen said we could come visit you anytime. In the meanwhile, somewhere in Canada was the real Makowiecki baby boy that we had to search for and bring back home. The end."

Jeffie clapped. "That was good. I liked it. Me a prince."

Grinning, Becky was amazed at how the story had just kept coming to her, and was very happy that Jeffie had liked it.

"Tell me your story now, please, Becky!"

Glancing to the left, Becky stared at the emerald green grass and the bright sunshine, longing to be out in the sun.

"Later, let's go back out," she said.

"No, I like it here, tell me your story," he said.

In the distance, Becky heard the squealing of bike

tires...and voices. The voices of Joey and Fred. By the way his body jerked, Jeffie heard them too. Maybe playing on the lawn wasn't such a good idea after all.

"My story? What's my story?" Becky hummed as she thought and thought. "Okay, this is kind of like the Oz story, except instead of going to Oz, I go to Hollywood," she said leaning back against a post.

"Hollywood? Where Lassie lives?" Jeffie asked.

"Exactly."

"So when do you meet Lassie?"

"Let me first get to Hollywood in the story. How can I meet Lassie if I don't get to Hollywood and become a star, so I can act with Lassie on her television show?"

"Oh," he said.

Settling back against the post, Becky began. "Strong winds, they blew me, faster than the fastest jet plane, to the magic middle of Hollywood, Hollywood Boulevard and Vine Street. On the sidewalks are the footprints and autographs of all the famous movie stars."

"Lassie too?"

Becky shrugged. "Probably. Lassie's pretty famous. Okay, so I followed the footprints and the paw prints on Hollywood Boulevard's sidewalk to Schwab's Drugstore. Lots and lots of movie stars have been discovered by talent agents while drinking colas and milkshakes at the drugstore's counter, and since today felt like my lucky day, I went in.

"I hopped onto a stool at the counter and ordered a chocolate fudge milkshake with an extra scoop of ice cream. I slurped it very, very slowly, because sometimes it takes time for the right talent agent to notice your star potential and come up to you and say, 'I'm going to make you a star. Now just sign on the dotted line of this contract.' I was real full after my milkshake, but I ordered another one because no agent had noticed my star potential...yet. I slurped very slowly. Then suddenly a short bald man, with a big cigar hanging out of his mouth and a suit jacket that didn't button over his big belly, sat down on the stool next to me. He ordered a coffee, took a copy of the *Variety* newspaper out of his jacket pocket, and read it. To get his attention, I slurped so loud that almost everybody seated at the counter looked over at me. Including him. I gave him a big smile, and then and there, he said to me, 'Kiddo, I'm going to make you a star!' 'Sure,' I said, 'I'm ready to sign on the dotted line.'

"He gulped his coffee, then hailed a cab, and we went straight over to the MGM movie studio. The head of the studio saw my star potential immediately, and signed me to a life-long movie contract. Since Becky Makowiecki wasn't a good movie star name...."

"That's for sure," Jeffie interrupted. "Nobody can say our name right the first time."

"Or the second or third time either, anyway, where was I? A new name. I changed my name to...Rebecca Davis, because Mummy's favourite actress is Bette Davis. And before long, I was a bigger star than even Hayley Mills."

"Who's she?" Jeffie asked.

"A big star."

"How come if she's a big star I don't know who she is?"

"You do so, you saw her in *Pollyanna*. Can I finish my story?"

"So finish it."

"The end."

"Jeffie, Becky, where are you? It's time for lunch," their mother called, standing on the steps above their heads.

"Prince Jeffrey is coming, hold your horses," Jeffie said as he crawled out.

"Rebecca Davis is at your service," Becky said as she crawled out.

Hands on her hips, their mother stared at them. "What did you say? What were you doing under there? The sun's outside and you two are under the porch like sacks of potatoes in a cold cellar. What were you doing under there?"

Jeffie and Becky looked at each other, and giggled.

"So don't tell me, I don't want to know, Mister and Miss Potato Head. You want to live like potatoes, see if I care. Such children!" she said, shaking her head as she went back inside the house.

Becky curtsied. "After you, your Majesty!"

Laughing, Jeffie went up the stairs with Becky following behind him, holding on to the tail of his shirt as if it was a train on a coronation cape.

WASHINGTON, DC, HAVANA & MOSCOW

"NOW CLASSSSS!" MISS PAYNE SPUTTERED, AS SHE TAPPED the dreaded pointer against a map of the world.

"Classssssss!" Linda hissed, back to imitating the Payne-in-the-neck in her old desk across the aisle from Becky, thanks to Becky's mother and Mrs. Friedman, who had called Mr. Lucas to insist that it was the best for Linda...and the worst for Miss Payne if she didn't see why.

Glowering exactly like Miss Payne, Linda glanced over at Becky, then jabbed her ruler around as if it was a sword, just as Miss Payne was doing now with the pointer. Her imitations of Miss Payne were funnier and meaner than before, and that was because, besides hating Miss Payne more than ever, Linda hated learning about the Cold War. So did Becky, but she couldn't decide what was worse...learning about it...or not learning about it.

It used to be that going to school was like wandering through a library where every book you pulled off the shelf was about something new and different. Like Ponce de León searching for the Fountain of Youth in 1513 on the island of Bimini and discovering Florida instead or about Emily Carr and how she became a sculptor and a painter. Now class was even worse than being at a military academy. It was like being trapped in Los Alamos, New Mexico, in the forties when those scientists were inventing the atomic bomb. They called it the Manhattan Project. The Kill Off Mankind project was more like it, Becky thought, since they knew what the bomb was for when they were inventing it.

"Classssssss!" Miss Payne said, beating the pointer against the world. "Who knows their geography?"

It used to be that geography meant following the route of the explorer Vasco da Gama travelling from Portugal around the Cape of Good Hope to India, or naming all the countries that belonged to the Commonwealth, but not anymore.

"Will one of you tell the rest of us where Washington DC, Havana, and Moscow are located?" Miss Payne demanded.

"Waaaaaaaashington, DC, the capital of the United States, is on the northeast coast," Linda sputtered out, in her Miss Payne voice.

Everyone stopped whispering, turned around and stared at Linda. Was everyone staring at Linda because she sounded an awful lot like somebody they knew and hated, or because she was answering on her own without Miss Payne dragging the answer out of her?

"Havana, the capital of Cuba, is a port city. Cuba belongs to the islands of the West Indies in the Caribbean Sea," Linda said proudly.

"Yes, that's correct, Linda, thank you," Miss Payne said,

sounding startled. "And can you tell us where Moscow is located?"

"Chalk two up for the dummy, duh!" Perry shouted out as Linda opened her mouth to answer. Like she'd been suddenly socked in the stomach, Linda slumped over in her seat.

"If any dummy knows that, how come you didn't know it yourself, dummy!" Judy shot back, and everybody started laughing.

That Judy, she had some mouth on her, Becky thought, wishing she could sock Perry out with words like Judy could.

"Are we finished with this?" Miss Payne said.

"Yes, we're finished, you can continue with your geography questions," Judy said, in a smart-aleck voice.

Becky and Linda looked at each other, then looked over at Judy with awe.

Miss Payne rubbed her nose, like she wasn't sure what to do next, whether she should take the pointer, and point it into the middle of Judy's chest or just ignore her and go on. Becky would love to see Miss Payne try, because Becky would bet two, no five, dollars that Judy would just grab the pointer and snap it in half.

"Linda, do you know where Moscow is located?" Miss Payne asked, in a pooped-out voice.

"Moscow, the capital of the Soviet Union, is located next to the Moscow River, in the western part of the country near Europe."

"Very good Linda. At least some of us in this class are studying their atlases."

Linda sat up straight and said, "I didn't learn that from an atlas. I learned it from my Uncle Jack, he's a travel agent."

Everybody laughed loud and long.

"Classsssssssssss! Who do you think you are? The audience for *The Ed Sullivan Show?* It's time to be serious. Very serious business is going on in those locations right this very minute, on October 23, 1962. Very serious business that will have a very serious effect on your futures!" she shouted, striking the map with the pointer.

When Becky thought of Washington, DC, she saw the White House. When she thought of Havana, she saw a package of Cuban cigars, and when she thought of Moscow, she saw the Red Square surrounded by beautiful old buildings as big as palaces and as decorated with gold as a birthday cake was decorated with icing.

"Classsssssss, here is Washington, DC." The teacher tapped on Washington on the map. "And here is Havana," she said, tapping on Havana. Cuba was so small an island that the pointer covered up the whole country. "And here is Moscow," she said, with one last tap.

"Do we know what is going on today in those places?" she asked in a sharp voice.

Nobody answered, as usual. There was just loud whispering, louder chair scraping and then loudest of all was the giant boom from Louie knocking his books off his desk.

"Anything more from you, Louie, and you will be visiting Mr. Lucas for a *very* long time," Miss Payne said, clicking her shark teeth, as she stooped over to write in the new black book she kept on her desk. It was a ledger book that an accountant used. Except, instead of Miss Payne keeping track of money, she was keeping track of every student's *misdeeds!* That's what she'd said to the class – *misdeeds*. The class had laughed at the word, but not for long, because Miss Payne said you were allowed one page of *misdeeds,* and when the page was full, you were permanently in the hands of Mr. Lucas. And since no one in the class could take being in the hands of Mr. Lucas even temporarily, especially Perry and Louie who knew from experience exactly what Mr. Lucas was like in the punishment business, everyone was trying to make sure their page never got filled up.

After Louie settled down, Miss Payne began to talk. Before long, Becky was listening hard. Very hard. The Soviet Union and Cuba were communist countries, the teacher explained. In communist countries, the country was run by a leader and the communist party. They were not elected by the citizens, as in democratic countries like Canada, England, and the United States. In communist countries, the country controlled everything and the people had no freedom. In democratic countries, the free citizens all had the same rights under the law, and elected politicians to represent them – in parliament in countries like Canada and England, and in the Congress and Senate in the United States. Democratic and communist countries didn't get along because each believed their system of government was the only right way to run a country. Since Cuba and the Soviet Union were communist countries, in the Cold War they were on the same side, against the United States.

Cuba was only ninety miles by sea from the tip of the state of Florida in the USA. This past summer, the United

States had got suspicious when many Soviet ships were sighted going back and forth from Cuba. So the Americans sent a U-2 spy plane to fly over Cuba. When the pilot saw missile sites with Soviet nuclear missiles aimed at the United States and Soviet bomb-carrying planes, he took photos of them to show the President and the top military generals.

"Did any of you hear the speech President John Kennedy gave on television last night?" Miss Payne asked.

"Nah, I was busy doing my homework," Louie said, and the class burst into laughter, knowing that – knowing Louie – he was busy *not* doing his homework. He always handed in his homework assignments late, saying that since he always got C-, why should he rush to get them in on time.

Miss Payne opened the black book again and flipped over to Louie's page. She picked up the pen and held it over Louie's page, like she couldn't make up her mind whether to fill in one more line or not. "How about anyone else?" she asked, closing the book, but leaving her pen as a marker so she could get to Louie's page fast...if she needed to.

"No way, I was getting my beauty rest," Perry said, making his face even more hideous by bulging out his eyes like poached eggs and humping his nose like it had been broken too many times like a hockey player's.

"The speech was on at seven o'clock," Judy piped in. "Is that your bedtime, baby Perry?"

After the class finished hooting, Perry shouted out, "Now our boy, Joey, he definitely needs some beauty rest!"

The class then turned to stared at Joey. Now, along with the Frankenstein stitches on one cheek, there was a huge bruise on the other, and both his lips were swollen. Becky knew exactly what from – his father's fists.

"Shut up!" Joey spat out angrily.

"Classssssss, we have heard enough," Miss Payne said, as she was frantically flipping through the black book, no doubt searching for Perry's, Judy's, and Joey's pages after she'd written on Louie's.

"We are asking you for the last time, did any of you hear the speech?"

Becky had heard maybe ten seconds or so when she'd come downstairs to get a glass of apple juice after supper. Before she could even ask her parents why President Kennedy was on television after the news was over, her father had leapt off the couch and over to the television, which he'd shut off suspiciously fast. He always did that when he didn't want her to see something on the news, like the trial in Jerusalem last year of one of the top Nazis who had worked for Hitler during the war, Adolf Eichmann. The whole time he'd been on trial, her father had guarded the television tougher than a Brinks guard on the lookout for bank robbers. She knew why then, because he didn't want her or Jeffie to know about World War II. Her mother would only say that Eichmann was on trial for war crimes, but what kind of crimes, she'd refused to say.

President Kennedy hadn't been talking about World War II, that's for sure. But maybe...about World War III, she thought, suddenly filled with fear. What else was she to think, after being given that to think about day in, day out, at school? When she'd asked her parents again why the President was on television, her father had told her he was just talking politics, like a politician. Knowing better than to push her father to talk when he had no intention of talking, Becky had gone on her way to the kitchen, got her apple juice, and tried to push her worry away. But she'd kept on wondering and worrying.

"I did," Judy said, standing up and turning around so she could speak to the whole class as if she was the teacher. "I heard the whole eighteen-minute speech. President Kennedy said the Soviet Union has been sneaking its missiles and bombers into Cuba for only one reason — so that if the Soviet Union wanted to attack the United States with nuclear missiles, they could strike first now, 'cause their missiles were close enough to do that. Their missiles can only hit targets a thousand or so miles away, but the American missiles can hit targets thousands of miles away, like Moscow even. President Kennedy didn't say that, but I thought I'd bring it in, in case you didn't know. Because it's important to know 'cause then you get why it's such a big deal when the Soviets put missiles in Cuba so close to the United States. Any questions so far?" Judy asked, looking around the classroom.

Everyone in the class, including Miss Payne, was frozen silent by the double whammy combination of fear because of what Judy was telling them, and amazement that not only could Judy remember everything that President Kennedy had said without any notes to remind her, but she could even add in other stuff that the President had forgot to mention.

"Everybody's got it? Good, so back to the speech. To make sure that no more Soviet missiles and nuclear warheads — you make a regular missile into a nuclear missile by attaching a warhead, that's a cylinder packed full with nuclear explosives, to the top of it. President Kennedy didn't say that, either, but I thought I'd bring that in too, in case you didn't know.... So, to stop Soviet ships from bringing missiles and warheads to Cuba, American military ships were going to 'quarantine' Cuba – surround the island, like border guards do. And President Kennedy said that if a missile was launched from Cuba, America would consider it an attack not just from Cuba, but from the Soviet Union, and so would declare nuclear war against both of them.

"Any final questions before I take my seat?" Judy asked, looking around. "So you all got everything? Good." She sat back down.

"Very, very good," Miss Payne said, not looking good at all after listening to Judy.

Gazing around the classroom, Becky noticed that nobody looked too good right now, as if they were thinking the same thing – nuclear war could destroy not just one village, one part of a city at a time like what happened in World War II, but a whole city, provinces, states, countries...the world. Millions and millions of people could die in minutes if the Americans or the Soviets went to war.

The teacher cleared her throat a couple of times, then put down the pointer. "Classsssssss, do not worry. Mr. Kennedy and Mr. Khrushchev are reasonable men. There will be a peaceful solution. Do not worry."

Why did people always tell you not to worry right after giving you something gigantic to worry about? If there was nothing to worry about, how come Prime Minister Diefenbaker had built the Diefenbunker? How come every hour on television there was a test of the emergency broadcast system? How come Mr. Lucas had turned the school into a military academy? How come the class was doing projects on atomic bombs and radiation sickness?

Miss Payne gave the class a big fake smile. "Let us move on to a new subject," she said, tugging the bottom of the map of the world that hung from the ceiling in front of the blackboard. Instead of rolling up slowly, it jerked up fast with a loud flapping noise like an explosion, and the world disappeared.

On the way home from school, Becky and Linda talked and laughed about everything under the sun...except what Miss Payne had told them. Linda did an excellent imitation of Perry making a face. Then Becky told Linda about her mother and Aunt Frightful, who always said, "Guess who died?" instead of hello. When Aunt Frightful had said it *again* last week Becky's mother had got so mad that she'd said back, "So you finally killed somebody and you're confessing to me?" Then Linda made Becky laugh when she started singing in Mrs. Lepinsky's voice, "Some henchanted evenainng, you vill meet a strangler!" Becky laughed, but her laughing had changed from funny laughing to the kind of laughing she did when she got scared and nervous.

When they reached Linda's house, they looked at each other. Twirling a strand of hair around her fingers, Becky took a deep breath. "You think...Linda?"

Linda shrugged, then quickly ran toward her house.

At home, Becky told her brain, enough already with the nuclear missiles and nuclear war, but her brain wouldn't listen.

"What's the matter with you?" her mother asked when Becky came into the kitchen and drifted around picking up and putting down stuff on the counter and the kitchen table. Her mother was beating a veal cutlet with a pounder to make it as thin and flat as paper, because that was the only way Jeffie would eat his. Finally, after picking up and putting down practically everything in the kitchen, Becky went over and stood beside her mother.

"So are you going to tell me or are you just going to stand there with a face as long as a rabbi's beard?" her mother said, tossing the pounder into the sink with the rest of the dirty utensils.

"Mummy, what did you think would happen when the war started?" Becky asked.

"Where does that question come from? From watching me fight with a piece of veal cutlet?" her mother asked, wiping her hands on a dish cloth. "You have to know right now?"

Becky nodded.

"Is there a reason you have to know right now?" her mother asked.

"I just wanna know," Becky said, then looked away.

"Okay, I got a minute. A Makowiecki minute. The veal, it can wait," her mother said.

They sat down on the kitchen chairs.

"Okay, what did I think when the war started? Let me

remember," her mother said, clasping her hands behind her head.

Becky already knew that World War II had begun on September 1 of 1939 when Germany attacked Poland. But it had started to begin long before that in 1933, when Adolf Hitler was elected Chancellor of Germany and the Nazi party came to power. Since, like her mother always said, Hitler always wanted to rule the world, like the devil rules hell, he set out making Germany strong and ready to go to war. And one of the first countries in Europe he planned to take over was Poland.

Like in a game of tug of war, all the countries in Europe were divided into two sides. On one side were the Allied countries, which included England, France, and Poland. On the other side were the Axis countries – Germany, Italy, and Japan. The Allies signed an agreement, promising to defend the other Allies if they were attacked by any of the Axis countries.

So when Germany attacked Poland with the help of Russia, not just two countries were suddenly at war, but five. Since the Germans had been preparing for war since 1933, when they attacked Poland they had so many tanks, bombers, fighter jets, rockets, machine guns, and artillery, and a big army, while the Poles had barely any modern war equipment. Her mother said it was like the Polish army was fighting a war in 1839, not 1939.

In the first week of September, one of the first battles of the war had taken place near her mother's village. All the people in the village had run away, hiding their stuff like her

Bubbe had in the basement of the store in the middle of the village, and hiding themselves in the mountain forests surrounding Krasnobrod, which was in a deep valley.

"What I thought was, the Germans would come, there would be a battle, and then they would go away, but it wasn't like that at all," her mother said. "Then after the Polish army lost to the Germany army, I thought the Germans would take over Poland and everything would slowly go back to the way it had been, except now we would be ruled by the Germans. People like us in villages like Krasnobrod, what did we have to do with governments and rulers and such things? We lived our lives, and that's that. Never did I think that what was to come was a world war, that Hitler would conquer one country after another, that so many millions of people would be killed, and that my family who had never travelled anywhere far, not even to Warsaw, would have to go so far away to survive."

"Did you worry about dying?" Becky asked, so quickly that all the words ran together.

Her mother shook her head slowly. "You would think so, but it's not so. All we thought about was how to survive to the next day, and to the next. And about food, we never stopped thinking about food, because we never had enough to eat."

Her mother came over to Becky and hugged her. "You know what, I'm still always thinking about food. The food I'm thinking about right now is those veal cutlets, which if I don't make them now, we'll have supper at midnight instead of at six."

Becky also stood up and helped her mother make supper. After supper, her parents always watched the CBS *Evening News* with Walter Cronkite at six-thirty. Mostly Becky didn't watch the news but went upstairs to read or do homework or play with Jeffie. Not this evening. She wanted to find out more about what was going on in Cuba, and who would know better than Walter Cronkite? And this time, she was not going to be shooed out of the living room by her father.

"The news? You're watching the news?" her father asked, as Becky plopped down beside him on the couch.

"Why?" her mother asked, giving Becky one of her long looks.

Becky just shrugged. If she said why, her father would shut off the television in a flash.

"There's nothing on the news for you," her father said. "Why don't you go upstairs and play with Jeffie?" Her father was shaking his legs, like he was just itching to leap up and switch off Walter Cronkite.

"Leave her alone, so she wants to watch the news," her mother said, looking at Becky as if she'd guessed why Becky wanted to watch, and thought she should.

The anchorman, Walter Cronkite, who always reminded Becky a bit of Captain Kangaroo, introduced the first story. A reporter standing in front of the White House talked about President Kennedy's speech, the part where the President said that the United States would go to nuclear war against the Soviet Union if a missile was launched from Cuba at any country in the Western Hemisphere. In the next story, a reporter standing in front of a picture of Red Square in

Moscow, gave the official Soviet response, calling the American naval quarantine "a piratical threat" that could "lead to disastrous consequences to all mankind."

Like the world broken up into radioactive pieces, Becky thought, her mouth going dry with fear. Lately that was happening so often that maybe she needed to carry around candies to suck, like Mrs. Lepinsky did in all her purses and pockets.

"That's Nikita Khrushchev!" she said, pointing to a picture of him that came on the screen.

With astonished looks on their faces, her parents stared at her.

Becky just shrugged again. "Miss Payne, at school today, when she was talking about the missiles in Cuba, she showed us pictures of Khrushchev, Kennedy, and Castro."

"See, didn't I know something was up?" her father said to her mother.

"Congratulations, you want a prize?" her mother said.

Her father faced Becky. "What did the teacher tell you that for? Why do you have to know?" Then he started speaking very quickly in Polish to her mother and she answered back just as quickly in Polish.

Becky didn't like seeing her parents fight, especially when it was over her.

"Mummy, Daddy," she said, but they were too busy arguing in Polish to hear her.

"So she knows, big deal," her mother said. "She should know what is going on in the world. She lives in it. If we only had known...."

Her father answered her mother back in even faster Polish. The veins in his neck were all pushed out and he was all red in the face, while her mother was all white except for the flash of her gold front tooth.

"Mummy, Daddy, stop it, right now!" Becky yelled at the top of her lungs.

Her parents stopped. Still, from the way they were giving each other angry looks, she knew they would start all over again once she was out of the living room.

"Look, look, there's some pictures of the missile bases in Cuba that the spy plane took, and of the missiles too!" she said, gesturing at the television.

There was one story after another about the missiles in Cuba. The television glowed and cast off a shaft of light, just like the light that had beamed off the alien spaceship that conquered earth in a creepy movie Becky had kind of watched through her hand, which had been covering up her eyes during the scary parts.

In a story about the political careers of Kennedy and Khrushchev, Becky was practically hypnotized by their voices and their waving hands and arms. Giving a speech before the Senate, John Kennedy's voice rose and fell, was soft then strong, and he moved his arms like a maestro. In a speech to the Supreme Soviet, the Russian parliament, Khrushchev's barking voice was as snappy as a dog straining on its leash. He looked exactly like those wrestlers her father liked to watch on TV on Saturday afternoons.

When the news was over, Becky jumped up from the couch, wanting to get out of the living room fast.

"Don't you worry," her father said, looking very, very sorry he hadn't turned off the television. "Everything will be fine. Those two, it's only big talk. Everything will be fine."

"Listen to Daddy, he knows," her mother said, her voice trembling all the same.

"I'm going upstairs to read a book," she said.

"Read a happy book, not one of those Cherry Ames nurse books with all the accidents and the hospitals, promise me," her mother said.

"Yup!"

"Read about the hobbit. What's his name? Bilko, no that's not it, I'm thinking of Sergeant Bilko. You know who I mean, anyway!" her mother shouted after her as Becky climbed the stairs.

"It's Bilbo Baggins," Becky mumbled, as she dragged herself up the stairs to her bedroom. From the bookshelf above her desk, she pulled out *The Hobbit* and lay down on her bed to read. But she couldn't even read one sentence. No matter how hard she tried, she couldn't keep the sentences and the story in her head, so she put the book back and lay down on her bed.

The death of the world. Her death. As she tried to imagine what it would be like to be dead, her heart beat so hard and so fast that it hurt even more than having the pointer jabbed into her chest.

There was only one thing to do. Pray to God, so she did. "Please God, make Khrushchev and Kennedy forget about wars and missiles and let there be peace on earth. I promise to be good. I will obey my parents...and even Miss Payne. I will watch out for Jeffie, never leave him alone. Just please, make Kennedy and Khrushchev forget about wars and missiles and make peace." She kept repeating that over and over and over.

THE FALLOUT SHELTER

"MY DAD WANTS TO KNOW IF YOU'LL COME WITH US ON Saturday to see *Stagecoach*. It stars John Wayne," Becky told Linda, who was standing next to her in the schoolyard at recess. "He says it's real good. He's seen it four times, maybe more."

"I'll have to check my social calender, but I think I can squeeze you in," Linda joked. "Suddenly I'm all booked up. My father's taking me to a Leafs hockey game in two weeks. Can you believe? He never takes me anywhere. You suddenly popular too?"

"Yup!" Becky said. She'd bet twenty dollars that every single person in the schoolyard had become suddenly popular too. Everywhere Becky went the last two days, people were making plans. It was like if everybody made enough plans for the future, there had to be a future for the plans to happen in. Becky hoped that Khrushchev and Kennedy were making lots of plans for their futures too.

"What do you want to do?" Becky asked, looking around

the yard. There were no games, just bunches of kids standing around talking. And there was one and only one thing everybody was talking about. Nuclear war and nuclear missiles. Now the first thing that everybody said, even before hi, was "What do you hear about what's going on?"

"Jump ship. Hit the road," Linda said.

"There's Judy, Elise, and Rhonda, let's go over there," Becky said, taking hold of Linda's arm and dragging her.

"Why are you pulling me? I was coming anyway," Linda said. "Where am I going to go? Timbuktu?"

Becky let go of Linda's arm. Her arm had grabbed Linda's arm practically on its own, as if her arm thought Linda just might jump ship and hit the road for real.

"That President Kennedy, he's so handsome," Elise said, sighing.

"Handsome," Judy groaned. "How can you think about something stupid like that? All I care about is that he doesn't put his finger on the nuclear button in the briefcase that military officer carries around handcuffed to his wrist."

Becky found herself nodding along. In that briefcase was the nuclear button the President would press to launch a nuclear war. Whether or not the President used it, that was what counted.

Elise flushed with embarrassment. Becky then felt bad for her, though she agreed with Judy that what Elise had said was kind of dumb, though she was right too, the President was very handsome. Maybe she should say something to her, but then if she said something, maybe Judy would think she was going along with Elise, and then Judy would think she was stupid too.

The recess bell rang and in the crowd of kids going back inside, Becky squeezed close to Elise and whispered in her ear, "I think he's very handsome too!" and was glad that she said it, though she felt sneaky for not having the nerve to say out it loud in front of everyone. Including Judy.

In class, everyone took their seats slowly and noisily, as usual. That used to drive Miss Payne crazy and she would shout over the noise that she couldn't understand why it was so difficult for them all to sit down fast and quiet. Today she waited until everyone was at their desks and kind of quiet before she began speaking. "Today, Allen Rosenzweig will be giving his presentation on fallout shelters. Allen!"

When everybody else had come to the front of the class to do their presentations, they had carried lots of stuff – papers, maps, pictures, and books. But runty Allen was strolling to the front carrying just a sheet of paper. That was Allen all over. He was a lazy and stupid dumbbell, and didn't care that he was one. No one ever wanted to do projects or presentations with him, because he never did his share of the work, and if you didn't want to get "D" for dumbbell like Allen always got, that meant you had to do most of the work, which explained why Allen was the only one in the class doing a presentation without a partner.

During most of the presentations, the class just listened, because they knew there wasn't going to be a test on how to build a bomb and what were the symptoms of radiation sickness, it was just "vital information for their well-being" according to Mr. Lucas, whom Miss Payne had invited to speak to the class about why they had to learn about the Cold War.

Knowing about fallout shelters was vital information, that was for sure, so this time, Becky took out her pen and notebook. She wasn't the only one. For a change, she hoped that Allen had done some work instead of no work. This was important stuff to know, and maybe this time even Allen got that.

He pushed up his glasses and looked down at the sheet of paper. That was a good sign that maybe there was something on the paper worth reading.

"A fallout shelter is a shelter from fallout," he said.

There were a few groans in the class. Becky loosened her grip on her pen, not willing to put it down, still hoping that Allen would have a couple pieces of information worth writing down.

"You go to a fallout shelter to be safe from radiation fallout," he said.

The groans got louder in the class. Giving up hope, Becky put down her pen. Just when everyone really needed vital information about how to get to or build a fallout shelter, there was Allen, standing there, not ashamed one bit about being such a lazy and stupid dumbbell.

"Yes, Allen, there is more?" Miss Payne snapped.

"In case of a real emergency, you must evacuate to your nearest fallout shelter," he read.

Those were the exact words the announcer said on television after the one-minute test of the emergency broadcast system. Everybody knew that and booed Allen. He'd done no work at all. Nothing. A couple kids threw spitballs and erasers at Allen, and got him!

"Miss Payne," he whined. "People are throwing things at me."

"Continue, Allen," Miss Payne said, stepping away from Allen like she was giving the class free aim at him. Some pencil stubs hit him on the legs and he grimaced like he'd been hit by boulders.

"A fallout shelter building is a building with the fallout shelter sign attached to it," he said.

"Is that all the information you have?" Miss Payne spat out.

He nodded and just stood there as everyone even Becky booed and threw things at him. "Miss Payne, everybody's throwing things at me," he said, as ducked to avoid being hit by a flying ruler.

"Allen, come see me after class. Return to your desk!" Miss Payne watched with a little smile on her face as Allen ducked and danced to avoid the stuff still being tossed at him as he went back to his desk.

There had to be a way to get vital information fast on fallout shelters. There could be a nuclear war with nuclear missiles any time. What was everyone supposed to do?

Miss Payne must know. Becky could ask her during the "Current Events Question Period." In all Grade Six, Seven, and Eight classes, Mr. Lucas had ordered the teachers to have a fifteen-minute question period every day. It was supposed to be like the one in the House of Commons where the New Democratic Party and Liberal Party Members of Parliament got to ask Prime Minister John Diefenbaker and his cabinet questions about how he and the Conservative Party were running the country.

The question period was scheduled next.

"Are there any questions today?" Miss Payne asked, then glanced up at the wall clock as she leaned back against her desk. Becky glanced at the clock too. It was eleven. The question period was supposed to be fifteen minutes long, but the teacher was making it shorter day by day. Yesterday it had been only eight minutes. That made it extra important that Becky get her question in right at the beginning. She began waving her arm faster and higher than anyone else.

"Yes, Becky, I can see you, you can stop waving," Miss Payne said.

"How come there aren't any fallout shelters in Canada all over the place like there are in the United States?"

"How come?"

"How come?"

"How come?"

The room became an echo chamber of "how comes" from everywhere and everyone.

Miss Payne shifted against the desk, almost losing her balance and some kids giggled. "Because..." she paused, clearing her throat so strongly that it sounded like she was gargling mouthwash, "...because Canada has no atomic weapons and no desire to get involved in a nuclear war with any country. We are a peaceful nation."

"But..." Becky shouted, forgetting even to wave her arm, "if radiation stays in the air, and the wind blows the air over Canada, what are we supposed to do?"

"Miss Payne, my father says..." Judy began.

Miss Payne wrinkled her noise like she'd smelled a skunk.

Every time Judy said "My father says," it meant she was about to tell Miss Payne that what she'd just said was all wrong, and that she, Judy, was going to say what was right.

"My father says that across Lake Ontario in New York state is one of the number one targets for the Soviet missiles – the US Bomarc missile base in Plattsburg, New York. So if there is a nuclear war, one of the first missiles will be heading for Plattsburg, and that means the radiation will be falling out all over Southern Ontario. So what are we supposed to do then?"

There was an explosion of noise in the class. Coughing and sneezing, scraping chairs and banging books, and lots of yeah, yeah, yeahs.

"Classssssssssss," the teacher said, making the gargling sound again. "If it is necessary, you can evacuate to your nearest subway station and stay in the subway tunnels."

Becky and Linda looked at each other and rolled their eyes. When Becky's father had taken them to see another of his favourite westerns, *Rio Bravo,* they'd taken the subway to the Carlton theatre. Even though it was a Saturday afternoon, the platform had been packed with people. And if that was just on a day some of the people in Toronto were going downtown to see movies or go shopping, what would it be like when everyone in Toronto was rushing to the subway to get safe from the fallout? Plus, how could everybody live in the subway? Where would everybody sleep? The tunnels were covered in tracks, so you couldn't lie down there to sleep, and what about food? There were only candy stands.

"Settle down, class," Miss Payne said over the noise. "A

nuclear war is not going to happen. Mr. Kennedy and Mr. Khrushchev will come to a peaceful solution. It's not going to happen. End of question period."

It's not going to happen, it's not going to happen, it's not going to happen, the teacher had said. But could she know? Only Kennedy and Khrushchev would know that. And it didn't sound so good from the letter that Khrushchev had written back to Bertrand Russell, a British writer and pacifist (whom Becky had never heard of before even if he was world famous). In his letter, Khrushchev had written that even though the Soviets would not "make any reckless decisions," the situation "was fraught with irreparable consequences." *That* was suppose to reassure Bertrand Russell and the rest of the world. Not in Becky's book.

When the lunch bell rang, Allen, moving like an Olympic racer, was the first one out of his seat and out the door. On the way home, the dull grey October sky was suddenly speared open by a ray of white sunlight. Becky and Linda froze, stared up at it and then at each other. Was that what a nuclear missile would look like?

"We've got to *do* something!" Linda yelled.

"Yeah, but what?" Becky whispered.

"There's got be *something!*" Linda yelled.

What was Linda yelling for? Becky wasn't deaf yet. "Ssh, ssh," she whispered as they passed Mr. Rutland's house. If Linda didn't stop yelling, in two seconds, Rufus would be barking and growling and circling them, and with Becky's luck, this might be the day Rufus decided it was time not just to sniff her but attack her, but good!

"Who cares about that crazy dog?" Linda yelled. "I'm not afraid of that crazy dog. Come and get me!"

Howling like the wild, crazy dog he was, Rufus bolted off the porch.

"See what you've done!' Becky hissed. "Run!"

And they ran. Good news for them, a car was coming down the street and Rufus stopped chasing them and went after the car. Panting, they stood in front of Linda's house.

"See you later," Becky said, hoarse from fear and running.

"We got to think of something!" Linda yelled and ran toward her house.

How could Linda still run when Becky's legs could barely carry her home. After finishing lunch, she went into the living room to watch cartoons on TV with Jeffie.

"There has to be *something*!" she said to herself during a commercial.

"What'd you say?" Jeffie asked, rolling from his stomach onto his back.

"Nothing, I was talking to myself."

"Becky's talking to herself, Becky's talking to herself. Like Bertie the Bogeyman!" Jeffie shouted out.

"Shut up!" she shouted back.

"You shut up!" he shouted back.

That was enough for today, and today was only halfway through! Ahhh! Becky sprang off the couch and ran upstairs.

"What's going on here?" she heard her mother ask Jeffie.

"Becky's acting crazy. Like Bertie," Jeffie told their mother.

From the top of the stairs, Becky shouted. "AM NOT!"

"Stop it you two! This very second. Not a single word more from either of you, do you understand?"

Becky groaned. That and the need for a plan were the *only* things she understood.

NORTH TONAWANDA

So far every plan Becky had tried out on Linda on their way back to school had got the same answer: "Stinky!" First Becky had suggested that the whole class sign a petition and send one copy to Kennedy and one to Khrushchev, telling them to sign a peace pact like all the countries had after World Wars I and II. Linda said that countries had to go to war first before they could sign a peace pact, not just threaten to go to war. And besides, would why would they bother reading a petition from a bunch of kids in Toronto? But Prime Minister Diefenbaker had written her back when she'd written him a letter, Becky had told Linda. He had to, Linda said, because Becky's parents were voters, and he needed their votes in the next election. Becky didn't believe that. She knew she'd written a good letter and that's why the Prime Minister had written her back.

After seven, no eight, stinky, stinky, stinkies from Linda, Becky gave up. She would keep her ideas to herself until she came up with a plan that even Linda would have to admit was an honest-to-goodness real plan.

An honest-to-goodness real plan came to Becky, not in school, of course – who could think in school with Miss Payne talking about the periodic table and everybody else either whispering or dreaming about something else as they sat slumped at their desks – but while watching cartoons with Jeffie. In between cartoons, there was another test of the emergency broadcast system. Rather than covering her ears with her hands like Jeffie was doing, she listened. And it was a good thing, because after the siren noise was finished, a man's voice announced that in case of a real emergency, Buffalo area residents were to evacuate to their nearest fallout shelter, and he began giving out the addresses.

Becky rolled over on the couch, faster than a barrel going down Niagara Falls, and grabbed the pad of paper and the pencil her parents left on the end table for phone messages. As quick as she could write, she scribbled down the locations of the Buffalo-area fallout shelters: 507 Delaware Avenue; 698 Elmwood Avenue; 116 North Tonawanda Boulevard. Crack! The lead in the pencil broke because she was pressing down too hard.

"Who ya writing now?" Jeffie asked, flipping over on his back to watch her. "Will ya get a picture back like you did from Lassie?"

"I'm not writing anybody," Becky answered, shaking her head so fast that her ponytail smacked her right in the nose.

Jeffie sat up. "Then what ya writing?"

She rubbed the side of her nose, which was stinging. "I am writing the addresses of some places."

"Places, why?"

"'Cause, in case we have to go there," she said, wishing the cartoons would come back on so Jeffie would just turn around and go back to watching.

"What's there?"

"A building, that's all," she said breathlessly.

"A building?" he repeated. "What kind of building?"

"Look! *Top Cat* is starting."

Only then did Jeffie turn his attention back to the television and Becky sighed with relief. She glanced down at the pad. So she had the addresses. But just where were those buildings in Buffalo? Her family would need a map of the city to find them. And how would they get to Buffalo in time? Buffalo was a good two-hour drive from Toronto. Her father would have to rent a car, and the traffic would probably be bumper to bumper, as heavy as during rush hour. Then what if the American border guards wouldn't let any Canadians across the border – like the time when her father forgot his citizenship papers when they were going to Crystal Beach for the day, and the guards made them turn around and go back to Toronto.

Having the addresses of fallout shelters was no help at all! Useless! Useless! Useless! Crumpling up the paper in her hand, she threw it onto the floor. If only the Canadian government had built some fallout shelters in Toronto. They could have built them on Centre Island, there was plenty of space there. Nah, that was no good. There were only a couple of ferry boats, and by the time they'd ferried all the people in Toronto to the island, it would have taken a day, or even two, and by then too many people would have already been exposed to fallout radiation.

There had to be something, but what was it? Then she remembered that after some of the tests, the announcer mentioned an address where people could write for pamphlets on how to build your very own fallout shelter in your very own backyard. That was the something!

When she couldn't find a pen on the end table, she went to the closet in the vestibule, to search through her father's jacket pockets for a pen. In his brown houndstooth sports jacket, she found one and skipped back to the living room.

"Commercial yet?" she asked Jeffie.

He twisted his head around and stuck his tongue out at her.

Ignoring him, she sat back down on the couch, eagerly waiting for the next test. Pen clutched between her fingers, she waited and waited, but it didn't come on for another half-hour, not until the end of *The Three Stooges*. When the announcer gave the address, Becky's hand was so cramped from clutching the pen that she could barely write. Messy or not, there it was: United States Office of Civilian Defence Mobilization, Buffalo, New York, Branch, 1601 Delaware Avenue, North Tonawanda, New York.

"What are you writing down?" her mother asked.

Startled, Becky quickly covered up the address with her right hand, then looked up. There was her mother standing near the television set.

"And you, Mister, how many times have I told you not to watch the television from so close? You don't have to be inside the set to see it!" Then she bent down and grabbed Jeffie by the feet. "What did I just say to you? Move!" Dragging Jeffie backwards by the feet, Becky's mother moved him three feet away from the television, near the couch.

"I can't see from so far," he whined.

"Tough. The doctor says there's nothing wrong with your eyes: 20/20 vision, you have. Better than anyone else in this family. Everybody else in this family watches from the couch with no complaints and nobody even sees as good as you do. What makes you so special?"

Becky moved her head around, trying to signal Jeffie not to argue back. But Jeffie missed the signal and her mother got it.

"What's going on with you? First you're covering up the pad of paper like there's something you don't want your mother to see, and now you're moving your head, like you're making a secret signal. Do I deserve this?"

Becky shook her head, no. She loved her mother but that didn't mean she couldn't have at least a couple of secrets from her. And writing away for a pamphlet on how to build a fallout shelter was going to stay a secret until Becky had somehow, someway, built one in the backyard. Only then would she show it off to her family as a big surprise, just like her parents had showed off her bedroom to her after they'd painted it lilac, hung up new violet drapes, and dyed her old yellow chenille bedspread nearly purple.

"It's just an address. I'm going to write a letter. That's all," Becky said, in the small soft voice she always used when she was lying.

"Mm," her mother said, eyeing Becky like she didn't believe her.

The doorbell rang and her mother went to see who was there. Saved by the doorbell! Whoo, Becky let out a big breath.

"You?" she heard her mother say. "Don't you have a key? Am a doorman?"

"I forgot it this morning," she heard her father say. "Is this the hello I get?"

They started to fight, and Becky felt bad because she had put her mother in a bad mood.

WHEN BECKY CAME DOWN FOR BREAKFAST the next morning, her father was already in the kitchen. The radio was on and he was bent forward, listening hard like he wanted to make sure not to miss a single word, both his hands gripping the coffee mug.

"How come you're not sleeping?" she asked him. He slept in on Saturday mornings. So did everybody except Jeffie, who knew better than to wake everybody else up at seven o'clock if he wanted to be allowed to watch Saturday morning cartoons.

"Couldn't sleep," her father said, right away stretching out his arm to turn down the volume on the radio like he didn't want Becky to hear. "Dreams, dreams, dreams! So many dreams."

If there were good dreams, her father told them to her. But when they were bad, he kept them to himself. These had to be bad, because her father didn't say anything, just sipped his coffee.

"How come you're up so early?" he asked, as Becky went to the cupboard to get a bowl and a box of Cheerios for breakfast.

"Couldn't sleep," Becky said, sitting down at the table, then standing again. "Forgot the milk."

"Sit, I'll get it," her father said, getting up and going to the fridge.

As he poured the milk onto her cereal, he gave her a sleepy look. "You're dressed. So early? Where are you going? *Stagecoach* doesn't start till three o'clock."

Her father was wearing his used-to-be-white but now splotchy-with-blue-spots bathrobe from one of her mother's washing machine accidents. On Saturday mornings, Becky didn't get dressed until later, but this morning she'd gotten dressed right away because she was going to mail the letter to North Tonawanda. The faster she mailed the letter, the faster she would get information on how to build a shelter to protect her family from fallout.

"I...I...was going to Linda's to remind her about the movie today," she said softly.

"The telephone doesn't work?"

"I didn't want to wake up all the Friedmans with the telephone ringing."

"Won't knocking on the front door wake them up?" he asked.

Why was everyone in her family a regular Perry Mason lawyer poking at her with questions when she was trying to lie? How come her lies always stunk?

"I didn't think of that," she said, her voice even softer. "I'll call Linda later."

It was only eight o'clock. She still had an hour to sneak out and put the letter in the box before the mail was picked up at nine. "You can put the radio back on. I don't mind," she said. If her father said yes, it meant what he was listening to on radio – about the missiles in Cuba – wasn't bad news. If he said no, it meant something bad had happened.

"I heard enough already," he said, turning the radio completely off. "A big weekend, you and Linda have planned. Today the movie with me. What a movie! You and Linda will like it. And tomorrow, roller skating at the arena and then dinner at Mrs. Lepinsky's. You know what a *balebosteh* she is – a house decorated like a magazine picture, and can she cook, like a chef in a fancy-pants restaurant." He cleared this throat. "Think about *that,* okay?"

If only Becky could, she would, but she couldn't. Not thinking about the missiles in Cuba was like having a picnic at the base of a volcano which was rumbling and ready to erupt. How could you enjoy the picnic when, any second, you could be burnt up by a river of hot lava?

After each spoonful of cereal, Becky meant to ask her father what he'd heard. It took twelve spoonfuls for her to get up the nerve. "Did you hear any news about what's going on in Cuba?"

Her father put down his coffee mug, then rubbed his cheeks. "A little something, but don't worry about it. There won't be a war. Just big talk."

Becky rested her spoon on top of her cereal bowl, her stomach tight as a fist. "What did you hear?"

"If I tell you, you're going to worry and get scared. So why do you want to know everything?"

"I just wanna know," Becky mumbled. "I just wanna know." Her father didn't want to tell her because he knew what a Chicken Little she was and he didn't want to make her into an even bigger Chicken Little. She remembered the day on Rushton Road when she'd decided not to tell Jeffie about the Gottesman brothers. And look what had happened to Jeffie because she hadn't said anything.

"I just wanna know," she said, louder.

"Okay, I'll tell you. But it's nothing. It sounds worse than it is. Okay?"

"Okay."

"Brand new photos from the American spy planes show that the missiles bases in Cuba are almost finished being built, and show missiles all ready to be fired."

That was just a little something! All the Cheerios Becky had swallowed rushed back up her throat. She swallowed down hard. "Will they go to war now?"

"They won't go to war. Nobody wants a war. Now, forget about it. Think about something else," he ordered. "Tell Linda to be ready about one-thirty. We'll go a little early to get good seats."

How could she think about something else? She forced herself to finish the rest of the cereal, even though she'd lost her appetite, but good. After her father went upstairs to shower, she snuck outside to mail the letter.

"GIRLFRIENDS, HOW ABOUT WE CELEBRATE even more with some wine?" Mrs. Lepinsky said, beaming a big smile at Linda and Becky. Using her best china, real silver silverware, and crystal goblets even, Mrs. Lepinsky had served them supper in the dining room.

"Why not?" said Linda.

"Sure," said Becky.

When Mrs. Lepinsky had greeted Becky and Linda at the door, they both had known something was up, because she looked dressed for a special occasion. She was wearing a flowery going-out-for-dinner dress and her real pearl necklace and pearl button earrings. She even had a lace hairnet over her bun. Dressed up so nice, Mrs. Lepinsky looked not *that* much older than Becky's mother. Okay, so her hair was all white, but it was as thick and shiny as Becky's. Okay, so her face had a couple of wrinkles here and there, especially around her eyes and mouth, but her cheeks were as smooth and rosy as Linda's. Okay, so her green eyes needed reading glasses to see anything close up, but they were as sparkly as emeralds. And her teeth, Mrs. Lepinsky had the straightest, whitest teeth, which seemed even whiter because of the ruby red lipstick she wore.

"You didn't hear?" Mrs. Lepinsky had said first thing.

Right away Becky had felt a bolt of fear, stronger than the lightning and thunder that had trapped Becky and Linda at the roller skating rink. It had been raining very hard and, since they didn't have an umbrella, they'd had to stay until the storm was over, so they'd come late to Mrs. Lepinsky's.

"Did something happen in Cuba?" Becky had said, her voice squeaky.

"No more missiles in Cuba! God bless!" Mrs. Lepinsky had said, clapping her hands. She'd heard on the radio that Premier Khrushchev had agreed to remove all the missiles from Cuba "in the interests of peace" and President Kennedy had welcomed his "statesmanlike decision" and then promised not to invade Cuba.

Mrs. Lepinsky had been so happy that she'd danced first with Linda, then with Becky. At first Becky had felt really happy, but the feeling didn't last long. Not that she wasn't ready to dance at the news, but the news only pushed her fear away a little.

It was over...for now. But the United States and Russia still had missiles aimed at each other. They were still in a Cold War, and President Kennedy and Premier Khrushchev still wouldn't go anywhere without their nuclear button briefcases. If that all remained the same, how could she stop being worried and afraid? Did Linda feel the same or not? It was hard to tell. Mrs. Lepinsky didn't look afraid, but then she wasn't afraid of much of anything after living through the Russian Revolution and two world wars.

"I hope you don't mind, it's just Manischewitz wine left over from Rosh Hashanah," Mrs. Lepinsky explained, as if the both of them were wine experts used to drinking good wine, not just sticky sweet Kosher wine. She poured a little wine into their goblets.

Becky and Linda smiled at each other. That was one of the things Becky liked so much about Mrs. Lepinsky. She treated everybody great. Not like Miss Payne, who treated Mr. Lucas and the parents better, and her students like second-class citizens and worse.

"Le'chayim!"

"Le'chayim!"

"Le'chayim!"

They clicked their goblets and took a sip of wine. But even as Becky was saying *"Le'chayim"* – to life – she was thinking the best way to guarantee a long *Le'chayim* for everyone she loved was to have a fallout shelter in the backyard. As long as there were still missiles and the Cold War, there was still a need to have a fallout shelter. Just in case, because you never knew. Becky wasn't about to go and forget about them just because the crisis was over...for now.

BECKY FIGURED IT WOULD TAKE FIVE DAYS to get the information on the fallout shelters from North Tonawanda. After six days passed, every noontime when she came home from school for lunch, she rifled the mailbox as her mother was opening the door. The first two times, Becky's mother just gave her a suspicious look and a loud "mm" when Becky handed her the mail. The third time her mother finally said something.

"Why the big rush for the mail? Who did you write that you don't want your poor mother to know about?"

"Nobody," Becky mumbled.

"So you won't tell me. I'll have to guess then. Let's see, you wrote back to Lassie, thanking her for the autographed picture," her mother said.

"The boy who plays Timmy on the show, he signed the picture, not Lassie."

Her mother groaned. "I know the dog can't write. I was making a joke. Ha. Ha. Ha. Just give me the mail, will you!" She snatched the mail out of Becky's hands. "Bill. Bill. Letter. And nothing for you!"

Never had Becky been so relieved not to get something

she wanted. At noontime, the next day, to beat her mother to the mailbox, she ran all the way home alone, since Linda refused to run, saying she was in no rush to get home for a macaroni and cheese lunch from a box.

Becky reached her house six minutes earlier than usual and tiptoed up the porch stairs. Still out of breath from running, she inched toward the mailbox, opened the lid slowly so it wouldn't squeak, and snatched out the mail. Bill for her father. Movie magazine for her mother, and a manila envelope for Miss Rebecca Makowiecki from North Tonawanda, New York. Kissing it, she unzipped her jacket, and shoved the envelope down the neck of her sweater, placing it next to her undershirt.

"Mail's here!" Becky shouted as her mother opened the door. She thrust the mail at her mother, kicked off her Oxford shoes, wiggled out of her jacket at record-breaking speed, then sprinted up the stairs.

"What's the matter with you? Why are rushing around like a chicken without a head?" her mother called after her.

Halfway up the stairs already, Becky turned to face her mother. "Bathroom! I have to go to the bathroom bad."

"So then go, fast, fast, who's stopping you?" her mother said. "Lunch is on the table. Wash your hands good afterwards."

"I know, I know!" Becky muttered. Because her mother was standing there watching her, Becky went to the bathroom. After counting to sixty, she flushed the toilet, then washed her hands. Opening the bathroom door, she stuck her head out, making sure the coast was clear. It was. She made a dash for her bedroom, hiding the envelope under her mattress.

She was almost too excited to eat her lunch, but she did anyway, because her mother had made Becky's second favourite lunch – a toasted Western sandwich, a glass of chocolate milk, a banana, and three chocolate chip cookies.

On the way back to school with Linda, all during the afternoon, and on the way back home with Linda, Becky hardly heard a single word because all she could think about was reading the stuff inside the envelope. At home, she headed straight upstairs to her room. She was tempted to close the door all the way, and not just halfway. But if the door was closed, her mother would know for sure Becky had to be doing something she didn't want anyone to know about.

Lifting up one corner of the mattress, she stuck her hand underneath and pulled out the envelope. Envelope in hand, she took her pen flashlight and headed for the closet and went inside, glad at least to have a closet door to close.

She cleared away a spot and sat down cross-legged. They'd sent two pamphlets: *Family Shelter Designs* and *The Family Fallout Shelter, 1962*. Beaming her penlight on them, she began to read.

The shelter had to be dug thirteen feet deep in the ground. Ten square feet of room was needed for every person using the shelter. That meant forty square feet for her family. And what about Mrs. Lepinsky? She couldn't be left alone. That meant fifty square feet and an awful lot of digging.

She read on. In the shelter you had to have a month's

supply of canned food and bottled water, a battery-operated transistor radio, eating utensils, clothing, pillows, blankets, medicine, and something called a dosimeter that you attached to the end of a broomstick and stuck out into the air to check the level of radiation, to see if it was safe yet to go back outside. How was she supposed to get all that and dig a giant hole in the backyard without anyone noticing?

Linda had to go in on this! This was an honest-to-goodness real plan. They could help each other digging out holes in their backyards for shelters. Too bad it wasn't summertime, because then they could have covered up the holes with some rolls of grass borrowed from Mrs. Lepinsky, who had gotten a whole new grass lawn, saying that, since she didn't know how much longer she was going to be here on this place on earth before moving to that place upstairs, she wanted to have a lawn as plush as carpeting. So she'd hired gardeners to scalp her lawn of its brown, dried-out grass, and had a new lawn laid down. But maybe, just maybe, Mrs. Lepinsky still had a couple of rolls of grass left over in her garage shed. Probably she did, because she never threw anything out.

Linda would go for this. She had to!

Flicking off the penlight, she put down the pamphlets and rested her head against her knees. What would it be like to be all together in a fallout shelter for a long time when everybody in her family always got so crabby, crammed together even on a short car trip? Maybe, though, everyone would stay polite in front of Mrs. Lepinsky.

The shelter would be there in the backyard, just in case. Just because her parents had aspirins, bandages, iodine, cough medicine, thermometers, Vicks VapoRub, calamine lotion, and castor oil, didn't mean they had to use them. All that stuff was there, just in case, because you never knew.

Having had enough of the dusty closet, she pushed open the door with one foot and crawled out. To get some fresh air, she opened the window wide and took in several big, deep, refreshing breaths of air. Elbows propped on the windowsill, Becky gazed out at the blue sky and white clouds speeding across it, then looked back down at the backyard, trying to decide where to start digging.

THE GARAGE SHED

"SPIT IT OUT, ALREADY," LINDA SAID, WHACKING BECKY hard on the back as if she was choking on a piece of food as they sat on the back-porch stairs at Linda's house.

It was now or never. Becky took a deep breath and glanced around Linda's backyard. Yes, the space between the flower beds and the oak tree seemed like the best spot to suggest for the fallout shelter.

"Remember how Perry said that after a nuclear missile or bomb exploded...." Becky stammered because she was so nervous.

"We all go kaput from the radiation in the air," Linda said, then stood up. She clutched her stomach, acted like she was barfing, then ripped at her hair and tumbled down onto the dried-up fall grass.

Did Linda think that pretending to die of radiation sickness was funny? Not in Becky's book. She was sorry she'd brought it up.

Linda sat up and dusted off some pieces of dried grass

from her pea jacket. "Not funny, huh?"

"Nope!" Becky said. Should she go on or should she just forget about it? But if she didn't say something about it to Linda and there was a nuclear war, what would happen to Linda and her family? She had to say something, even if Linda laughed at her.

Linda sat back down on the step next to Becky. "Having your own fallout shelter, that would help, wouldn't it? I saw a picture in *Life* magazine of a family sitting all together in a fallout shelter they'd built in their own backyard. It looked like a cold cellar, except it stored people, not food. You know the Mayor, Nathan Phillips, he has one, just over on Oriole Parkway, and so do the owners of the Eaton's stores in Forest Hill. So I wrote to Ottawa and got two pamphlets. One's called *Eleven Steps To Survival* and the other is called *Fallout Shelters*. What do you think? It's hard, but it would be easier if you helped me make one in my backyard, and I helped you make one in your backyard."

Startled, Becky nearly fell off the edge of the step. It was like a telephone line was running between her brain and Linda's brain, passing ideas back and forth without them having to say a single word out loud.

"I wrote away to North Tonawanda and got two pamphlets too."

"Really?" Linda said. "Great minds think alike, huh, and not like Allen Rosenzweig."

Becky laughed. Miss Payne had given him a week-long detention for not doing any work on his fallout shelter presentation, and worse, she'd put him in the detention room run by Mr. Lucas.

"So then let's do it," Linda said, studying her backyard.

"How about over there?" Becky mumbled, pointing in the direction of the oak tree.

"That's what I was thinking too!" Linda said. "Inside the garage shed. The floor is just made of dirt, so we can dig and nobody can see what we're doing until we're ready to show them. And the shed can be the roof of the shelter. If we just made it in the backyard, how would we build a roof for the shelter?"

Linda was right. What kind of roof and protection would they have gotten from Mrs. Lepinsky's leftover rolls of grass? The sheds were perfect, because neither of their families owned cars, only rented them when they were going on a vacation, so hardly anyone ever went into the garage sheds.

For the next hour, they figured out how they were going to get stuff for their shelters. Since Linda's mother mostly bought only canned and boxed food, because she hated to cook, Linda was going to, day by day, steal cans and boxes and store them away in the shed. Since Becky's mother hardly ever bought canned and boxed food, because she loved to cook, Becky had to start going shopping with her to get her to buy some.

Most of the other stuff, like pillows, blankets, cutlery, can openers, flashlights, batteries, and clothes could be stolen one by one and stored away.

Linda and Becky couldn't stop giggling as they told each other how they were going to steal the stuff. The only big thing they had to get was the dosimeter, but they'd figure that out later.

"Why are you two laughing like hyenas?" Mrs. Friedman said, coming out onto the back porch. "I could hear you both, even with the radio on."

That only made Linda and Becky giggle some more. "Go ahead, laugh some more. What are you doing out here anyway? It's chilly and it's already getting dark."

"We were just admiring the view," Linda snapped back.

"You are *such* a comical girl. Aren't I lucky to have you to be entertained by!" Mrs. Friedman said, then slammed the back door shut as she went inside.

Becky peeked over at Linda, whose face had gotten all red like she'd been slapped by her mother. Linda got up. "It's kind of chilly. Why don't I come over to your house tomorrow, and we can compare pamphlets and make more plans."

"Sure," Becky said, standing up to go home. Thrusting her right arm out like a knight did before he went off on a grail quest, she said loudly, "Canned food, here I come!"

Linda made a face. "Just wait until you have to eat it every day!"

WITH CANNED FOOD ON THE BRAIN, two days later, when her mother mentioned she was going food shopping to Dominion and did Becky want something special from there, Becky surprised her mother by asking to come with. Her mother gave her the long look, then told Becky to get Jeffie ready to go.

In the store, Becky stuck to her mother like a shadow. After only ten minutes, though, Becky was already getting a bad case of wandering feet. Her mother was always *so slow!*

She looked at this, she looked at that. She compared this price with that price. Sometimes when Becky couldn't stand her mother staring and staring at two different brands, she was really tempted to grab any one box out of her mother's hands and just toss it into the shopping cart. Those times when she wasn't just tempted but ready to do it, she would leave her mother and wander up and down the aisles. That was why she hardly ever went shopping with her mother anymore, except when her mother needed help carrying the groceries home.

But this afternoon, no matter how slow and how picky her mother was being, Becky was going to be patient for once, and be on the lookout for the chance to get her mother to buy canned food.

So what if the Soviet ships were now taking the missiles back to the Soviet Union? Something was still up, because why else were the television stations still running the test of the emergency broadcast system every half-hour, and why else was Mr. Lucas still ringing the siren, and why else was the class still ducking and covering under desks, and why else were President Kennedy and Premier Khrushchev putting an emergency telephone hotline in their offices? She bet she wasn't the only one with nuclear war and canned food still on the brain.

There was no canned food in the first aisle, only fresh fruit and vegetables, so Becky had a little time to let her eyes and thoughts wander just a little as her mother was busy picking grapes off bunches and tasting them so she could choose the sweetest tasting bunch to buy.

Since Jeffie had no mission except to get out of Dominion as fast as possible, he began yanking on the back of their mother's camel car jacket. "Hurry up! Come on! Let's go!"

Their mother swallowed a grape, then without a word, she swooped up Jeffie and placed him in the front seat of the shopping cart.

"This is for babies. I'm not a baby!" he cried out.

"Mm," their mother said, and went back to picking off grapes, until finally, finally, she chose two bunches of seedless green grapes. It was a good that there was nothing to pick off oranges, apples, bananas, tomatoes, lettuce, cucumbers, and potatoes, because otherwise they would be stuck in Aisle One forever and forever!

Aisle Two was filled with drinks. Instead of picking up a bottle of Orange Crush and begging her mother to buy it, Becky picked up something she'd never even noticed before – bottled water.

"Can we get this?" she asked.

"What? Are you crazy? I'm going to spend money on water when I can get it free from the taps? What's come over you lately?" her mother said.

Shuffling from foot to foot, Becky tried to make up a half-decent excuse for why she wanted to buy water. But she couldn't even make up a crummy one, so she just put the bottle back on the shelf. Next to it she noticed a bottle of seltzer water. Ah! She could sneak away a couple of bottles of the seltzer water her parents had delivered every two weeks. Becky didn't like it much, it made her burp, but mixed with raspberry syrup, it wasn't *too* bad.

She silently trudged alongside her mother as they went up and down Aisles Three, Four, and Five. When they reached Aisle Six, where all the canned fruit, vegetables, and meat were, she took a deep breath, preparing herself to fight with her mother.

She picked up a can of peaches. "Can we get this?"

Her mother raised her eyebrows. "Okay. Peaches are out of season. Check the price, then throw it in!"

Becky scratched her head. So that was how to do it! She had to chose fruits and vegetables you couldn't get in the fresh fruit and vegetable section.

Next she picked up a can of corn. "Can we get this?"

Her mother raised her eyebrows even higher. "You hate corn in a can."

"I changed my mind," Becky whispered, looking over at Jeffie, who was slumped over in the baby seat like he was napping.

"That brand is too expensive. Pick up the one beside it."

Whew! This was hard work, Becky thought, as she tossed the can into the cart. Near the end of the aisle were the canned meats. Becky picked up a can of Spam luncheon meat.

"Can we get this?" she asked.

"What's gotten into you?" Her mother now sounded very annoyed. "You pick up cans of vegetables and fruits you never wanted to eat when I bought them before. Now suddenly they're appetizing? Okay, I don't mind buying them, if they're fruits and vegetables out of season. But if I can afford to buy fresh, why should we eat garbage in cans? Spam! I wouldn't feed Spam to a dog!"

Jeffie lifted up his head and barked.

"Stop it, you, this very second!" Becky's mother said, giving Jeffie a very strong *you're going to get it if you don't listen to me* look.

"But Mummy, Aunt Rifka served it to me and Evelyn once for lunch," Becky said.

"She would," her mother said. "That's Rifka all over. She's as cheap as they come. Why are you giving me that look? You think I'm cheap too, don't you?"

Becky slowly shook her head, no. A couple of weeks ago, she and her mother had gotten into a giant fight in Aisle Five when her mother wouldn't let her buy a package of chocolate chip cookies. Even after her mother had promised to bake her a fresh batch later at home, Becky hadn't stopped calling her mother "Mrs. Cheap."

All the way home, her mother had given her a long lecture on the difference between being careful with money and being cheap. Being careful with money meant that for pennies of the cost of a bag of chocolate chip cookies, her mother could bake a batch that would taste much better. Being cheap meant you bought something you knew didn't taste good just because it was cheaper.

Becky put back the can of Spam. Rather than spending her allowance on comics, potato chips, chocolate bars, and caramel candies, she was going to have to save it so she could buy Spam and canned vegetables.

EVERY DAY when Becky went over to Linda's to check how Linda was doing with getting stuff for the shelter, she felt worse and worse. After just a week, Linda had a grocery store aisle worth of canned food. Canned fruit cocktails. Canned peas and corn. Canned tuna and salmon. Boxes of cereal, cookies, and crackers. Linda had even come up with an idea for how to get bottled water. She was taking empty orange juice, milk, and cola bottles out of the garbage, washing them out and pouring in water! To sterilize the water, you put in Halazone tablets, Linda had read in one of her pamphlets, and she'd already sent off a postal money order to the address of the company that sold them, ordering enough tablets for both of their families.

Why hadn't Becky thought of that?

From her family's guest room, Linda had gotten pillows, sheets, and blankets, and she'd already filled one suitcase with changes of clothes for her family. Next, she was going to steal some cutlery, knives, and a can opener.

After just a week, what did Becky have to show in her garage shed? Not enough food for even two meals, and pretty crappy ones at that. Two cans of peaches. One can of green beans. A box of Ritz crackers and two boxes of Cheerios. A bottle of Aspirin and a bottle of calamine lotion. She had only managed to sneak out one old feather pillow, which every time you put your head down on it shot out a stream of feathers, a torn bedsheet, and a can opener so dull you had to have the strength of Hercules to open a can with it.

Linda had even come up with an idea to get extra money to buy more supplies and a dosimeter. On the school bulletin board, she'd seen a sign that the *Toronto Daily Star* newspaper was looking for paper boys. If a stupid and lazy dumbbell like

Allen Rosenzweig could have a paper route, why couldn't she and Becky?

It was another genius idea from Linda. How come she wasn't coming up with any genius ideas? Becky would have to work harder and think harder so her family's shelter would be all ready and waiting...just in case. If that meant getting better at stealing things from their house, she'd do it. If that meant delivering newspapers, even though strange dogs might chase after her, she'd do it, carrying a can of her mother's hair spray, if she could steal it, to spray at any biting dogs.

AT LAST BECKY HAD COME UP WITH AN IDEA. Since Mrs. Lepinsky was going to be staying with the Makowieckis in their fallout shelter, it was important to find out what kind of food she could eat and to steal some of her clothes so she'd have a couple of outfits to wear until it was safe to go back to her house.

As Becky sat with Mrs. Lepinsky in her living room, asking questions about her diet, saying it was for a school project, Linda was upstairs, going to the bathroom for the fifth time but really stealing Mrs. Lepinsky's clothes and stuffing them into Becky's and Linda's schoolbags.

"What a bad stomach Linda has today," Mrs. Lepinsky said in a worried voice. "Linda, sweetheart, how are you doing? I know just the thing to settle your stomach. Warm milk with cinnamon, I'll make some."

"No, no, no," Becky said, pressing her hand down on Mrs. Lepinsky's arm. If Mrs. Lepinsky got up, she would catch Linda stuffing her clothes into the schoolbags. Becky would have to iron them all when she got home, because Mrs. Lepinsky would never, ever, wear anything with a wrinkle in it. Plus, Becky knew that Linda hated drinking warm milk as much as Becky did. It tasted horrible and, worse, heating it up made a thick film sit on top of it which stuck to your teeth.

Linda came into the living room, wiping her washed hands on her overalls. "I'm feeling much better. Where were we? Your dinner menu."

She plopped down on the couch next to Mrs. Lepinsky and picked up her notebook.

"Mrs. Lepinsky can't have salt in her food," Becky said.

"High blood pressure," Mrs. Lepinsky said. "I haven't had a pinch of salt in who knows how many years."

There was lots of salt in canned vegetables and meats, Becky knew, that's why she hated eating them so much. There must be canned foods without salt. She had to check that out.

"Mrs. Lepinsky, she can't eat too many sweets either," Becky added.

"High blood sugar," Mrs. Lepinsky explained. "I haven't had a pinch of sugar since...last Tuesday. I cheated and had a cherry danish. It was delicious."

There was lots of sugar in canned fruits, Becky knew, because her cavities always stung from the syrup. They had to find canned fruits without so much sugar.

"Do you take any medicine?" Becky asked.

"Medicine? I eat medicine. High blood pressure pills.

Heart pills. Stomach pills. Don't ask," Mrs. Lepinsky said.

Linda had to steal some of those too. Becky wiggled her shoulders as a signal, hoping Linda would get it.

"Itchy back?" Mrs. Lepinsky said. "I just got a manicure, so my nails are nice and sharp. Turn around and I'll give you a good scratch."

Linda bolted up from the couch. "I have to go to the bathroom again!"

"Maybe you should TAKE SOME PILLS for it when you get home?" Becky shouted after her.

"I'M GOING TO TAKE SOME PILLS, don't worry about it," Linda said, leaping onto the stairs.

"You don't have to wait until you go home, I have a pill you can take," Mrs. Lepinsky said, as she scratched Becky's back. Nobody gave as good a back scratch as Mrs. Lepinsky. "Linda, sweetheart, look in my medicine cabinet, and take one of the oblong yellow pills in the bottle that has Dr. Steinberg's prescription on it. It will settle your stomach one, two, three!"

Linda stopped four steps up and hung over the bannister. "I will, thanks. That's where I'm going. Straight for your medicine cabinet."

EACH TIME THE DOORBELL RANG at Linda's house, Linda and Becky jumped off the couch, thinking it was Frank Dimaggio, the head paper carrier, come to interview them. So far, an Avon Lady selling cosmetics, a Compton's ency-clopaedia salesman, and a vacuum cleaner salesman had rung the doorbell. No wonder Becky's mother was always complaining that between running after Jeffie and running to answer the doorbell, she ran more in a day than a marathon runner. After the milkman had rung the doorbell to give the Friedmans their weekly bill, Linda didn't sit back down, but instead paced back and forth in the living room...leaving so many footprints in the carpeting it looked like a school band had marched through.

"The footprints...." Becky said, not wanting to give Mrs. Friedman another reason to pick on Linda.

"I have to vacuum later, anyway," Linda said. "Where is he already?"

"Maybe he's not coming."

"Sure he's coming. Why wouldn't he come?" Linda said, yanking back the drapes and smashing her face against the front window.

"Maybe he already has enough paper boys," Becky said, tugging at her overalls. Boy, was she ever sweaty! To make Frank think she was bigger and stronger than she was, she'd put on a pair of thick leotards, an undershirt, and a long-sleeved shirt under her overalls. She'd looked herself over in the bathroom mirror and flexed her arms like Popeye the sailorman. Good! She looked strong enough to toss a newspaper near a porch and not like the skinny shrimp she was. She looked almost as strong as Linda, who was four inches taller than her.

"You all right?" Linda asked noticing Becky stretched out on the loveseat trying to cool off. "Your face is all red and shiny. Why are you wearing so many clothes?"

"I'll explain later," Becky mumbled.

The doorbell rang and Linda dashed to the door.

"I'm Frank Dimaggio, and you must be one of my new paper boys."

"I'm Linda Friedman and Becky Makowiecki's on the loveseat over there. Do we get the jobs?" Linda asked as she led Frank, who was a roly-poly man not much taller than Linda, into the living room.

Frank laughed, and Becky saw that he had a gold front tooth just like her mother's and so gave him a big smile.

"Now that's just the kind of greeting I like to get," he said, coming over to Becky and shaking her hand. She squeezed his hand tight so he would think she was strong enough, but he didn't seem to notice. She took a deep breath, ready to answer all his questions, but to her astonishment, after they all sat down on the couch he did all the talking. He talked, then talked some more, then gave Becky a route on Arlington and Winnett Avenues – thank her lucky stars, not on Rushton Road – and gave Linda a route on Atlas and Winona Avenues. He got up from the couch.

"You know Becky, tossing newspapers is like doing sports. You get hot fast. Dress warm, but not too warm, otherwise you will get as sweaty as a construction worker," he said, smiling, his gold tooth shining.

Blushing, she promised not to overdress.

When Frank was gone, she and Linda whooped and danced around the living room.

"We have our own paper routes!" Linda yelled out.

"And soon our own dosimeters!" Becky said.

"Look what you two have done to the carpeting! Foot-marks everywhere!" Mrs. Friedman said angrily as she stomped toward them. "How many times have I warned you about this?"

"Mrs. Friedman, we're sorry about all the footmarks," Becky mumbled, not sorry at all, but sometimes you had to say things you didn't believe, like she always did when Rufus was circling her and growling and she said nice doggy, go away, nice doggy.

"What's sorry? Is sorry going to do the vacuuming of the carpet?" Mrs. Friedman spat out.

"Wasn't I going to vacuum today anyway? So what's a few more footmarks to vacuum?" Linda muttered.

"Don't you talk back to me!" Mrs. Friedman said, raising her arm to hit Linda, then she dropped it and stomped out.

"You better go now!" Linda whispered.

"See you tomorrow, *Star* paper boy," Becky said. As she walked home, she wondered how come Mrs. Friedman acted so mean for nothing to Linda? And how come Miss Payne acted so mean for nothing, and how come Mr. Gottesman was so mean when he was punishing his sons, and probably other times too, making them be just as mean for nothing? Her head began to spin so fast with how comes that she had to stop walking and hold onto her head. "No more how comes for today!" she told her brain.

She knocked on the door of her house and her mother answered. "Look at that face! He didn't take you as paper boys?"

"Yeah, he took us," Becky said, with a big sigh.

"So how come you look like you just came from a funeral?" her mother asked.

"How come? How come? How come?" Becky grumbled.

"What did I say?" her mother shouted as Becky ran past her and up the stairs. Right now, all she wanted to do was lie on her bed with her pillow over her head to block out all the how comes she had no answer for.

EVERY DAY AFTER SCHOOL and early on Saturday mornings for the past two weeks, Frank had come to Becky's house in a station wagon filled with bundles of newspapers. He would give Becky her bundle, and with the papers in Jeffie's wagon, off she'd go to deliver them. She had tried tossing them for a couple of days, but since she had trouble even throwing a softball straight, the newspapers had landed on driveways, on flower beds, in the middle of lawns, but never where they were supposed to land – on porches. So she'd ended up carrying them up to the porches, and that was fine with her...unless the people had a dog. But knock on wood, she hadn't been bothered by any dog...yet. Becky liked being a paper boy and earning her own money. The money was really helping her supply of food grow.

On her third Saturday as a paper boy, after delivering her papers, Becky went over to Linda's to check out her garage shed. Now Linda had enough food to open a restaurant. Sitting on a blanket in the corner of Linda's shed, they munched on Kit Kat chocolate bars. Across from them were two brown suitcases, one filled with clothing, the other with linens and towels. Next to them was a big shopping bag filled with potato chips, cookies, chocolate bars, and candies – another genius idea from Linda. Why only eat canned peaches, peas, and Spam? Linda had said.

"This is so great," Becky said, looking around, feeling jealous.

"You think so?" Linda said proudly. "Not bad. Not bad at all. Maybe I won't wait for a nuclear war and just move in here anyway."

Becky nodded. That's what she would do if she had to live day in and day out with Mrs. Friedman.

"You know what I was thinking," Linda said, licking the last bits of chocolate off the wrapper.

Ohhhhhh! Another genius idea was coming from Linda, Becky just knew it. After all the years Becky had spent making up escape plans in her head, you would think that once she was in the middle of a real plan, she would be bursting with ideas. But no! If it wasn't for Linda's genius ideas, Becky would still be working on some stupid plan about borrowing a roll of grass from Mrs. Lepinsky's shed to cover up a giant hole in the backyard.

Maybe she was only a dreamer, just like her father always said. All the escape plans she'd made – more even, she'd bet, than the world-famous prisoner, the Birdman of Alcatraz – and she'd never yet escaped to anywhere.

"The ground's going to freeze into a block of concrete soon, you know that, don't you?" Linda said.

Becky nodded, even though she had totally forgotten that it was now the beginning of December and winter was around the corner.

"So if we want to start digging, we have to do it soon. Very soon!"

"Do you want to begin now?" Becky asked.

"Can't. Too many people snooping around on the weekends. We'll start on Monday right after delivering the *Star.* One day we'll dig in your shed, the next in mine," Linda said, then got up.

Becky got up too. As they were leaving the shed, Becky clutched Linda's arm. "I got the phone numbers of some stores that sell dosimeters. I'll call them and find out how much they cost, so we'll know where we can buy the cheapest one."

"Good idea!" Linda said.

Even that good idea wasn't really Becky's. It came from watching her mother compare prices in grocery stores.

"Monday, we dig!" Becky said, sticking out her hand to shake Linda's.

"Monday, we dig!" Linda echoed.

ON MONDAY AFTER FINISHING HER PAPER ROUTE, Becky slipped into the house and changed into her digging clothes: an old red sweater, a pair of leotards, and on top of them, a new pair of jeans her mother had bought for her. They were so loose around the waist that she could drop a book right down her legs, if she wanted to. Her mother believed in buying clothes several sizes larger so Becky and Jeffie could grow into them. Becky hoped she would be around to grow into these jeans. And the only way to make sure of that, she thought, giving her jeans a sharp tug, was to get her fallout shelter built fast.

She went to get Jeffie who was lying on his back on his bedroom floor, racing Dinky cars on his stomach and along his arms.

"You ready yet? You said you'd help, remember?"

After leaving Linda on Saturday, she'd taken Jeffie to Tom's Variety store and told him how she and Linda were going to be building fallout shelters in their garage sheds, in case there was a war. It would be just like a tree house except, instead of being up high in a tree, the house would be in the ground like a cellar. After buying Jeffie a Coffee Crisp chocolate bar, a Joe Louis cake, and seven Kraft caramel candies, he'd agreed to help, and most importantly, to keep it a secret till they were done.

"Don't feel like it. Do it yourself!" he said, as he zoomed a car up his arm to his shoulder.

She'd spent some of her hard-earned fallout shelter savings bribing Jeffie with food. It better not have been a waste of money.

"You promised!" she said, getting mad. "Just forget about it!"

He sat up. "Okay. I'm coming."

Becky helped him get dressed in warm clothes. Then they went outside to their backyard where Linda was pacing back and forth.

"What took you guys so long? Geez, it's already getting dark. And it's cold out here," she said, rubbing her hands together.

"Ask HIM!" Becky said, pulling Jeffie toward the garage

shed. Before she opened the door, she turned to him. "Remember, this is and this stays a secret!"

He made a face at her. Becky pushed the door open, and just as she was stretching to reach the metal chain to put on the single light bulb, she felt Linda tug her back.

"No, no, no, the light will show under the door and give us away!"

Linda was right. But once the door was shut, it would be as pitch black as a cave in here. How could they see where to dig then?

"It's too dark here!" Jeffie complained as Linda shut the door.

"Only for a second," Linda said. "I have a flashlight in my pocket. It'll give us enough light for digging, but not enough to give us away, especially if I place it at the back." She flicked it on.

Yet another genius idea from Linda! Jeffie got all excited when Linda shone the light all around the shed. He ran around, touching everything, not that there was that much to touch. Compared with Linda's shed, which was now as filled with stuff as a department store, Becky's shed looked like, well, a garage shed with some canned food and candy, some bottles filled with water, a shoebox with knives, cutlery, and a can opener, an old suitcase that wouldn't close with clothes in it, two pillows, a blanket, and three sheets.

"Just wait till you see Linda's!" Becky said to Jeffie, handing him a gardening spade. She and Linda grabbed two shovels propped against the side of the shed. Then Linda went over to Becky's supply of canned foods and, choosing a large can of peaches, she rested the flashlight on it so it would beam light at them while they worked.

Just as Linda had said it would be, the ground was already getting solid from the cold, making it hard to shovel up. After only ten minutes of digging, all of their backs and arms hurt. Plus, there was all that dirt! What were they going to do with it?

"Garbage bags for the dirt, that's what we need," Linda huffed, taking a rest.

Becky decided to take a rest too, and so did Jeffie. For a couple of minutes, they stood there, panting.

Through all the panting, Becky heard something. Something that sounded like footsteps.

"Somebody's coming!" Becky hissed. "What are we going to do?"

How come nobody ever came out to the garage shed… except when the three of them were in there, digging it up?

"Think fast!" Linda said, gulping. "What should we say?"

"That we're digging a hole to go into after there's a war," Jeffie said.

"NO!" Becky and Linda hissed together at Jeffie.

"I got it!" Becky said. "We'll say what I said to Jeffie. That we're making a tree house in the ground for the winter."

Before Linda or Jeffie could say whether they thought that would work, the garage shed door swung open, banging against the wall.

"What's going on here?" Her father strode into the shed. He reached up and yanked on the light bulb. The brightness blinded Becky and she blinked her eyes several times until they adjusted to the light. With a feeling of dread, she watched her father slowly look around, taking everything in.

"Why's all this food here? And a blanket and pillows, and a suitcase?"

Becky opened her mouth, but nothing came out. She looked over at Linda and Linda opened her mouth, but nothing came out there either. Of all the people to find them in the shed, it had be her father! Becky felt like she had the stinkiest luck on the whole planet earth.

Dropping his spade, Jeffie went over to their father.

"So is somebody going to speak? Or are you all going to stand there like mutes?" her father snapped in a louder voice.

"Hey, Pilgrim," Linda said, and gave Becky's father a little smile which disappeared when Becky's father glared at her, not saying a word back.

"Daddy," Jeffie said, tugging on their father's sleeve.

Becky's heart dropped right to her knees. That blabber-mouth, he was going to tell their father everything. She put her index finger over her mouth, then she shook her head, making her braids fly. But Jeffie wasn't paying any attention to her. He was looking at their father.

"Daddy, we're digging a hiding place," Jeffie explained.

Linda softly groaned and Becky clutched her shovel for support, her knees shaking like anything. This was finished. She was finished.

"A hiding place," her father said in his sarcastic voice, which like always, made her stomach do somersaults. "What for? Did you rob a bank lately? Is the hole for the loose change which is always missing from my pockets lately?"

If she didn't have the shovel to lean on, Becky would have

fallen over, her legs were shaking that much. She was the one who had been taking all the loose change from her father's pockets.

Jeffie giggled. "No, it's a hiding place...for us."

Becky could hear Linda hemming and hawing, trying to get some words out. "It's a tree house, a kind of hideout, like in a western, Pil...grim," Linda swallowed the words when Becky's father scowled at her, then again at Becky.

Becky glanced around the shed. It could be a tree house kind of hideout, and all the stuff, the cans, the blankets, the cola bottles filled with water, could be tree house supplies. Why not? Just as she was getting up the nerve to go on with the tree house story, her father put his hand on Jeffie's head and said, "Somebody here is going to tell me the truth, right Jeffie? This is a tree house like I'm the Prime Minister."

He left Jeffie's side and went over to the cola bottles which he tapped with the toe of one of his shoes. "What's this for? Water in bottles? Since when do any of you drink water?" Then he went over to the pile of cans and picked up a can of peas. "Peas? Since when do you eat peas?" Holding the can of peas in one hand, he went over to the suitcase and took out a beige short-sleeved shirt. His shirt. "I was looking all over for this shirt. Why is it here in a suitcase?"

He came over and stood in front of Becky and Linda, still holding the peas in one hand and his shirt in the other. "Now once and for all, who is going to tell me what is going on here?"

Becky and Linda looked at each other. It wasn't going to be either one of them. Becky stepped closer to Jeffie, one hand behind her back so she could pinch him to remind him not to spill the beans.

"Ouch! What did you do that for?" Jeffie squealed.

"I have all the time in the world to wait," her father said, his voice getting lower and lower like it did when he was very, very angry. "Nobody is leaving here until I get the truth, do you hear me? Don't give me any more garbage about a tree house. Why are you digging a hole like a grave?"

Becky gazed at the hole. Her father was right. It *did* look exactly like a grave. She shivered all over. How come a place that was supposed to protect you from dying from radiation looked more like a grave than a shelter? And how come none of them had seen that when they were digging, when her father saw that right away?

"Is somebody going to tell me or not?" her father said, saying every word slowly and clearly.

Forcing herself to stop looking over at the hole and thinking *grave, grave, grave,* Becky glanced over at Jeffie, who was moving his mouth around like he was getting ready to spill the beans. She tried to get her face to say to him, please don't do it, but his mouth kept opening and closing and opening....

"Daddy, it's a hiding place. For us. When the missiles fall. Becky got plans," Jeffie said.

In a flash, her father dropped his shirt and the can of peas and gripped Becky's arms so tightly he was really hurting her. "What missiles? What plans? What are you up to?" he yelled, shaking her.

Becky had never been so frightened of her father in her

life. "Nothing," she mumbled, glancing over at Linda, who looked as frightened as Becky was feeling.

"Pilgrim, Pilgrim," Linda whispered, as she lightly tapped Becky's father on the arm.

He jerked her hand off and Linda's face crumpled like she was going to start crying. "Answer me right now, do you hear me?" he asked. "What are you up to now?"

"Nothing," Becky mumbled, hardly able to speak or even breathe she was so scared.

Jeffie went over to their father, and tugged on his pant legs. "Let go of Becky. Let go of her!"

"Answer me!" her father yelled, the lines around his mouth an inch deep now.

He started to shake Becky back and forth and the shaking made her feel like she was going to throw up the shortbread cookies she'd eaten just before coming out to dig. She had to tell her father. He wouldn't stop shaking her until she did.

"It's a fallout shelter. To save us from the radiation from nuclear missiles and bombs, in case there's a nuclear war between the Russians and Americans," she cried out.

"Are you insane?" her father roared. Still holding onto her with one hand, with his other hand he slapped her across the face, first on one side, then the other, as Becky sobbed and struggled to get away.

"How dare you fill Jeffie's head with such nonsense! I'll give you a fallout shelter!" He raised his hand to slap her again.

Before he could, Linda leapt on him, grabbing his raised hand and kicking him in the shins. "You let go of Becky! Let go of her! You're hurting her!"

Then Jeffie joined in, pounding his fists into their father's thighs. "Mummy, Mummy, come quick! Daddy's killing Becky! Stop him, Mummy! Mummy! Mummy come quick!" he wailed.

Her mother came running into the garage shed. "I heard shouting from the kitchen. What's going on here?"

Everybody froze, even her father, and turned their heads to look at Becky's mother.

She shouted at Becky's father in Polish. He shouted back even louder in Polish. She shouted back some more, then finally Becky's father let go of her and Becky, stumbling on the can of peas, fell to the ground, crying. Linda and Jeffie came over, crouched beside her and patted her on the back. Pushing past Becky's father, her mother knelt and took her into her arms.

"What happened?" she murmured, stroking Becky's head. The closeness of her mother made Becky start sobbing all over again.

"Him!" Linda said, pointing at Becky's father. "He slapped and shook Becky. Just because we were building a backyard fallout shelter to save us all from the radiation. For trying to save her family and Mrs. Lepinsky, what does he do, he goes completely nuts! I'm making a fallout shelter too. We're not the only ones, you know. The mayor has one. Prime Minister Diefenbaker has two – one in his house and the Diefenbunker! If they can live after a war, why can't we too?" Linda shrieked, then began to wail, and Jeffie joined in.

Becky raised her head from her mother's shoulder to look

over at Linda. Wiggling an arm loose, she reached over and took hold of her hand. And this made Linda wail even more. Then Becky sobbed harder and so did Jeffie.

Her mother opened her arms wide. "Come children, come to me!" Linda and Jeffie moved closer so that Becky's mother could hold all three of them together. "Children, shush, shush!" she murmured over and over as she held them. When they all stopped wailing, she raised her head and started speaking in Polish to Becky's father.

Her father flung back Polish words at her mother like he was throwing stones. "You encourage her...always...with those crazy ideas of hers!" he yelled, switching back to English. He strode over to the cans, kicked over a stack of them so that they rolled all over the shed.

Her mother spoke back to her father in Polish. Becky didn't want to look at him, but she kept lifting her head from her mother's shoulder to sneak peeks at him. He looked like an angry lion at the zoo, stalking back and forth in his cage, growling. She saw Jeffie and Linda doing the same thing as her, watching him, then looking away, then watching him again.

"Your daughter. Your son. Your children! You always take their side! So take them, your children!" her father yelled and stormed out.

Becky felt her mother stiffen. As her father went through the door, her mother yelled after him, "What did the children do so wrong? Nothing. Absolutely nothing." Her mother's voice got hoarse and she coughed hard.

In all the years, Becky had never seen her mother get so

angry at her father. "Mummy, I'm sorry. Me and Linda, we got real scared about there being a nuclear war, so we thought we'd build our own fallout shelter to live in until it was safe."

"Why did he have to go and hit Becky like that. He's nuts!" Linda cried out.

"Linda, please," her mother said, sighing. "Don't say things like that when you don't know the whole story."

"Why did Daddy have to hit me like that? He's just like Mr. Gottesman! We didn't mean to do anything bad." Becky shook all over and her mother held her even tighter.

"Shush, shush. You all meant good. I know. Daddy...."

"I hate him! I hate him! I hate him, Mr. Gottesman the second!" Becky shouted, then burst into wails.

"Me too! Me too!" Jeffie shouted, and wailed along with Becky.

"Children, please!" her mother said, sounding close to crying herself. "Don't ever say that. Not never. You don't believe me now, but Daddy loves both of you very much. He's not like Mr. Gottesman. Not at all. You have to understand...."

"You're wrong! I don't believe you!" Becky interrupted. "I hate him!"

"Me too!" Jeffie wailed.

"He's horrible!" Linda wailed.

"Children, please! No more. You're breaking my heart!"

UNION STATION

Becky sat cross-legged at the top of the stairs, listening for the sound of her father leaving for work. Only then would she go downstairs to have breakfast before school, and not one second before, even if it meant eating cold Cream of Wheat and dried-out toast. Ever since her father had hit her in the garage shed three days ago, she hadn't talked to him. She wouldn't even look at him unless she had no other choice. But that wasn't working out too good, because all it did was start more fights with her father where he yelled at her and she pretended she was somewhere else without a father who hated her.

So now she was avoiding him, and that was almost working except for suppertime. But then everybody was too busy talking and passing food, talking and cutting the food, and talking and swallowing the food, to bother her about not talking to and not looking at her father. So far, anyway. She heard the sound of the closet door squeaking and heavy footsteps on the hardwood floor. At last, her father was getting his coat and leaving for work!

"Beckelah, where are you? You'll be late for school. Come eat already. Daddy's in the vestibule, come say goodbye!" her mother called out.

"I'm not dressed yet," Becky called back. When was her father going to leave already? She was hungry and her legs were falling asleep from sitting cross-legged for so long. Straightening out her legs, she saw that two pleats on her kilt were stuck together by bubble gum! Trying to get it off, she picked at the gum with her fingernails, but it wasn't so easy when you hardly had any fingernails. Then the sound of heavy breathing made her glance up. There was her father at the foot of the stairs, staring up at Becky, who was dressed from top to toe.

Becky didn't know what to do, this being one of those awful times she had no choice but to look back as her father looked at her. Then he shouted her mother's name and started speaking in Polish. From the slap, slap, sound of slippers, her mother was running to the vestibule from the kitchen. She came and stood beside Becky's father at the foot of the stairs, and for the longest minute, they all looked at each other.

Her mother put her hand on her father's arm. He flung it off, turned and slammed the door as he rushed out.

"Beckelah, why are you still doing this to Daddy? He's sorry. He's very sorry, you know that," her mother said.

Becky didn't answer. Complaining in Polish to her mother about her, she'd bet, then slamming the door, no, her father didn't seem sorry to her. Not one bit.

"Fine, be like that," her mother said, sighing. "At least come down and have a little breakfast. You'd better hurry, before Jeffie finishes his and starts eating yours!"

A BRISK WIND BLEW Becky back a couple of steps. Clutching the collar of her navy pea jacket around her throat, because she'd left her scarf in her bedroom, she looked over at Linda, whom the wind hadn't budged. Not an inch.

"No chance of the wind blowing me. I'm too fat. That's what my mother keeps reminding me of at every meal. 'Do you really need to eat that *too?* Just look at you, just look at you!'" Linda blurted out as she trudged beside Becky on the way to school.

"You're not fat!" Becky said. That Mrs. Friedman, how come she had children when she didn't want any? Linda wasn't fat in Becky's book. A wrestler was fat. Linda was just kind of chunky.

"You know what she said to me after your parents told her about the fallout shelter in the shed?" Linda spat out. "She said I was just hiding the food so I could eat it all by myself because I'm such a pig."

"I can't believe that!" Becky said. How could Mrs. Friedman think that when Linda had worked so hard on her shelter so she could save her family?

"Well, believe it!" Linda said. "You speaking to your... father yet?"

Becky shook her head, no.

"Good!" Linda said. "Never speak to him again. I'm giving

my mother the silent treatment too...not that she's noticed yet."

"Mm," Becky said, her face getting hot. She was embarrassed that Linda had seen her father hit her like a Mr. Gottesman, and she didn't want to talk about it.

"Did Frank call you from the *Toronto Daily Star?*" Linda asked.

Becky nodded. Her mother had told he'd called, but she hadn't called back. Now every time she delivered papers it made her remember why she'd taken on the paper route, and then she remembered what had happened with her father, so the whole time she was delivering papers she was miserable with remembering. Too bad, the only thing she wished she could have inherited from her father was his ability to forget as easily as Miss Payne erased her chalk writing off the blackboard. And did she inherit that? No! She had a memory that never stopped!

"He wanted to know if you and me could take on some extra streets during the Christmas holidays, because some of the other carriers are going on vacation. I said I would. Will you too?"

"Sure," Becky said, though she didn't want to. But if she didn't, Linda would be stuck having to do all the extra streets by herself. "I'll call Frank after school and tell him I'll do it too!"

The school bell rang just as they reached the fence, and they had to run to make it to class in time. After hanging up their coats, they rushed down the aisle between the desks only to be stopped by Judy's outstretched arm.

"Watch out!" she whispered. "The rat Miss Payne ate for

breakfast didn't agree with her. She's already sent Louie to the principal's office for...."

"Judy, what have we told you about talking?" Miss Payne hissed.

"That if I continue talking, I will shortly be keeping Louie company in the principal's office. I think that's what you said, wasn't it?" Judy said right back at Miss Payne like she was just daring her to try it.

"We're glad, very glad, you understand," Miss Payne said. "Now everybody rise for 'God Save the Queen.'"

It came over the PA system and everyone sort of sang along. Then as Mr. Lucas was reciting the Lord's Prayer, as he did every morning, there was a noise.... Was it a fart?

"Classsssssssssssssssssss!" Miss Payne hissed, stretching out one arm to clutch hold of the pointer. Once she got it, she thrust it out like a sabre. "No noises during the Lord's Prayer. Do we understand?"

The class understood. Or else the pointer was going to be drilled through somebody's chest until it came out their back.

"Today we will be performing a reading of the school play, Gore Vidal's *Visit To A Small Planet,*" Miss Payne announced with a big sigh of disappointment. No one from their class had even tried out for the annual school play at the end of February. After all the presentations on nuclear war and missiles, no one was too sure there was going to *be* a February, so why bother having to memorize a lot of lines when you could be packing in as many fun things as you could, just in case the end was really coming?

So, since none of her class was represented in the play,

Miss Payne was making them perform it in class. Even if Becky hadn't known Mr. Lucas had chosen the play, she would have guessed, because everything he chose was science fiction. This time it was a supposed-to-be-funny play about an alien who comes from outer space to earth and how the human beings he meets are weirder than any alien on any other planet in the universe.

Miss Payne directed the play like an animal trainer at the circus. And the more she directed, the more the class acted like stampeding circus animals.

"Do we have any volunteers?" Miss Payne asked.

Judy's arm shot up.

Miss Payne looked all around the class for another raised arm. But nobody raised their arm.

"Judy, please come to the front of the class," Miss Payne said, snapping each syllable out like somebody shooting elastic bands. "But we need more volunteers. Judy can't perform the play alone."

"Oh yes I can, I can do a one-woman show, using different voices for all the different parts," Judy said, bowing to the class as they clapped and whistled in agreement.

From the sour pickle expression on Miss Payne's face, it was clear that one voice from Judy was more than enough for Miss Payne. "Volunteers, please!"

Becky crouched down at her desk, and so did Linda and Marty Rappaport. Becky hated to perform, because she could never do anything right when too many people were watching. Linda hated to perform because of the Scrabble game her eyes played with her whenever they felt like it.

Despite all the tutoring Linda had got from the rabbinical student, she wasn't doing much better in school. Her parents had taken her to a pediatrician, then an eye doctor, and both of them had said there was nothing the matter with Linda. They both had told the Friedmans that Linda should just *apply* herself to her schoolwork. Ha! As if Linda didn't already. Becky would like to see how they'd *apply* themselves if their eyes played the Scrabble game with them. And Marty, he hated to perform because of his stutter.

"Becky, Marty, Linda, up to the front of the class," Miss Payne said, choosing them all, Becky bet, because their crouches had said *please don't choose me!* so of course she did.

"We will be performing the scene from act I when the alien arrives," Miss Payne said, looking them over to choose who was going to play what role. That was easy. Since three of them were lousy actors, the big role of the alien named Kreton should go to Judy. Becky looked over at Judy and mouthed, "You play Kreton!" Judy nodded.

"I can play Kreton, I know the role almost by heart," Judy said. Was Miss Payne in an extra torturing mood or not? If she was, she would make Linda or Marty play Kreton just to torture them, and give Judy the smallest role to torture her. But maybe having to listen to Linda and Marty would be even worse torture for Miss Payne. Clinking her shark's teeth, she slowly walked in front of them.

"Becky, you play Reba Spelding; Marty, you play Conrad Mayberry; Linda, you play Roger Spelding; and Judy, you play Kreton; and start at the beginning of the scene on page twenty-three."

Becky skimmed through the scene. Good, good, she had only a couple of lines. But, oh no, Linda had lots of lines. Linda's head was bent over the playbook and she was silently saying her lines. "Judy," Becky whispered. "Linda!"

Judy looked over at Linda and back at Becky, waving her hand in an *I'll handle this* signal.

Like she was some famous actress, Judy smoothed down her short brown hair, straightened her striped Oxford shirt, and did a couple of throat clearings. Then she began to read her part very, very slowly – so that when Linda read the part of Roger, it would just seem like they were speaking clearly for the people in the last rows of the auditorium, like Miss Payne was always ordering, and not as if Linda was having trouble reading her part.

They reached the section where Kreton was asking the Speldings about what year it was in earth time and where he'd landed.

"1962," Linda read out loud, "...and you're in the state of...Ver..."

"Virginia," Becky whispered.

"Virginia," Linda said. "s.a.u."

"Is that a country in outer space?" Perry jeered. "Did you come from there?"

""We all know where you came from wormface – under a rock!" Judy said, bouncing the playbook against her leg.

"Judy, watch your tongue!" Miss Payne spat out. Judy turned from eyeballing Perry to eyeballing Miss Payne.

"They are just letters. Read them in the right order, Linda," Miss Payne said.

"USA," Becky whispered.

"Rebecca, stop it! What have we told you about whispering to Linda? It must stop, once and for all. Linda, please go on!"

"USA," Linda mumbled. Then the next line she said in the scene, if Becky hadn't had the playbook right in front of her eyes she wouldn't have been able to tell what words Linda was trying to say.

"What language is that?" Joey shouted.

"Mongolian," Perry jeered. "The mongoloid is reading Mongolian." Everyone was hooting, and Linda's face became as red as her hair.

"Kreton...." Becky whispered, sliding closer to Linda.

"Rebecca, that is enough from you! Your constant, repeated, blatant whispering only highlights Linda's inability to read correctly. It does not hide it. Linda, this will not do, not at all! Please tell your mother at lunchtime, we want to speak to her after school today. Linda, go back to your seat, the rest of you, continue reading the play."

Between Marty's stuttering of his lines and Becky's mumbling of hers, she bet nobody could get what was going on. Finally, finally, finally, the noon bell rang. That torture was over, but another one began on the walk home for lunch. Becky kept saying she was sorry every two minutes or so. If she hadn't been such a crummy whisperer, Miss Payne wouldn't have kept hearing her, and Linda wouldn't be in such trouble. She'd made everything worse for Linda. Everything. Linda said it was okay, but it wasn't okay.

After lunch when Becky went to pick up Linda, Mrs.

Friedman came to the door, and told her that Linda had a bad headache and wouldn't be going back to school that afternoon, then slammed the door shut.

Becky stood there, staring at the closed door. Had Mrs. Friedman slammed the door in Becky's face because Linda had told her mother and her mother blamed Becky? Should she knock on the door again or just go back to school? Lifting her hand to knock, she stopped. What if Mrs. Friedman told her that Linda never wanted to speak to her again?

Becky turned and went down the porch stairs and down the walkway to the street. She walked a block, then spun around and headed home, feeling too sick to sit in school for the rest of the afternoon.

"Mummy, let me in!" Becky said as she knocked hard on the front door for the third time. How was she going to get in when the sounds of her mother vacuuming the carpet, and the television were so loud? Just as she was about to kick the door, it swung open and there was her mother, holding onto the vacuum cleaner hose.

"You? What are you doing here?"

"I told you somebody was there!" Jeffie shouted from the living room.

"So if you can hear and see so good that somebody's at the door, why are you on top of the television again, tell me that?" her mother shouted to Jeffie.

"Because I like it!" Jeffie shouted back.

"Because I don't like it, if you're not sitting next to the couch in two seconds, say bye-bye television watching for a week," her mother shouted, then turned back to face Becky.

"You look terrible," she said, dropping the hose with a clunk, and stretching out her arm to put the palm of her right hand on Becky's forehead.

"You're a piece of ice. The freezer should be so cold," her mother said. "The way you picked at your lunch, I should have known." She helped Becky off with her coat and scarf. "Come, I'll cut you a big piece of cheesecake, then you'll feel better fast."

Becky shook her head. "I'm tired. I wanna sleep," she said, so pooped out she could barely stand up.

"Becky's back?" Jeffie shouted. "Why?"

"Get off your stomach and stand up on your legs if you want to know why," her mother shouted back.

As her mother was helping Becky up the stairs, Jeffie followed behind. "What's wrong, Becky?"

"Nothing's wrong, I don't feel good, that's all." She wished her mother and Jeffie would just leave her alone.

"Later she'll come downstairs and play with you, okay?" her mother said.

"Okay," Jeffie said, then hopped down the stairs. At the bottom, he paused. "When later?"

"Later, how's that for an answer?" her mother asked.

"Okay!" Jeffie said. "What do you want to do then, huh?"

"Jeffie!" Becky and her mother said at the same time. When they reached Becky's bedroom, her mother rubbed the back of Becky's neck before she went in. "So later you'll tell me what's bothering you?"

Becky gazed up at her mother. How did her mother know she wasn't sick?

"You think a mother can't tell the difference between a child who's sick and a child who's worried sick? What kind of mother do you think I am?"

"My kind of mother," Becky said, her voice slurred.

"So my kind of daughter, you *will* tell me later, right?"

Becky nodded, then lay down on her bed and fell asleep. When she got up, she went back downstairs and helped Jeffie build a fort with his Lego set. It was a good thing that building a fort was easy and didn't take any thinking, because all of her thinking was about Linda. Should she call her...or not?

"That wall's crooked," Jeffie complained, as he got up and walked around the fort. "And it's got holes!"

"Do it yourself then!" Becky complained back, then took a look. Jeffie was right. Her side of the fort resembled a piece of Swiss cheese. So she pounded the Lego blocks tighter together until there were no holes in the wall. "Okay?"

He shrugged. "So what do you want to make now? A tower? A bridge?"

"Whatever, you decide."

As Jeffie circled the fort, Becky went back to thinking about Linda. Maybe she should call her now.

"So what are my two *mieskeits* up to now?" her father joked. When her father was in a good mood for a joke he teased them by calling them his two *miskeits,* which was Yiddish for ugly persons.

Startled, Becky glanced up and met her father's gaze. Right away she glanced away.

"I'm not a *mieskeit,* you're a *mieskeit!*" Jeffie said, hugging their father's legs. Jeffie had forgotten about what happened in the garage shed. Becky was never, ever going to forget.

"So what about you, Becky? You a *mieskeit* or not?" her father said, kneeling down beside her. Though she could smell his Old Spice aftershave mixed with the oil he got on his fingers from twisting wires into mattress springs, she pretended he wasn't there. As she stared down at the carpet, she heard her father's breathing and felt his eyes on her, almost like a hand touching her.

"How long is long?" he asked angrily, then stood up.

"Supper's ready!" her mother called out, coming into the living room. Her father spoke to Becky's mother in Polish and she answered back in Polish. Her father's voice got louder and louder, and her mother's higher and higher as they argued and argued. Jeffie and Becky looked at each other. She wished she could just run out of the room, but that would make her parents argue even more.

The phone rang, and Becky leapt up and grabbed it on the end table. It was Mrs. Friedman. "How's Linda? Can I talk to her please?" Becky said, panting into the phone receiver.

"If you think you can get her to talk, good luck to you," Mrs. Friedman said. "Linda! Linda! Come to the phone. It's Becky. She wants to talk to you. LINDA! Did you just hear what I said? Are you deaf along with being dumb?"

She was making things worse for Linda. Again. Why did she always make things worse? "It's okay, Mrs. Friedman. I'll talk to Linda later," she mumbled into the receiver. "Do you want to speak to my mother?"

Her mother came over and took the receiver from Becky.

"Hello, Miriam. No, I'm not busy. Not exactly. Just hold on a minute!" Placing her hand over the bottom of the receiver, she whispered to Becky. "Go turn off the oven, and set the table please. We'll have supper a little late today. Miriam has something important to tell me."

What was it? Becky wanted to know, so she stayed beside her mother, who kept making shooing away signals to her as she said, yeah, yeah, I know, I know, huh, yeah, yeah, into the receiver.

"Excuse me for a minute, Miriam," her mother said. "What did I tell you to do? If you don't turn off the oven, the meatloaf will shrink to the size of a peanut. Go and do it now!"

So Becky went. After turning off the oven, she set the table, then plopped onto a kitchen chair. Finally, her mother rushed into the kitchen and went right for the stove. Putting on a pair of oven mitts, she bent over and took out the meatloaf and potatoes, then stuck a giant fork in them. "Stones, we'll be eating stones for supper," she said with a sigh.

"Mummy, so?" Becky said, her heart pounding.

Her mother came over and gave her a quick hug. "It's not a story for now. Ira, Jeffie, come, the overcooked supper is on the table."

Even if the meatloaf hadn't been tough as rubber and the potatoes hard as marbles, Becky couldn't have eaten much.

After helping her mother clean up, Becky went upstairs and tried to do her homework. She opened her geography book, began to draw a map of Venezuela, then got tired of doing it and opened her history book. She read about the fur trade in Canada in the eighteenth century, but the words wouldn't travel from her eyes to her brain, and that made her remember Linda and how her eyes played the Scrabble game with her.

When was her mother going to come and tell her what Mrs. Friedman had said? Fed up with trying to do her homework, she got up from her desk and went to the window, opened the drapes, and leaning her forehead against the window pane, gazed out at the night sky. The quarter moon was as bright as a street light and as thin as a swing. All around it were dancing dots of stars. Tonight, gazing out at the moon and the stars wasn't making her almost believe that maybe, maybe, there was more to life than what the eye could see.

"A beautiful night, no?" her mother murmured, as she came in and stood beside Becky.

"Yeah," Becky said softly.

"What does it matter if it's beautiful out there, and it's not beautiful down here, not at all?" her mother said. "Come, we'll have a talk about Linda, and then I'll tell you a part of my story I never told you before."

Becky turned away from the window and sat down on the bed leaning against the headboard next to her mother, who was already there with her feet propped up on a pillow.

"Miriam, she had a talk with Miss Payne and Mr. Lucas. Then when Mr. Friedman got home from work, they talked. And the end of all this talk is that the Friedmans agreed with Mr. Lucas that Miss Payne's class is not the right one for Linda. There's another class at Dufferin Public School that might be the right one for Linda, and so tomorrow, Miriam is going to take Linda there to meet with the principal and teachers, and see what's what."

"Can I go there too? Maybe it's the right one for me too? Miss Payne stinks!"

"I agree, Miss Payne, pleasant company she's not. But as a teacher, she's not so bad...for you and the other students that can keep up. Linda needs a teacher that will give her special attention and extra time. You can still see her every day after school and on the weekends. Things will work out for Linda, you'll see."

"I should have helped her more!" Becky cried out.

"You helped Linda. But sometimes we can't help people, no matter how much we want to. Like your Daddy, this I know too, too well," her mother said, her voice coming out all pinched like someone had put a tight hand on her throat.

Her mother stroked her throat. "So many years and so much time gone by, and still the words to tell this story, they stick in my throat like they don't want to come out and be heard. This story, every word of this story, it still hurts me. I'll never forget," her mother said, sniffing back tears.

"What, Mummy, what?" Becky asked.

"Remember when the Germans burned down Krasnobrod?" her mother asked.

Becky nodded. All that was left of the houses was charred wood and ashes, and with all the fences burnt down, cows, horses, and chickens were on the loose. The dirt roads were clogged with families leaving Krasnobrod to find a new and safe home.

"Now, maybe a week after the German soldier kicked me

in the face, Zaide and Bubbe packed up what little we had to pack up and we got ready to go somewhere, anywhere else. Me, I didn't feel too good. My nose was all swollen so I couldn't breathe through it. The soldiers, the sounds of rifles and guns shooting day and night, the dead people you saw everywhere – terrible, it was just terrible. All I wanted to do was sit down, close my eyes, and cover my ears. But my parents made me get up and go. So I did, but I was like a sleep-walker. You could have pinched me, hit me, anything me, I would have felt nothing. A little ways outside Krasnobrod lived my Bubbe with her eldest son, my Uncle Moishe, a bachelor. Where she lived, the houses, they didn't burn down. But now I think, better they would have.... Right before we got near to where my Bubbe lived, my father, he saw a Russian man with a horse and cart. Since there was a family already in the cart, Zaide went over to the man to ask if he would take our family too. The Russian man agreed after Zaide traded the boots he was wearing and his leather belt for a ride for us on the cart."

Her mother paused, stroked her throat, then cleared it. She put her hand on top of Becky's. "On the side of the road, who do we pass but my Bubbe, standing beside Uncle Moishe? My mother told the Russian to stop the cart, and she got out and talked to her mother. The back of my mother was to me, and my Bubbe was facing me. She took a step to the left and gave me a look, then patted her apron pockets. I knew she was searching for candy to give me, so I hopped off the cart and went over to her. My mother stopped talking and my Bubbe smiled and dug her hands deep into her pockets until she found two candies, which she handed to me. I thanked her and she leaned forward and kissed my head, then my mother took me back to the cart.

"We climbed back on, and the Russian whipped his horse, and off we went. I looked over at my mother. Why wasn't Bubbe coming with us if it wasn't safe to be here anymore? So what if the cart was packed full with our family and another, and their valises? I could have sat on my Bubbe's lap and held a valise in my lap. Did my mother ask Bubbe to come with? Had Bubbe refused because even if we had made room for her, there would have been room only for her, and she would have had to leave Uncle Moishe behind all by himself? Questions, I had a mouth full of questions, and a heart filled with fear. I wanted to ask my mother why we were leaving Bubbe behind, but I was afraid. Not a good thing for a child to be always afraid of a mother...."

"Like Linda's afraid of her mother," Becky murmured. And like she was sometimes afraid of her father. ·

Her mother sighed. "Yes, like that. So though my mouth was filled with questions, I didn't speak. I just watched, as long as my eyes could watch, my Bubbe and Uncle Moishe standing on the side of the road as we drove away.

"We didn't take Bubbe with us. Why? I squeezed the candies she gave me so tight they made dents in my hands. Why didn't I help her? Why didn't I say to my mother, shame her even, how can you leave your mother like that on the side of the road? Did you even ask her to come with? Now I know I was afraid not just to ask questions, I was afraid to hear my

SHERIE POSESORSKI

mother's answers. My mother, she thought mostly just with her head, and sometimes, and that time was one of those sometimes, you have to think what's best first with your heart and then let the head think up ways to make what's in your heart come true. The head, it can be too hardheaded, too practical...seeing only what's there, and nothing else.

"With my whole heart, I wanted to help my Bubbe. I wanted her with us," her mother said, panting like she was going to cry. She panted and panted, then was quiet.

"Your poor Bubbe!" Becky said, feeling like crying too.

"My poor Bubbe. I should have said something to my mother. I carried those candies in my pockets for who can remember how long. Every time I squeezed them, I saw Bubbe standing there on the road, and my heart, my heart. My Bubbe, she was killed a month later, we found out after the war from people from our village...don't know by whom. What happened to Uncle Moishe, we never learned. So many years, and I never could ask my mother why we just left Bubbe like that," her mother said, shaking her head.

"You, my darling daughter, you tried the best way you knew how to help Linda. You did. I know you don't believe it, but in the end, this will help Linda. You'll see. Me, it's another story. It's not good enough to want to help my Bubbe. I should have said something. I should have done something. For this, I cannot forgive myself. Look at the time," her mother said, glancing at the alarm clock on Becky's night table. "I talk any longer and today is going to be tomorrow."

She got up from the bed and bent over and kissed Becky. "Sweet dreams," she murmured, then left.

THERE WAS LINDA in a swing flying so high and so fast it seemed like it was going to shoot her like a slingshot across the playground and into the dark ravine. "Linda, Linda!" Becky tried to shout, but her voice was gone. Next she tried to dash toward the swing to grab hold of Linda, but her feet wouldn't budge. It was like they were glued to the ground.

"*Shaineh maideleh!*" Becky twisted her head around to see who was calling out "pretty little girl." It was a very old lady walking out of the ravine. Older even than Mrs. Lepinsky. On her head was a red-and-white scarf, and her face had more wrinkles than Becky had ever seen on a face. Who are you, what do you want, Becky tried to say, but her voice was still gone. As the very old lady came closer and closer, holding on with both hands to a cane, like it was the only thing holding her up, Becky suddenly felt happy to see her. The very old lady was smiling at Becky, and she had a nice smile, even though she was missing teeth here and there. Her blue-grey eyes, Becky had seen them before. But how could she know somebody's eyes and nothing else about them?

"*Tayer maideleh, ech hob dos tsuker far du!*" "My dearest girl, I have some sweets for you." Who used to say that? Taking one hand off the cane, still smiling at Becky, she stuck her hand into the pocket of her apron. "Bubbe!" Becky shouted, her voice coming back as loud as a bullhorn. It was her mother's Bubbe. Her shout frightened Bubbe and she lost her grip on the cane and started to tumble down. Becky leapt forward to try to catch her. Over her head, she saw Linda's body rocketing through the air like a missile.

The alarm clock rang. Becky bolted up in bed. Her

pyjamas were soaked with sweat, as if she'd been running and running on a hot summer day, and her mouth was all dried out. The morning light peeking through the drapes was pulling her dream away and Becky tried to pull it back. There had been Linda in a swing, she remembered, then what? A very old lady...with a cane and candies. Her mother's Bubbe. But try as she might, the light tugged her dream away, leaving Becky only with the feeling of being sad and not knowing what to do about it.

"Are you up yet?" her mother shouted from somewhere.

"I'm up, I'm up!" Becky called out as she got out of bed and headed for her closet. She grabbed the first things she saw, a white sweater with sleeves so long they hung down to her knees, a brown jumper, and a white blouse.

Tossing them on her bed, she left her room to go to the bathroom. In the hallway, she heard her parents arguing downstairs.

"You spoil her, Hannah, that's why she's like this," her father said bitterly. "You, it's you that lets her get away with such nonsense." He then yanked open what sounded like the door of the front closet.

"Ira, Ira, Becky's only a *child*. So she got carried away with the fallout shelter in the garage shed. Weren't you afraid there was going to be another war? I was. I still am. She was only protecting us. Is that such a bad thing?"

Carried away, carried away, the words rang and rang in her ears. More than anything else in the world, Becky wished that right now she could be carried away from everybody and everything.

"I said I'm sorry to *her* twenty times, so help me God, but she won't even look at me," her father shouted.

"What do you expect? You scared her to death with your slapping and screaming!" her mother said in a sharper voice.

"You think you're the only one who loves the children. So help me God, I should drop dead...." her father said, then switched to Polish.

Her mother answered him back in Polish.

Then Becky heard the sound of the front door being slammed shut, followed by her mother sobbing.

She got everybody in trouble. Linda, and now her mother. All she ever did was make trouble for people. Troublemaker, troublemaker, that's what she was. She quietly returned to her bedroom.

"Becky, are you up? Get ready fast or else you'll be late for school!" her mother called out.

"I'm up," Becky called back. "I'll be down soon."

"Up and down soon, that's my girl," her mother said, making a joke but sounding unhappy all the same.

Becky glanced at the clothes she'd tossed onto her bed. Instead of putting them on, she trailed the shaft of light peeking out of her drapes to the window. Flinging open the drapes, she stared out the window. The sky was a patchwork quilt made up of clouds of all shades of grey. In the distance was a whirling funnel of black clouds. It was a perfect escape to Oz sky...if only there was an Oz to escape to. If only Becky could think of a place to go where there wasn't any trouble.

Everyone would be better off without her, because she was a troublemaker. She had to go away – run away – to a place where she couldn't cause any more trouble. But where? She'd figure that out once she got out of the house.

"Becky, are you dressed yet? If you're not, I'm going to come up and dress you myself," her mother shouted.

"I'm getting dressed. I'm coming. Give me five more minutes, okay?"

If her mother came up, Becky would have to leave without taking anything with her. In less than a minute, she was dressed. That gave her four minutes to pack. But what? She went to her closet and took out her overnight case. In it, she quickly stuffed a nightgown, a pair of jeans, and a sweater, then stopped when it hit her that the overnight case was big. If she took it with her now with her schoolbag, it would be like wearing a big sign saying, "I'M RUNNING AWAY!" Forget that! She took her clothes back out and put them away, just leaving out her nightgown which she stuffed into her schoolbag.

What else? There wasn't room for much else. Money, that's what else. Her *Toronto Daily Star* carrier money. She dashed to her dresser and took her envelope with the money out of the top drawer. How much did she have? Only nineteen dollars saved up from her paper route? And what about her paper route? She'd better call Frank sometime later and say she was sick or something and couldn't do it anymore. Where was the card with his name and number on it? Ahh, she'd taped it onto her desk. She dashed over, copied his phone number onto the envelope to remind her to call.

"BECKY, IF YOU ARE NOT DOWN HERE BY THE TIME I COUNT TO TWENTY, I'M GOING TO COME UPSTAIRS AND CARRY

YOU DOWNSTAIRS. DO YOU HEAR ME?"

How could she not hear her? Next door Mrs. Lepinsky probably could hear too. What else? What else? A book. She grabbed *Emily's Quest* and put it in.

Clutching her schoolbag, she dashed downstairs to the kitchen. There she found her mother sitting down at the table, sipping tea from a glass mug. On a plate in front of her were the cubes of sugar she liked to hold between her teeth and crunch as she drank down the tea. Her nose and eyes were all red from crying.

"Sorry I'm so late," Becky mumbled, pulling out the kitchen chair, sitting down and picking up the spoon to eat the bowl of Cream of Wheat.

Raising her head, her mother glanced at Becky. "That sweater! Good, so you're dressing properly...for a change."

That heavy, long, white wool sweater, Becky hardly ever wore it. Not only was it too big, but it was an old lady sweater. But today who knew how long she was going to be outside before she got to where she was going, wherever that was, so the old lady sweater would keep her dressed properly...for running away.

"Where's Jeffie?" she asked as she spooned down her Cream of Wheat like it was cold ice cream, which it almost was now after sitting so long on the table.

"He's in bed still," her mother said, fumbling through her housecoat pockets for a tissue to blow her nose. "I think he's getting a cold. I asked him what he wanted for breakfast, and he said nothing, he's not hungry. When he says that, you know he's not feeling good."

Before she ran away, she should she go upstairs and say goodbye to Jeffie, Becky thought, gulping down a glass of milk. She stood up. "I'm going back upstairs for a sec to say goodbye to Jeffie."

Her mother stood up and gave Becky the long look. "Why do you have to say goodbye? Are you going away on a voyage? You'll see him after school. Anyway, he's probably sleeping and you'll wake him up."

"Yeah, I guess so," Becky said, flushing. Her mother was a mind reader even when she didn't know it.

They went to the vestibule where her mother stood watching while Becky put on her coat, scarf, and boots. She was sorry she wouldn't get a chance to kiss Jeffie goodbye, but if she made a big deal about it, her mother, the mind reader, would know for sure something was up.

"Be careful, watch out!" her mother said like she said every morning. Becky hugged her tight and said a secret goodbye. Her mother kissed the top of her head. As Becky opened the door to leave, her mother tugged her back. "Hold on, your lunch money, I have to get it. Remember, today the school is showing a movie in the gym at lunchtime. Don't buy junk."

When her mother returned with two dollars, Becky took the money and put it in her coat pocket. She would put it in the envelope with the rest of her money later, otherwise she might lose it and she couldn't afford to lose even five cents right now. Becky then clutched onto the material of her mother's faded-blue flowered housecoat that she always wore, even though she had a new one hanging in her closet.

"Trying to rip my *shmatteh* into pieces for cleaning the floor, are you now? Your father says if he sees me wearing it one more time he's going to take a pair of scissors and start cutting it into rags. I told him, just try Mister, you just try," her mother said, smiling but still looking very unhappy.

"Gotta go, I'm late," Becky mumbled.

"You're telling me? So go already! And remember, no junk for lunch and don't sit too close to the screen, you'll ruin your eyes. Be careful."

Becky nodded and went out the door. In case her mother was watching from the living-room window, which she did sometimes, Becky went up Arlington Avenue toward school. Like they had a life and a mind of their own, her feet went straight for the porch on Linda's house. Linda. No more walking to school together. Not ever. She spun around and ran down Arlington until she found herself at St. Clair Avenue and Vaughan Road. There, out of breath, she rested against the red-and-white streetcar stop pole.

Should she take the streetcar east or west? Which was best? Where did she want to go? Anywhere. Nowhere. Back home, that's where she really wanted to be as the nippy nearly winter wind pinched her cheeks and nose. The rest of her was warm, that was one big advantage of wearing lots of too-big clothes. But if she took her scarf and wrapped it around her face, she'd look like a bank robber, and the last thing she needed was for people to notice her, so she'd just have to freeze until a streetcar showed up.

The streetcar going east toward Yonge Street came. By this time, Becky didn't care which way the streetcar was going, as long as it was warm inside. She dropped her money into the fare box.

"Where you off to on a school day, Miss?" the streetcar driver asked. He was very fat and parts of his bottom were sticking off his seat. How come the seats didn't come in different sizes? It must be very uncomfortable to sit on a seat that was too small for you every day for the whole day.

"I'm going...to the doctor," she whispered the lie.

"Without your mother?" he said, twisting his head to look at her.

She nodded.

"Good luck at the doctor, Miss," the driver said, and smiled at her.

Becky made her way to the back of the streetcar. When the streetcar reached St. Clair subway station, since mostly everybody else on the streetcar was going south on the subway, Becky went south too. She was mushed between so many people she couldn't see where she was going. With both hands, she hung on to the pole for dear life because each time the subway stopped with a lurch at a station, people bounced into other people. Station by station, the subway was emptying of people, and at the last stop, Union Station, there were just a couple of people with suitcases left.

Becky walked behind them as they climbed the stairs up to the train station. For a place that you didn't stay in long because you were going someplace else, it was beautiful enough to want to stay in, looking like a combination of a ballroom and a cathedral. On the top level of Union Station was a huge hall with a curved high ceiling, fancy tiles on the floors, big arched windows on each side, thick Roman pillars, and the names of places etched in stone tablets in the walls. In the centre was a huge board with the train schedules on it. Trains were leaving soon for Ottawa, Windsor, Montreal, even New York City, and Chicago. It would be nice to go to New York and see the Empire State Building and the Statue of Liberty. But she had only twenty-one dollars. Was that enough for a ticket to New York City?

"Your mother and father gone off and left you alone?"

Becky felt a hand on her shoulder, looked around and shivered. The hairy white hand belonged to a man with a little moustache and a bald head.

She pulled away, but the man's ugly hand stuck to her shoulder.

"My father, he's over there," she mumbled, pointing to the crowd of people standing in line to buy train tickets.

"I could buy you a strawberry milkshake, how would you like that? We could be back by the time your father gets your tickets. He won't even know you're gone." He smiled, which made his little black moustache look like a shrinking caterpillar.

Meeting a bald, short man while she was sipping a milkshake at Schwab's Drugstore, that had been part of her story to Jeffie about becoming a Hollywood star. In her story, it had been a happy and exciting moment. But that wasn't what Becky was feeling now. The man was creepy, and she didn't like the way he kept squeezing her shoulder tight with his hairy hand and smiling at her. Becky knew that smile. That was the same mean, evil smile that the outlaw Liberty Valance had smiled just before he took out his gun to shoot the hero in the movie *The Man Who Shot Liberty Valance.*

"A place I know across Front Street has the best milkshakes, you'll see," the man said, licking his lips.

How stupid did this man think she was? Did he think she was some dumb nine-year-old that would go off with him for some lousy free milkshake?

Becky opened her mouth, but when she needed words more than she'd ever needed words before, none came out. Without her even noticing, the man had slipped one arm around her waist, and was firmly moving her along in the crowd. His touch was as sickening and scary as having a cobra snake wrapped around her. Her body got all stiff like it did when it was freezing cold outside.

Outside the station, the man paused to catch his breath and Becky tried to wiggle free, but his grip on her waist and shoulder remained tighter than a cobra's. A man selling hot dogs and pretzels rolled his cart closer to them. "Warm up with a wiener!" he sang. The steam coming out of his cart surrounded her, and miracle of miracles, the hot steam unfroze her body. With all her strength, Becky jerked her shoulder free of the man's hand and, squirming like an eel, broke free.

CENTRE ISLAND

NEXT TO UNION STATION WAS A TRAFFIC TUNNEL. THOUGH it was dark and gloomy, Becky ran into it, coughing as she ran, from the smell of gasoline fumes. Was the man running after her? The honking of cars and trucks driving through the tunnel was so loud that she couldn't hear any footsteps, and she wasn't about to stop even for one second to look around.

When she reached the end, she paused and looked back. There was nobody there! Resting against the tunnel wall, Becky puffed and puffed, trying to catch her breath. Never, ever, in her whole life had she been that scared.

"Toot! Toot! Toot!"

Becky looked up and around. She'd run all the way to the harbour where the ferry boats to Centre Island were docked.

"Toot! Toot!" The horn on the ferry blew again. That's where she would go. Centre Island. She always loved going there in the summertime, and she especially loved the little houses on Ward's Island. Every time she saw them, she wished she could live in one of those houses.

If she wanted to catch the ferry boat, she'd better move fast. Taking a deep breath, she darted across two roads and up a hill to the dock. At the dock, she bought a ticket and made it onto the ferry just as the guard was closing the gate.

Though it would be nice to stand outside on the top deck to watch as the island, its trees now naked brown, came closer and closer, Becky headed inside to the bottom deck and sat down, because she was like her mother. All the boat had to do was give a little jiggle and there went her stomach.

Usually she sat on the wooden benches near the port-holes, but since she was alone she decided it was safer to sit on the bench next to the life jackets.

"All aboard! First stop, Hanlan's Point!" a man bellowed.

Hardly anyone was on board. So far Becky had counted only seven people, none of them sitting on the bottom deck. She was all alone.

The ferry pulled out of the dock, and her stomach moved along with it.

"Stop it!" she whispered, slipping one hand underneath her coat and pressing down on her stomach. Did her stomach listen? It tossed, it turned, it made her head spin, and the milk and the Cream of Wheat from breakfast leapt back into her mouth. All this, and the ferry had only been sailing for two minutes!

How had her mother been able to stand being on a boat for a whole two weeks when her family had come to Canada? She'd been so seasick she couldn't eat and could barely even sip water. The only thing that had made her feel better had been her daily trip to the library on the top deck of the ship. On a couch in the library, she'd escaped her seasickness and everything else while reading. She could still remember every single book she'd read on the trip, and the best one of them all had been *The Wandering Jew*. That book had been something, something, her mother had said.

"You don't look too good, can I get anything for you?"

Still pressing hard on her stomach, Becky looked up into the rosy face and hazel eyes of one of the ferry's deckhands.

"No thank you, I'm fine," she mumbled, edging back toward the wall, fearing that the deckhand might be just like the horrible man at Union Station.

He stood from his crouch, and saluted her. "Charlie Anderson, at your service, and what would your name be, young lady?"

"Becky Makowiecki," she said. The second she said her name, she knew she'd made a mistake. She should have made up a name. Some escaper she was turning out to be.

"Becky, I have just the thing for your stomach. Peppermint mints." He pulled a roll out of his jacket pocket and handed it to her. Charlie seemed like he was all right, so she unravelled the paper and took out one mint.

"Thanks!" She popped it into her mouth and bit down on it.

"No, no, no, it works best if you suck on it," Charlie advised.

Becky sucked on the mint, which was now in two pieces. Like her father, she was a candy chomper, and not a candy sucker. Her father.... She didn't want to think about her father.

"No school today?" Charlie asked.

This time Becky was prepared to lie. "There's school, but my class is practising a play and I'm not in it because I forget the lines, so my mother said I could visit..." Becky mumbled.

"You're visiting Jimmy Richardson!" Charlie exclaimed.

Becky nodded hard and thanked the heavens that her mumble had sounded like somebody's name.

"Charlie!" a deep voice yodelled.

"My skipper calls!" Charlie said, smiling. "Pleased to have met you, Becky. Say hello to Jimmy, and remember, mints are not bubble gum to be chewed, but scintillating sensations of peppermint to be savoured! Got it?"

"Got it!" Becky said, smiling back.

The boat docked at Hanlan's Point, and when it began to move on, the mint really helped and Becky was able to take her hand off her stomach.

"Centre Island!" Charlie bellowed.

Centre Island. That's where her family got off when they came to the beach for picnics. All of a sudden, she decided to get off here, instead of Ward's Island, and dashed off the boat. She waved to Charlie from the dock as the ferry pulled out, then turned around to go. But where?

Centre Island was as still and deserted as the moon. The hot dog stands near the dock were boarded up. The rippling of flags on the poles was the only sound to be heard. Shivering, Becky looked right, left, then ahead. The sky was metal grey, the grass coated with slivers of frost. Now, what was she going to do here, outside, with nobody in sight?

Ward's Island, there had to be people there. She walked fast to the left, and as she walked she passed the tiny Centreville amusement park. Like everything else on Centre Island, it was empty. The roller coaster ride had no roller coaster. The cars in the bumper car ride weren't there. Even the animals in the farm were gone. Right now, Becky would have given anything to see somebody. But there was nobody anywhere. Not even a squirrel. By the time she reached the boardwalk leading to Ward's Island, she was running. The wind had picked up, and the waves were slapping so strongly against the wall barrier along the edge of the boardwalk that it was drowning out Becky's clop, clop, clop on the loose boards. Why she was running, Becky didn't even know. It wasn't like there was somebody chasing her. She felt as if she was on a deserted island, which she was, except for a couple of seagulls circling overhead.

So far, escaping wasn't anything like she'd thought it would be. It was like running along a road where you didn't know what was ahead or where you were going or if you were ever going to feel safe again. The only point of escaping was to get to a someplace better, wasn't it? In summer, Centre Island was a someplace better. In December, unless you were a seagull, it wasn't. How many escape plans had she made, too many even to remember every single one, and now she'd finally gone and escaped, and she'd done it with no plan at all!

Off in the distance she sighted the tiny houses on Ward's Island and picked up speed. When she reached the first row of houses, she began to walk slowly, staring at each house as she played the house game. That's what her mother always played with her and Jeffie on the walks they took around the neighbourhood. Whenever her mother saw an interesting house, she would say, "I wonder who lives there?" Then the three of them would try to guess what the person was like. Once they'd passed a house where the green paint on the door and window frames had been peeling off, and the windows had been so thickly covered with dirt that you couldn't see in. The grass on the lawn had been knee high and pieces of old newspaper had been stuck to the branches of the tree in the middle of the lawn.

Their mother had guessed that a lonely widower lived in the house. Since his wife had died, he didn't care about anything anymore, so that's why the house was so neglected. Becky and Jeffie had guessed that a mad scientist lived in the house and was too busy in the basement doing experiments on squirrels, pigeons, and raccoons to care about cutting the grass and cleaning the windows with Windex.

She felt like crying as she remembered. No crying! Besides, it was so nippy outside that if she allowed herself to cry, the tears would freeze solid on her cheeks, and she would get frostbite, and then she'd *really* have something to cry about.

More than anything she wished, she hoped, she prayed, that in one of those houses lived a kind house lady that would invite her in and give her something warm to drink and eat. She stared at a thin house painted blue, but nobody came out. She stared at a green house with a deck chair on the front lawn, but nobody came out. She turned right and began walking up the next lane with houses. She stared and stared at the houses, but nobody came out. Her nose dripping from the cold, she lifted her arm to wipe it on her coat sleeve. When she put down her arm, there was a white terrier looking up at her. He seemed like a friendly dog, not a biter or a chaser, so she bent over and patted his head and scratched his ears, and as she did, the dog licked her nose. Never had she been so happy to see a dog!

"Izzy, Izzy, Ishmael, where have you gone? You knew I was making lunch, and off you went anyway. My beef stew is going to be steaming hot, and yours, if you don't show your snout shortly, will be cold and stringy." The man's voice was a bit weak and old sounding, kind of like Mrs. Lepinsky's, but with an English accent.

Beef stew. If Ishmael didn't want his, Becky would gladly eat it for him, because she was very hungry and very cold. Ishmael yapped, then ran up the lane. Then he sat down, turned his head, and yapped again, as if asking Becky, aren't you coming with me?

Becky took three steps, then froze, remembering the horrible man in Union Station. What if Ishmael's owner was like him? But what if he wasn't? What if he was nice and friendly, just like Charlie Anderson? Should she follow Ishmael or not? How come when she wished for things, like right now she'd been wishing and hoping for a house lady, when her wishes did come true, they came true but never in the way she'd wished for?

Ishmael yapped and yapped, sat down and waited.

"Okay, I'm coming," she said, and Ishmael got up and trotted toward a house at the very end of the lane. Becky took a deep breath. If when she saw the man he gave her the creeps like the Union Station man had, she'd run faster than she'd ever run in her whole life, before he could clamp a hand on her.

Ishmael sat down in front of a white picket fence, twisted his head around, and yapped at Becky. The fence surrounded the funniest looking house Becky had ever seen. Unlike all the rest of the midget houses on the lane, this house was tall and skinny, and tilted to one side. The shingles on the roof were royal blue, and right under the roof was a porthole window like the ones on the ferry boat. The bricks were faded yellow, and the large front windows were criss-crossed like those on a church. On the porch was a brown rocking chair and a little table, and on the lawn an anchor sat surrounded by a tangle of bare shrubs.

Becky closed her eyes, trying to picture the house man that lived here.

"So you've brought me a visitor, have you now, Ishmael?" the man said.

Becky opened her eyes and blinked twice in surprise. Standing right there was the house man she'd pictured. He was tall and thin, just like his house. His head was mostly bald, except for a fringe of white hair, his eyes were as blue as the ocean, and he had a bushy grey-and-white beard.

"Let me introduce myself. Captain James Richardson, but you can call me Jimmy, everybody does. Pleased to make your acquaintance." He stuck out his hand over the fence gate. Behind his wire-rimmed glasses, his blue eyes twinkled.

So this was Jimmy Richardson, the man Charlie

Anderson thought she was coming to visit. Plus, he was *just* the house man she'd pictured. This must be a sign. A good one. But still Becky was a bit frightened as she stuck out her hand. What if she was wrong?

"My, my, you must be very cold," he said as he gently shook her hand, then let it go.

"Pleased to meet you...." she said shyly, her teeth chattering. "My name is Rebecca, but everybody calls me Becky."

"Well, Becky, would you care to join Ishmael and myself for lunch? You probably heard that beef stew is on the menu. That should take the chill out of your system, but if it doesn't do the trick, dessert will – it's waffles with hot chocolate syrup."

"Thank you for inviting me, Captain Richardson," Becky said, as he swung open the gate for her and Ishmael. As she walked in, her legs began to quiver. If she was wrong about Captain Richardson, how would she get out once she was in the house? She'd made so many dumb, stupid mistakes lately that she wasn't so sure anymore if she was doing the right thing.

"Jimmy, please. Nobody calls me Captain Richardson since I left the navy," he said as he walked slowly up the porch stairs. "Darn arthritis! It makes me legs as stiff as a mast."

He opened the door wide and stepped aside so Becky and Ishmael could go inside, and what an inside it was! It was just like the inside of a boat. The walls were covered with pictures, the same as in Mrs. Lepinsky's house. Except here the pictures were of catamarans and schooners, cargo ships, mail steamers and ocean liners, sailors in ports all over the world, and family pictures instead of paintings of Russia and family photos. On the mantelpiece above the fireplace were models of ships; in the bookcase were books on boats, travelling, the navy, and explorers. A life preserver hung on the wall beside a roll of thick rope. She was almost sure now that coming inside was the right thing to do, but still her teeth were chattering and her legs quivering.

"You may say, and correctly I would say, that I have a love of all things nautical," Jimmy said, smiling. The door swung shut, and Becky shuddered.

"I think we could all use some hot stew to warm up. Whether it's tasty too, I'll leave that up to you and Ishmael to decide."

Becky and Ishmael trailed behind Jimmy. In the kitchen, she sat down on a bench beside a long wooden table, and Jimmy brought a plate of steaming hot beef stew and set it down before her while Ishmael yapped at his heels.

"I haven't forgotten you, old boy. We have a guest, and the guest gets the first serving, not rascal terriers!"

The steam was rising up from the stew and warming Becky's face. It smelt tasty, very tasty. Carrying a tray, Jimmy came back to the table, and set his plate, a basket of toasted buns, and two glasses of hot apple cider on the table. He then sat down on the bench opposite Becky.

"Thank you," Becky said, now more shy than scared.

"No, thank you. It's not often I am blessed by company, other than Izzy's and my neighbours, once the summer is past. So what brings you to Ward's Island? Let me see if I can guess. At home, there's nothing but sadness and trouble. So you thought you would go on the lookout for a fresh, new land."

Becky looked at him. That sounded kind of familiar. Then it hit her, and she grinned at Jimmy. "That's kind of what Professor Marvel said to Dorothy in *The Wizard of Oz!*"

"It doesn't take a crystal ball to see that you're running away," Jimmy said. "But you don't want to say why, do you lass?"

Choked up, Becky shook her head.

"Then, how about I tell you tales of me own life?"

Relieved, Becky dug into the stew as Jimmy told her his story while he ate. He was born in Manchester, England, in 1889, and his father worked in a cotton mill there. His mother died when Jimmy was four, and Jimmy was raised by his older sister Annie. Not wanting the life his father had, at the age of sixteen Jimmy had run away and joined the British merchant navy. It wasn't a military navy but a trading navy that carried mail, cargo, and supplies from England to almost every country in the world that had a port, because back then England had the most trade routes. Serving under the "Red Duster" – that was the nickname for the merchant navy's ensign flag – had been a grand old adventure.

It seemed like Jimmy had travelled everywhere – even to such faraway places as Burma, India, Malaysia, New Zealand, and Singapore. He'd done practically every job you could do on a boat. As a junior mate and cadet, he'd loaded and unloaded cargo, and swabbed the decks and cabins – that was why, he joked, his house was so shipshape. During the First World War when his cargo ship had been refitted as a hospital ship to transport wounded soldiers home to England, he'd served as an assistant to the nurses and doctors. On leave in France, he'd met and married Nicole, and they'd had a daughter, Margot.

After only a hour, she knew more about Jimmy's past than she knew about her father's. "My father never talks about his past like you do," she blurted out.

Jimmy arched his thick white eyebrows and glanced over at Becky like he was expecting her to say more, but she couldn't. Instead she asked Jimmy a bunch of questions about the places he'd visited, asking him to describe Sydney in Australia and Tokyo in Japan.

"I've talked my tongue into a dryness the equal of the Kalahari Desert's, and you haven't said much about yourself yet, lass," he said, taking a long gulp of cider.

Shrugging, Becky glanced away from Jimmy. She didn't want to talk about herself, not at all. When she glanced back, she saw Jimmy was getting up from the table. He opened the kitchen door to let Ishmael out, then came back to the table with the waffles and chocolate syrup.

Becky licked the flakes of waffle off her lips as she leaned forward to listen to Jimmy's adventures as the captain of a small mail steamer on the East Africa service. After his retirement, he and Nicole had moved to Bath in England where they'd lived near the sea in a little cottage until Nicole died. By that time, Margot had married and settled in Toronto. So he'd picked himself up and moved to Toronto, and here he was, close to Margot and his two granddaughters...and the water, so to speak.

"And only I am escaped alone to tell thee...me story,"

Jimmy said as he stroked his beard.

That sounded awfully familiar too. Then it hit her and she grinned at Jimmy. "The Bible...the Book of Job!" She couldn't believe she actually remembered something from Mr. Elkin's Hebrew School class, because she mostly doodled and twice had fallen asleep.

Ishmael began to scratch at the door, and Jimmy got up to let him in. He picked him up and placed him on Becky's lap, and she stroked his white, matted fur.

"You wouldn't think that such a rascal as old Ishmael could be so cuddly as he sheds hair and dirt and goodness knows what else in your lap, but he is – aren't you Izzy, old boy?"

Ishmael licked Becky's hand.

The chimes on the kitchen clock rang three times. "If you want to be catching the ferry back, you need to go soon. The ferry stops coming to Ward's Island in the late afternoon. If you can catch the 3:30 ferry, you can make it home before your family will even know you were gone. You will come back and visit me and Ishmael soon, won't you?"

Becky nodded hard. After thanking Jimmy for everything, she got ready to leave. When Becky saw how much effort it took Jimmy just to walk with her to the end of the lane, she made him go back home and raced the rest of the way to the dock. The ferry boat was pulling out of the dock as she got there.

Since the next one was an hour later, she decided to go back to the Centre Island dock and catch the ferry from there. As she walked along the boardwalk, her dread grew....step by step. She could never have stayed here alone on a nearly deserted island with no inside place to sleep except hot dog stands and no food to eat. She'd almost asked Jimmy if she could stay with him, but she knew he would have said no, and would have called her mother and when her mother found out she'd gone to Centre Island, everything would be even worse than it was already. There was nowhere to go...except back home. But she couldn't go home.

Where could she go? If she went to Linda's, Mrs. Friedman would sent her home faster than it took bread to pop out of a toaster. Plus, maybe after yesterday, Linda might not even want her to move in. Mrs. Lepinsky would let her move in for sure, but how could she hide out in the house next door to her own? She could go to Judy's, but she'd only been there once, and how could you ask to move into somebody's house after only one visit? She didn't want to go home, but how could she not go home? What should she do? Where should she go once she took the ferry back to Toronto?

At the end of the boardwalk was a beach. In the summertime, it was so crowded with people that when Becky and her family came there was barely enough room to spread out their blanket. Now the beach was empty except for several swooping seagulls and...Becky squinted. Was there a person on the beach? She squinted some more. Yes, there was a person sitting on a blanket facing the lake. Beside the person was a picnic basket. Curious, Becky crept closer and closer to the beach. A couple of golden rays from the sun broke through the clouds and zoomed around the beach like those giant klieg lights the movie studios used at movie premieres when big stars were arriving. One ray hit the person, and the shoulders of the person glittered as if the sun had hit a piece of metal.

How could it hurt to take a couple steps onto the beach just to see who the person was? Becky put one foot down on the beach, then the other. With good company, maybe Becky could figure out a way to stay on Centre Island just like Robinson Crusoe and Friday had on their island. Maybe the person had run away too! Or maybe the person was like the horrible Union Station man and Becky was about to do something not just dumb and stupid, but really dangerous. Another ray hit the person and lit up the back and shoulders of the person's coat. The coat was made of black-and-white wool, and on the shoulders were epaulettes with metal snaps. Russian soldier shoulders, that's what Becky called the ones on her mother's black-and-white wool winter coat.

Black-and-white coat? How could it be? Becky took a few more steps, took a deep breath, and shouted, "Mummy! Mummy!"

The person jerked, then turned around. It was her mother!

"Mummy, Mummy!" Becky cried, stumbling as she tried to run quickly on the sand.

"Becky? Becky? Is that you? How can it be you?" Her mother said, scrambling up.

Reaching her mother, Becky hugged her tight. "You fell from a star," she sang.

Laughing, her mother hugged her back. "And Krasnobrod is the name of the star," she sang back.

"What are you doing here?" they both said at the same time.

"Getting away," her mother said.

"You too?" Becky said.

When they let go of each other, her mother checked out Becky from head to toe. "You okay? You've been here all day?"

Becky nodded.

"That miserable piece of business that calls herself your teacher, wait, wait, will she get it from me! Did she call this morning to tell me you weren't at school, like she's supposed to do? You okay? Don't ever, ever, do something like this again, Becky! Nothing bad happened to you, did it?"

This was another one of those times when the best truth wasn't the real truth but either the "kind of" truth or hardly any truth. Nothing bad had happened, really...since she had managed to run away from the man at Union Station. Just now wasn't the time or the place for the real truth.

"Nope," Becky said, shivering as she remembered the disgusting feel of the man's coiled-cobra grip.

"You're cold. I have something to warm you fast. A thermos I have, filled with tea and lemon. It's not hot chocolate, but's it hot. Okay, not hot, but lukewarm. So sit down with your mother on the blanket and tell me what you did today," her mother said, sitting back down on the blanket.

Becky plopped down, very, very, curious about how and why her mother had come to Centre Island, of all places, and all prepared with a blanket and a thermos. Becky sniffed, smelling the delicious cinnamon sugar smell of Buffalo buns.

Knowing her mother wouldn't tell her a single thing until Becky told her "kind of" everything, she did, leaving out the Union Station man.

"This Captain Jimmy, I have to give him a call to thank him. What an adventure you had today! But you must never,

ever, do this again! Something terrible could have happened to you! You're a very lucky girl. And who would think that a mother and a daughter would end up escaping to the very same place. My place!" Her mother patted the sand beside the blanket.

"Your place?" Becky squeaked. "How come you were escaping? Who's taking care of Jeffie? What...."

Her mother held up her hand in the famous Makowiecki stop-sign signal. "Okay, slow down with the questions. Mrs. Lepinsky is babysitting Jeffie who, thank goodness, doesn't have a cold. You know how miserable he gets when he can't breathe through his nose, and can't taste food. And my place.... First you tell me, why did you come here, of all places?" her mother said, wrapping one arm around Becky. They were both sitting facing Lake Ontario. The wind had died down, and the rays of the sun were hop, skip, and jumping over the small wave crests as they broke on the shore.

"We always come here in the summer and have a good time. So I just came, that's all," Becky said, shrugging, giving her mother the "kind of" truth. Centre Island had popped into her head because it was there in front of her at the end of the Union Station tunnel.

"Mm," her mother said. "You know, maybe, maybe, it was the hand of God pointing this way, if you please, the way God did to my family, God Bless, so many times during the war."

Maybe there *was* more to it than she'd thought. The St. Clair Avenue streetcar going west could have come first instead of the one going east, but it didn't. She could have followed the people going north on the subway, instead of the ones going south, but she didn't. She could have gotten off any subway stop before Union Station, but she didn't. Gazing up at the sky, she saw a wiggle of sunlight poke through the racing clouds...like a pointing finger.

"How come you came here today?" Becky blurted out, wanting to know more than ever. "How come this is your place? Why wouldn't you tell me already?"

"A mother, she has certain, certain...*prerogatives,*" her mother said, smiling.

"Night school word," Becky chanted.

"One of those certain *prerogatives* is to find out if her darling daughter is safe and sound so she can relax a little. Relaxed, the mother answers questions. Nervous, the mother asks questions. Got it?"

"Yes, madam!" Becky said, sticking out her tongue and saluting.

"Watch the tongue, you know I hate the sticking out of the tongue. Only toads catching flies stick out tongues. The rest of us, we keep them in our mouths where they belong!"

"Yeah, yeah, so finish asking your questions so I can ask my questions."

Her mother groaned. "Such a mouth! You ran away today...because of Daddy and Linda, didn't you?" she said in a softer voice.

Becky glanced at her mother, then back at the lake. "I'm a troublemaker. I make nothing but trouble. For Linda at school, and for you at home with Daddy." Becky rested her head against her mother's shoulder while her mother patted her on the back. After a few minutes, Becky lifted her head and sat up.

"Better?" her mother asked, then hit her forehead with the palm of one hand. "One thing for sure will make you feel better, a buttered Buffalo bun and some tea, no?"

"Yes," Becky said, not wanting to hurt her mother's feelings by saying no, even though she was really stuffed from Jimmy's food.

Her mother unscrewed the thermos and poured tea into two Styrofoam cups, then took a bun out of her picnic basket and ripped it into two, giving the bigger half to Becky like she always did.

"So are you going to tell about how come you're here, already?" Becky asked.

Sliding her hands up and down to shake all the crumbs and sugar off them, her mother looked over Becky. "You should know by now, that me and Daddy, we don't exactly talk to each other or to you or Jeffie in a quiet voice. We shout, we yell, we scream, but that's the way we...we...COMMUNICATE!"

"That's two night school words today," Becky teased.

"And so what? I should save the words like an evening dress only for special occasions?"

Becky shook her head, no.

"As I was *communicating* to you, don't you worry yourself about me and Daddy. It's *you* and Daddy that...."

Now it was Becky's turn to put her hand up in the famous Makowiecki stop-sign signal. She didn't want to talk about her father, not now, not ever.

"Okay, okay," her mother said, sighing. "I'll let it go for right now, but we have to talk about Daddy. And Linda, I know you will miss Linda like anything, but in the long run, maybe this school and class will help her catch up, so you and Linda can be in the same class together next year."

"Really?" Becky said.

Her mother shrugged. "Maybe, maybe not. But there's plenty of time to be together after school and on weekends."

Her mother was right, but still, she would miss Linda and she couldn't stop feeling that somehow she should have helped her better.

A golden shaft of sun hit her mother like a spotlight.

Becky pointed one arm at her mother, the way Ed Sullivan did when he was introducing a singer, magician, or comedian on his Sunday night show. "So are you going to COMMUNICATE ALREADY how come you are here with buns and tea?"

"Here with you, both of us, at my place," her mother said with a smile. "How you should end up running away to my place...funny, but maybe not so funny when you think about it."

"So tell me already, Mummy!"

"This is a long story, so maybe you should give a stretch too," her mother said, then stretched and stretched until she found a more comfortable sitting position.

"*All* your stories are long," Becky said.

"You show me somebody whose life is a short story, and I'll show you a person who hasn't lived their life. Even the hobbits, do they have short stories? No! Four giant-sized books, because they've had such lives, those hobbits."

Becky groaned. "Okay, okay, begin already, please! Tell me first why this is your place."

"My place. First I have to tell you the part about when I was expecting you. Daddy and me, we were living with your Bubbe and Zaide, Rivem and Chaim, on Major Street. Daddy and me, we slept in the attic."

"The attic, just like the one the Little Princess stayed in," Becky added.

"Except we didn't have a nice rich man's servant bringing us Persian carpets and *tsatkes,* but we did have a big hole in the window screen that brought in flies, *oy* such flies," her mother shuddered. "So many flies, ants, spiders, and even sometimes bumblebees in that attic. Such hotness in the summer, and the noise in that house! Fight, fight, fight!"

"What was worse? The fighting or the bugs or the hotness?" Becky asked.

"Worse, was everything all together. It was too much for me. Daddy was working two shifts, from seven in the morning to nine at night, to save up money so we could put a down payment on a house for us all to live in after you were born. I was working from seven to two as a buttonhole maker in a children's clothing factory. After work, why go home to bake and swat bugs in an attic! So I took a book, a Buffalo bun, a thermos of iced tea, and three times a week after work, I went to Centre Island to this beach. A sip of tea, a bite of Buffalo bun, and some dreaming about the day you would be here and all of us would be in our very own house, and I was a new person."

What a coincidence that the very first time Becky had run

away, she ended up in the very place her mother had escaped to! But was it just a coincidence?

As her mother, who was the slowest eater on earth because she liked to *relish* (another night school word her mother liked to use whenever she had the chance) every single bite, still chewed on the last piece of her Buffalo bun, Becky was wondering why this beach was a favourite place of her mother's. So when her mother was finished eating, Becky asked.

"This beach," her mother said. "You want to know why this beach? This is where I met Daddy. My family, they came here for a picnic. Rivem, Chaim, and I were playing with a beachball. Out of the corner of my eye, I saw a very skinny man with a full head of wavy brown hair, watching us. When we finished playing, he came over, introduced himself and asked if he could borrow our beachball, because the ball he and his friends brought got a hole in it and all the air whooshed out. So I lent him the ball, and when he brought it back, he asked me out on a date. It was on the day I was having my birthday party, so I invited him to come too, and you know what he gave me as a gift – Chanel No. 5 perfume. Imagine!"

Her mother was blushing! Becky couldn't believe it. Her mother! "So was it love at first sight?" she asked.

"Yes, it was," her mother said with a big smile. "For me, for Daddy, and for the both of us when we first saw you, then Jeffie."

Becky scowled.

"Don't give me that face!" her mother said. "You don't know how much Daddy wanted to have his very own family.

Daddy loves all of us. Us includes YOU! If you think Daddy isn't eating himself up alive since he hit you in the shed, you're badly mistaken!"

"So why did he hit me then and go so nuts?" Becky felt all her anger and hurt come crashing back.

"Daddy, when he saw you were all digging a hole, he.... You know how he yells at you and Jeffie to cross the street quick when he sees a car coming down the road. He looks like he's mad at you, but he's not mad. He's just scared. When he saw that you were all digging a hole, he remembered things.... So Daddy, he acted like that. To understand, you have to know about the camps in the war. I don't know," her mother said, rubbing the back of her neck. "To tell you...or not to tell you, what's right, I don't know."

Leaning against her mother, Becky was silent. Did she want to know about the camps? Every time her mother got close to the camps part of the story, the way her mother spoke and looked filled Becky with fear. Becky was always kind of relieved when her mother said she wasn't old enough to hear about the camps. But today, even though Becky was filled with fear again, she didn't want to run away either.

"I'm old enough to hear," she said softly.

"Oh, Becky, nobody is ever old enough. I wasn't, when I heard. I was thirteen. In Leninibat," her mother murmured. "You remember how we got there?"

Becky nodded solemnly. "After the Russians let you out of the Siberian labour camp north of Novosibirsk, you only knew where you *didn't* want to go."

Her mother rolled her eyes as she remembered. "The

snow desert north of Novosibirsk was as far north as my family wanted to go. North was the Arctic Circle. It was freezing cold enough, thank you very much, below the Arctic Circle."

"You couldn't go west back through Russia to Poland, because the Russians were fighting back the German armies, who were marching on Moscow," Becky continued. "And you couldn't go east to live in China, because you didn't have visas."

Her mother nodded. "After just being freed from being arrested, we didn't want to go and get ourselves arrested again and put in a Chinese prison, thank you very much."

"So that meant there was only one direction left, south," Becky announced.

"South sounded very good to all of us," her mother said. "One of the guards at the camp told us if we wanted hot, hot, hot, which of course we did want, after cold, cold, cold, we should go to live in one of the Russian republics near Asia. So we did. We went south on barges, trains, and the faithful-but-very-tired-out feet and arrived in the republic of Tajikistan...."

"Which bordered Afghanistan on one side, and China on the other," Becky interrupted.

"Right, but then when isn't your remembering right?" her mother teased. "We wanted hot, hot, hot, and that's what we got, hot, hot, and more hot. We went from every day very much below zero in Siberia to every day a hundred degrees above zero. We settled in the town of Leninibat."

"There, you rented a one-room house from a Russian Arab who was born in Iran."

"Naieh, such a kind man," her mother said, so softly that Becky had to lean close to hear. "Naieh, he was the one who told our family about the camps. He had been a soldier in the Russian army, and during a battle, he was captured by the Germans. They sent him to the biggest death camp, Auschwitz.

"In 1942, the Germans, town by town, city by city, were rounding up the Jews in the countries they conquered and taking them on trains to the death camps they'd built in Poland."

Her mother paused, licking her lips like her mouth had gone suddenly dry, like Becky's always did all the time when she got a bad fright. Death camps, her mother had said. After all this time of wanting to know why her mother would never talk about the camps in Poland, now that Becky knew why, she wished like anything she didn't have to know.

"When Naieh was taken off the train at Auschwitz, what he saw there...in his worst nightmares, he would have never imagined, he told us. The people arriving at the camp – Jews mostly, some prisoners of war like Naieh, Slavs and Gypsies – they were divided into two groups. The ones that looked strong enough to work, like Naieh, they were put in one line. In the other line went young children, many women, the weak looking and the sick."

Her mother was shaking so much she could hardly talk. Becky reached over and put her right hand on her mother's back and rubbed it. Then her mother took a couple of deep breaths like a runner did to get the strength to make it to the finish. "This line was marched to a separate building. They were put in a room, told to undress, and then taken to what the Germans told them was a giant shower room. Except it wasn't a shower room, it was a poison gas chamber, and the people were gassed to death, then their bodies were burnt in crematoriums. All day long, as Naieh fixed fences and repaired barracks, whenever he raised his head to look at the sky, there was always a black snake of smoke there, for the crematoriums ran all day and all night long."

Becky tasted salt on her lips. She'd been listening so hard she didn't even feel the tears pouring down her face. Her chest got so tight she could hardly breathe. "Were there lots of camps?" she asked, her voice all scratchy.

"There were six death camps. The Germans killed six million Jews and eleven million people altogether from all over Europe in them. Naieh was in the camp for three months, and then he escaped with a couple of other prisoners of war and made the long journey back to Leninibat. Everywhere he went, he would tell people in farms, villages, on the roads, the Germans, they are killing all the Jews in Europe and many others too. The Germans, they are gassing them to death in death camps. But only a few people would believe him. Lots of people called him a crazy man."

"Why wouldn't people believe him?"

Her mother sighed and reached over to hold Becky's hand. "Because, because, there's lots of becauses. Because sometimes the only way we can survive terrible things and terrible times is not to look any farther than the end of our noses. We don't see it, we don't hear it, we don't know, then we're okay. It's like thinking about dying. If you think too much about dying, sometimes it can make it very hard to live, so you don't think about it, you push it away. Also, some things are so terrible we do not want to picture them in our heads. Like what happened to the people in the camps."

That was the way Becky felt right now, holding on tight to her mother's hand, wanting to say something, but not knowing what to say.

Her mother squeezed Becky's hand as they stared out at Lake Ontario. The dark blue twilight sky was spreading over the lake like spilled ink on a desk. Near the shore remained grey-and-white clouds, and here and there, a faint beam of sunlight danced on the water.

"My family, we lost all words too when Naieh told us his story," her mother said sadly. "What can you say about such things?"

With a sick feeling, Becky wondered if her father had been in a camp. The question lay like a weight on the tip of her tongue. Becky noticed that her mother kept glancing over at her like she was waiting for that very question. Straightening up because her legs were falling asleep, Becky took a big, deep breath of lake air.

"Daddy, was he in a camp?" she asked.

"No," her mother said softly. "Ever since Daddy hit you, a hundred times a day, I have gone over this in my head. Should I tell you Daddy's story? No, I say to myself. Daddy's story, it is his to tell or not to tell. But one part of it, I must tell you so you can understand why Daddy went so wild when he saw you digging a hole for a fallout shelter.

"Daddy and his older brother and parents, they lived in a

town called Ostrowic in the south of Poland. The Germans came to Ostrowic in the spring of 1943 to take all the Jews in the town to a death camp called Treblinka. Into a few cattle cars, they shoved everybody, and in the crowds and in the confusion, Daddy got separated from his family and he got shoved into one cattle car, and his parents and brother into another.

"There were so many people in the car he was in. People stood so jammed together that they couldn't even move their arms. There wasn't enough air to breathe. Some people, they began to cry out. Then more and more people cried out. In the middle of nowhere, the train stopped. The Germans, they came and slid open the door in the car Daddy was in. Never had air seemed so fresh and everybody in the car breathed in the air like it was the sweetest of flowers.

"'There's too many of us in here!' one man called out. 'Are there?' a German officer said. 'So get out!' Three more German officers with machine guns and shovels appeared and shouted to the people, 'Get out! Get out!'

"About a third of the people in the car got out, Daddy among them. The Germans marched them over to the edge of a forest and ordered a group of men and women to undress. Then they shot them dead and ordered four boys, Daddy among them, to dig up the ground for a mass grave. As Daddy and the boys dug and dug, they heard the Germans order another group of men and women to undress. Daddy knew that after he and the boys finished digging this grave, he would be soon digging another and another...and then his own.

"When the German officer watching the diggers walked

over for a minute to talk to the officers doing the killings, Daddy quietly put down his shovel and ran through the forest, running faster and faster and faster, every second expecting bullets to be shot at him. But there was such confusion there, Daddy was able to run away deep and far into the forest."

Becky saw her father running through the forest. When her father had run so far and so deep into the darkness of the forest that she could no longer see him running, then she saw what her father had seen when he came into the garage shed, and gasped, a sliver of cool air piercing her lungs like an icicle.

"What happened to Daddy's parents and brother?" she whispered, salty tears burning down her face.

"After the war, Daddy found out they were all killed in Treblinka," her mother said, wiping tears from her eyes.

"And Daddy, how did he survive alone for two years till the war ended?" Becky asked.

"More I cannot tell you. It is Daddy's story, and it is his to remember or to forget," her mother said gently.

"Daddy went through so much, and all by himself," Becky said, feeling terrible for her father. You never knew somebody else's problems, her mother always said. So maybe when Abie the Butcher mixed up the order and gave you chicken thighs instead of chicken necks and shouted at you when you complained, maybe he wasn't thinking straight because he was so worried about his wife who was in the hospital. So that's why, her mother always reminded Becky, first put yourself in somebody else's shoes and walk around in them before you get hotheaded. That was easier said than done, because when Becky's head got hot with anger, her anger burst out like cola out of a bottle that had been shaken, just like it had with her father.

Now that her mother had put Becky in her father's shoes, she understood why her father had become so upset that he'd hit her, and though it still really hurt her, she also knew that seeing her digging had made him remember things that really hurt him too. When she and her mother got home, she would give her father a big hug and tell him she loved him and was sorry for staying mad at him for so long.

In the quiet, Becky heard the sound of seagulls chattering as they dipped and dove above the lake. The waves lapped against the shore as regular as a ticking clock. She looked around the deserted beach.

"What's up?" her mother asked, bending her face so close to Becky's that their noses were practically touching.

"I was just thinking about you and Daddy escaping all that and coming here to this beach at the very same time to meet," Becky said.

"Life is very strange," her mother said. "Filled with miracles and coincidences and always the hand of God. Like what happened with Uncle Benny and Pocking."

"Tell me again," Becky said. She loved this part about Uncle Benny in Toronto. It was the best part of her mother's story. Right now, after hearing about the camps and her father, more than anything, Becky wanted to hear the happy ending of her mother's story.

"Again?" her mother teased. Imitating Becky, she squirmed around, and they both laughed.

"Again," Becky said firmly. "I'll never forget. When the war was finally over in 1945, your family left Leninibat and travelled back to Eastern Europe. Since your family didn't have anywhere to live, your family and thousands and thousands of other Jewish families who had no homes anymore went to stay in Pocking, a displaced person's camp run by the American and British armies in Germany."

"Now the Pocking camp was famous right to Berlin for having lots and lots of girls," her mother said, smiling. "So lots and lots of boys travelled from Berlin to Pocking to get dates. My girlfriend was dating one of these Berlin boys, and one night, she asked me to double date with her. Sure, I said. When Leib, my date, showed up, and my girlfriend introduced me, he said, 'Repeat your name.' So I repeated it. 'My name is Hannah Simkovsky.' 'Simkovsky,' he said, then pointed at me. 'In Berlin, they're looking for your family. You're the Chicken Palace family!'"

Becky got so excited that she had to butt in. "The Chicken Palace poster. In the offices of all the Jewish refugee organizations in Berlin was hanging the Chicken Palace poster – the poster your Uncle Benny had sent from Toronto."

"I should have kept one of those posters. But so anyway, my smart daughter, what did the Chicken Palace poster look like?"

"Your Uncle Benny owned a restaurant that only served chicken. He called it The Chicken Palace. On the poster was a picture of Uncle Benny standing in front of his restaurant with all his waiters and cooks. In big print on the bottom of the poster, it said, 'Looking for Yakov Simkovsky and his family. Anyone with information, please write, Benny

Simkovsky, The Chicken Palace, 362 Yonge Street, Toronto, Ontario, Canada.'"

"Uncle Benny was Zaide's older brother," her mother continued. "He had moved to Toronto in 1932. He was well off. Before the war, he used to send our family clothing and money. During the war, Zaide lost his address."

This was so wonderful that Becky had to butt in again. "After Leib finished talking, you said, nice to meet you, but goodbye. You ran back fast to your parents to tell them the fantastic news about Uncle Benny. When you told them, everybody jumped up and down and laughed and cried and praised God."

"My goodness," her mother said. "Are you sure you weren't there? You know my story better than anybody else in the whole wide world. Then what?"

Becky's chest swelled with pride. "Zaide and Bubbe travelled to Berlin to see the poster. They got the address, they wrote Uncle Benny. He got papers for you to come to Canada, and when you came here, he had a house all ready for you on Major Street. Then he helped you all to get jobs. The happy ending."

Becky clapped and so did her mother. When they stopped, they hugged and her mother murmured, "Uncle Benny, he was a very good man, may he rest in peace."

A whoosh of wind sprinkled sand all over Becky and her mother, getting in their eyes. When Becky rubbed it out, she was surprised to see a half moon in the inky blue sky.

"My goodness, it's nearly evening. When the tongue rolls out the magic carpet to the past, it's a long trip, and who should know better than you, you who have travelled so many times on that carpet to my past. I will have some explaining to do when we get back home, to your father and to poor Mrs. Lepinsky who is probably wishing she was back in Minsk rather than chasing Jeffie around the house. But we had an adventure today, no?' her mother said.

Becky nodded as she went over everything that had happened to her. Funny, on some days a big nothing happened, and then on some days, like today, everything happened. Just think! Today she had been miserable, sad, scared to death, and excited before she had reached her own happy ending, right here, in her mother's favourite escape place, the Centre Island beach.

"Escape, escape, the story of the world is the story of escape," her mother said as she gazed out at Lake Ontario, now as dark as a blackboard. The tips of waves were sparkling like stars on the black water. "I came to this country to escape from escape. But you can't escape from escape."

Becky leaned her head against her mother's shoulder. "There's always things to escape from," she said, sighing. "Nuclear war and nuclear missiles. The Gottesman brothers."

"And what about encyclopaedia salesmen, don't forget about them," her mother joked. "That last one, he chewed off both my ears. It's time to put a sign in the window, 'Encyclopaedia salesmen, we have a whole set from A to Z. Do not ring the doorbell, if you know what's good for you!'"

Becky giggled, then looked over at her mother. Her mother's nose was red from the chill in the air, and her hair was standing up every which way from the wind, and as she smiled at Becky, her gold tooth glinted like a jewel.

"There's small and big escape stories. There's funny and scary escape stories. There's happy and sad escape stories. The story of the world is the story of escape," Becky said, and her mother nodded.

The wind had died down and the sky and the water had joined together to form one never-ending horizon.

"Well, it's time, my darling daughter, to end today's escape story," her mother said, holding out her right hand to help Becky up. "If we want to have a happy ending, that next ferry boat, we'd better be on it, and on the way back home."

Grasping hold of her mother's hand, Becky stood up and shook the sand off her while her mother rolled up the blanket and placed it on top of the basket. Then with one last glance over her shoulder at the never-ending horizon of the lake and sky, she turned to her mother and they began walking toward the ferry dock.

ABOUT THE AUTHOR

S HERIE POSESORSKI is a Toronto-based author,
editor, and book reviewer who is a graduate
of the MFA writing program at Columbia
University in New York, and a former editor
for Harlequin Enterprises. She is the author of
two previous novella publications, and has had
book reviews and personal essays in a variety of
publications across Canada and in the United
States. *Escape Plans* is her first book-length
publication.